Bianca Gillam is a London-based author and armchair expert on 80s and 90s rom-coms. Her poetry has been published in a variety of publications and her lifelong interest in asking people how they met their partner has amassed an impressive collection of 'meet-cutes'. She formerly worked in publishing, where she had the joy of editing a wide variety of brilliant authors; she was inspired by the books she published to write her own.

BY THE SAME AUTHOR

Bad Publicity

off script

bianca gillam

BLOOMSBURY PUBLISHING
LONDON · OXFORD · NEW YORK · NEW DELHI · SYDNEY

BLOOMSBURY PUBLISHING
Bloomsbury Publishing Plc
50 Bedford Square, London, WC1B 3DP, UK
Bloomsbury Publishing Ireland Limited,
29 Earlsfort Terrace, Dublin 2, D02 AY28, Ireland

BLOOMSBURY, BLOOMSBURY PUBLISHING and the Diana logo
are trademarks of Bloomsbury Publishing Plc

First published in Great Britain 2026

Copyright © Bianca Gillam, 2026

Bianca Gillam is identified as the author of this work in accordance
with the Copyright, Designs and Patents Act 1988

This is a work of fiction. Names and characters are the product of the
author's imagination and any resemblance to actual persons, living
or dead, is entirely coincidental

All rights reserved. No part of this publication may be: i) reproduced or
transmitted in any form, electronic or mechanical, including photocopying,
recording or by means of any information storage or retrieval system without
prior permission in writing from the publishers; or ii) used or reproduced in
any way for the training, development or operation of artificial intelligence
(AI) technologies, including generative AI technologies. The rights holders
expressly reserve this publication from the text and data mining exception
as per Article 4(3) of the Digital Single Market Directive (EU) 2019/790

A catalogue record for this book is available from the British Library

ISBN: PB: 978-1-5266-7648-1; EBOOK: 978-1-5266-7649-8

2 4 6 8 10 9 7 5 3 1

Typeset by Six Red Marbles India
Printed and bound in Great Britain by Clays Ltd, Elcograf S.p.A

To find out more about our authors and books visit www.bloomsbury.com
and sign up for our newsletters
For product-safety-related questions contact productsafety@bloomsbury.com

For Andrew,
without whom this book wouldn't exist

Prologue

The call came in at 3 p.m. on a Tuesday.

I had imagined this moment so many times, the daydream sustaining me through a hundred late-night bar shifts and a thousand miserable auditions. Through sleepless nights wondering what, exactly, was so wrong with me that I'd decided to pursue an acting career, sacrificing financial and emotional stability and any chance I might have had at a 'normal' life for one filled with anxiety and rejection. Through call after call to say that they'd gone with someone else, my stomach swooping in a downward arc of disappointment that was becoming so familiar I now picked up the phone ready, poised like a carriage at the top of a rollercoaster.

But despite it all, the hope persisted.

That this time, it would be different.

That this time, it would be me.

I'd imagine where I'd be, what I'd say. How it would feel, to know I finally, finally had a chance at making it as an actor.

And when it came, I wasn't ready for it.

And I certainly wasn't ready for what happened next.

'What?' I said on the phone to my agent, my heart hammering so hard it felt like it might burst out of my chest.

'You heard me right. They want to do a screen test.'

'A screen test?' I repeated the words as if I was hearing them for the first time.

'A screen test, Lara. On Monday. Their two leads have dropped out, so they're on a bit of a time crunch to replace them. They have a new male lead lined up, but they're looking for a female lead pretty immediately. Can you get time off work?'

I hesitated for a second. I'd just taken on a 9–5 because the regular bar shifts I'd been working no longer covered rent for my box room in a shared house on the outskirts of London. But of course, that didn't matter in the moment. I'd find a way.

'Of course,' I said.

'Great,' she replied smoothly, a glimmer of excitement under her professional tone.

Natalie was an up-and-coming junior at one of the biggest agencies in London. She had spotted me performing in a small pub theatre a few years ago, when I'd been at the lowest point of my career, and had signed me the following week. I'd called my mum and cried down the phone, saying this was it: I'd finally got my big break.

But a few years had passed since then and nothing had happened, aside from the occasional local theatre production and some advertising work. I'd been stalling, increasingly struggling to justify this career choice. My confidence that I'd make it if only I kept trying tempered by the lack of evidence that I ever would.

'Nat,' I said, beginning to shake. 'Is this actually happening? I'm not lucid dreaming, right?'

'It's happening,' she said, sounding as astounded as me. We were silent for a few seconds, our shared excitement filling the space. A small, bright flame lit inside me, spreading warmth through my limbs.

A screen test was huge – way further than I'd ever been in the process before. This audition had been a complete shot in the dark – for a screen adaptation of one of my favourite books, about a female detective investigating a string of murders in 1800s London. As dream roles went, it was pretty much at the top of the list. And it had hit me harder than I thought it would, to find out I'd lost out to someone else. Even though at the time I'd reasoned I'd had a snowball's chance in hell of getting it anyway.

But now, through fate or circumstance, I was one of the few front-runners for the role.

Perhaps, just perhaps, this would be it, I thought, a spike of joy travelling up my spine. The break I'd been waiting for while I tried desperately for years to keep my eyes focused on the next audition, the next tape, the next shot. *You only have to get lucky once*, my dad had said to me when I'd first started.

For a half-second, I allowed myself to imagine a future of financial freedom and creative liberation, my dreams being fulfilled over and over again.

Then Nat spoke again and my stomach dropped to the floor.

'The new male lead is Avi Kumar – that's who you'll be testing with.'

'Sorry?' I said, shaking myself back to reality. Surely she couldn't have said that name.

She repeated herself, the words hitting me this time. Each one landing like a dart to my chest.

Shit.

Avi Kumar: one of the world's most famous men, gracing the cover of *GQ* as its Man of the Year last year. Described as 'the Darling of Hollywood', cast in everything from Marvel films to rom-coms to period dramas, hailed as responsible for ushering in a new generation of male British actors.

But I didn't know that Avi Kumar.

I knew the funny, dishevelled Avi Kumar I had met when I'd first moved to London. Who'd shown me the ropes at the theatre pub where we'd both worked as struggling actors – the same one Nat had found me in – and who had taught me to pull the perfect pint. Whom I'd shared my dreams with… because they'd been his, too. Whom I'd felt like I could be myself around, perhaps for the first time in my life.

Who had broken my heart and left for Hollywood, disappearing from my life slowly, then completely. Leaving me wondering what, exactly, I'd done wrong.

'Right.' I practically choked. *Oh, God.*

'You'll be great,' Nat said, worry entering her tone. 'I know he's a huge name, Lara, but—'

'It's fine,' I lied. *If only she knew the half of it.* I had imagined this moment so many times. Finally being in a room with Avi. Finally being able to ask him all the questions that had burned in my mind for months afterwards, as I'd watched his career take off, his face everywhere I'd looked.

But the audition wouldn't be the place for that. It would be a chance for me to prove myself. To finally get the career of my dreams.

I just never thought it would be like this.

And I felt suddenly, inexplicably… terrified.

'I know him, from before he was famous,' I continued, levelling my tone so she couldn't hear the emotions burning through me. 'So I was just a little shocked to hear the name, that's all.'

'You know him?' she said, sounding shell-shocked herself. 'How did I not know this, Lara?' she asked, clearly meaning *we-very-much-could-have-used-this-connection*.

'We haven't spoken in a while,' I said, regretting mentioning it now. I suddenly felt a little faint. 'Since he got famous, actually.'

'Ah,' she replied, seeming to sense that it was a sore subject and that she shouldn't press further. 'Well – you're in the room now. He might be a big name, but you're there too. And that's all that matters, in the moment. And the notes I have from other clients are that he's very professional to screen-test with, if that helps.'

It didn't help – it didn't help at all.

'Thanks, Nat,' I said anyway, my heart pounding at the thought of seeing him in person again.

For a hair's breadth of a second, it was almost enough to make me want to call the whole thing off. But I had promised myself I'd give this everything I had.

No matter what.

I just didn't know how it would feel, to see him after all this time.

'So, Monday then,' Nat said, clearing her throat. 'I'll email you the details.'

'Looking forward to it.' I was half lying. I still felt like I was about to vomit with nerves – at the thought of seeing Avi, or about the audition, I wasn't sure.

But even still, excitement coursed through my veins, my hand shaking as I hung up the phone.

Shit.

This could be it. This could finally, finally be it.

And in that moment, determination washed over me.

Avi Kumar or no Avi Kumar, I was going to do everything it took to get that part.

I

The first week after the phone call with Nat feels like a daze. She sends me the script and for the next few days I become a woman on a mission – running spreadsheets by day at my desk job at the paper company; reading scripts late into the night in a caffeine-fuelled haze. Surviving on fumes. I've always believed in controlling what you can, in circumstances like these – faced with such an unpredictable career, all I have until the moment in the room is the words on the page. Knowing them as well as I can. Burning them into the furthest reaches of my mind until I can recite them in my sleep. And this audition will be less predictable than most, given the fact that Avi will be there. So I can't afford for there to be any other variables.

This is what my life has been for the last few years: a double life. A life that consists only of work and auditions. Scrunched-up scripts in my bag, on the bus. Calls with Nat. Attempt after attempt to get to the next role, the next part. Trying to do everything I can to reach the impossible dream that I've nurtured carefully since I was a teenager and my parents convinced me to audition for the school play in an effort to encourage me to be more sociable. But then, suddenly, struggling to fit in seemed not to matter so much. Because when I was on stage, being someone else, I felt free.

The Saturday night before my audition the following Monday, I sit in my room, flicking through the book the film is based on.

It's an old detective series, first published when I was a teenager. I haven't opened this particular copy in a while – this is the first one I bought and usually I save it for the memories. Some of the glue in the spine has worn out, so pages have a tendency to fall out, and I had to buy myself a new copy to read and reread. I remember the first time I picked the book up in a shop, intrigued by the lock and key on the cover. Then opening it and becoming obsessed. The books tell the story of Amelia Blackthorn, a female detective determined to forge her own way in the world. People think she's too sharp-edged, and sometimes she doesn't quite fit in. But she always solves the case with a mixture of grit and determination, and not giving a flying fuck what the Victorian men around her think. Together with her assistant, Jackson – the part Avi will be playing – they're like a more modern, female-led Sherlock and Watson, combing the streets of London for unsolved mysteries. The plot of this film would be the first mystery she solves: a series of ritual killings of young women in London, which is traced back to a secret society operating out of a gentlemen's club in Pall Mall.

It's brilliant and pacy, and full of intrigue. A dream role. But that isn't why it's special to me. It's special to me because it's the book – the series – I used to hide under my desk at school and secretly read once I finished my work. No matter where I was, no matter where we moved to or how little I felt I was fitting in, I could turn to its pages. Everything else melting away as soon as I entered the world of Amelia Blackthorn. Strong and brave Amelia. Unapologetically herself. An alter ego I could inhabit when Lara Francis didn't feel like enough. And, still, it's been the book I return to as an adult. When I need guidance, or wisdom. Or just a sense that I can do something.

I pull the book down from the shelf and flick through its opening pages, waiting for that feeling to come over me – to find Amelia's strength of will. Her resolve, her determination.

But instead, something falls out.

I pick it up, thinking it's going to be a page from the book. But it isn't. It's a list – one I made when I was sixteen. At the sixth school I went to. The one I was bullied at.

When I get out of here, I will:
1. *Pursue acting with everything I can, not letting anything get in my way*
2. *Get my first role in a film*
3. *Not care about what anyone thinks (especially Alison)*

I smile at the last one – because it's about my sister. Who did, and still does, have many opinions about my life. Ones I still find it hard not to care about sometimes, even more than a decade later. I scan down the list one more time, a feeling passing through me – of nostalgia, of determination. But before I can dwell on it for too long, there's a knock at my door.

'Hello?' I call out. It'll probably be my flatmate Hannah, who runs the drama club at her school. I feel a twinge of guilt and anticipation; she's been waiting for me to respond to her request for me to come and give a talk to her students about being an actor. A talk I have been avoiding giving her an answer about – because, until this moment, I didn't really feel like an actor. More like someone who was repeatedly trying and failing to achieve a dream that might end up being out of her reach entirely.

It's not Hannah, though. Spencer, my other housemate, pops his head in. He's a musical-theatre actor, and the one who posted the spare-room advert for this flat on Facebook a year ago.

'Tea?' he asks. He's holding two cups.

Spencer is almost as laser-focused as I am, often having to cancel social arrangements to make auditions. We might not have evolved beyond professional allies over the past year, but I feel like he has my back. Sometimes he'll even step in to run lines with me when I need a scene partner for a self-tape. It's nice to live with someone who understands how much you need to give for a career in show business to work.

'Thank you,' I say, a flicker of warmth passing across my chest at the gesture.

'We missed you at fajita night the other night,' he says, and I feel a little bad. Spencer never expects me to attend the monthly flatmate dinners – especially when I have an audition to prepare for. But I said I'd try and make this one, and forgot.

'Sorry,' I reply, gesturing to the script. 'Duty called.'

'Do you have an audition?'

'Oh,' I say. I don't often share details of my auditions with my flatmates, because I don't like to jinx it. But Spencer looks so hopeful for me that it spills out. 'I've got a screen test, actually.'

'Lara, that's amazing!' he says, sitting down on the end of my bed.

I nod, then sit silently for a few seconds as he waits for me to offer more. But nothing comes. Most of my life is spent wondering what to say next. I'm never very good at these kinds of situations. Small talk has always been my sister Alison's strong suit.

'Well,' he says, after I don't offer anything else. My heart clenches a little as he gets up from the bed and moves towards the door. 'Good luck with it.'

'Thank you,' I say, my throat dry.

Spencer nods and steps backwards, shutting the door. And I turn my eyes back down to my script, my heart beating a little faster than it was before. Running my eyes down it, looking at the dialogue I'll be reading – opposite Avi. His character

Jackson's lines seeming to leap off the page in this moment. And in the next second, something has me self-destructively pulling out my phone. Googling Avi Kumar. Pictures pop up: him strolling down the streets of London, him stepping out of a bar in LA.

I wonder if he got what he wanted, I find myself thinking, out of the blue. He always used to say he wanted to be a theatre actor one day. So when he got that first big movie role, I was surprised by how immediately he seemed to acclimatise to that lifestyle. Postcards from LA appearing every couple of weeks with updates about his life. It was a ritual we'd started — when he first moved I asked him to send me the cheesiest postcard he could find and after the first few he just kept going. I'd return the favour, stopping by tourist shops on my way home from the pub. Picking up pictures of London buses, of Big Ben. To remind him of home. His looping handwriting used up all the space available, telling me about award shows. Incredible moments he had on-set. *It's great out here, Lara*, he wrote once. *I can't wait for you to see it too.* It lasted for six months. Until he came home to visit and everything fell apart. And after that, the postcards dried up completely.

I look towards the bed, to the box I've shoved under it. The stacks of postcards in it. Cards I've kept all this time. And I almost reach for it. But I stop myself.

Then I'm in my texts, scrolling through, finding the last conversation I had with him.

Last night was a mistake.

The same flash of hurt piercing my chest when I look at it now as it did back then.

Don't be sentimental, Lara, I think.

But it's hard not to be – because aside from being on stage or in front of a camera, there is only one other time in my life when I remember feeling that free.

And it was when I was with him.

The next day I arrive a few minutes early to meet my sister for lunch. We're meeting at our usual café: a local, around the corner from where she works. I'm a little nervous because I didn't tell her about the screen test, but my mum drew it out of me in a recent phone call and sent a message in the family group chat, wishing me luck tomorrow. So she knows and she'll be furious with me, probably. I always find the balance so tricky with Alison: too much information about my life and she seems to delight in telling me where I'm going wrong, too little and she is hurt that I don't share enough with her.

I decide to do some audition prep to keep my mind off things. But I've etched the lines so entirely into my brain over the last few days that I could probably recite them in my sleep. So in the moments while I'm waiting for her, I might as well attempt something new.

An acting teacher once told me that the best way to get into a character is to pretend that they can only live while you're inhabiting them. And so I close my eyes, breathe, and imagine Amelia coming to life.

I take a deep breath, trying to get into Amelia's character. Stepping into her shoes. Visualising her standing in front of me, walking forwards into her energy.

I sink into it, straightening my spine. Imagining someone pulling a thread from the top of my head to the ceiling. There's her confidence, her ability to walk into the room and own it. The feeling I'm always trying to channel, when I need it. Thinking of her when I need a boost, or when I'm feeling socially out of place. This time, taking that thought a step further – rather than just channelling her energy, I'm trying to become her.

Opening my eyes, immediately I feel more exposed – like people must be looking at me, wondering who I think I am to sit so confidently. But I breathe out, staying with it. With her. The waiter comes over and I order a coffee – delivering the words as if they were a line in a script, smiling as I do. They return my smile, and something lights up in me momentarily.

'Hey!' A voice comes from near the door, a hurricane of bright colour hurtling towards me. And I'm suddenly, horribly embarrassed by what I'm doing. I thud back into my body – Lara, again. My sister, Alison, standing opposite me.

And by the look on her face, I have some explaining to do.

'So you're telling me,' Alison says, hands on her hips, 'that you have a screen test for a film tomorrow, and I'm only hearing about it from Mum and Dad in the family fucking group chat?' Her tone is bright, as per usual, but there's something underneath it. She's pissed off. Still, I can't help but smile when I see her. Alison and I don't always get along, but her energy is addictive, like sunshine – she breezes into every room and lights it up instantly, leaving it brighter than it was before. I've always been jealous of it.

'I didn't want to jinx it,' I say, brushing aside the guilt of not telling her. But this kind of boundary is necessary, because I know she's never understood why I pursued this career. Can't wrap her head around why I'd want to voluntarily subject myself to the same instability we had as kids. And I get it. Our dad lost his job when I was young and our family had moved to five different towns by the time I was eighteen, fracturing our childhood into pieces. She's protective. The trouble is, her protectiveness often comes across as judgement. It's hard, when I'm with her, to feel like I'm doing anything right in my life. Any problems I come to her with are always of my own creation.

'Always so superstitious,' she says, the hurt overlaid by sarcasm, and my heart pinches slightly.

'I'm sorry, Ally,' I say, my voice soft.

'Alright, I'll ignore the fact that I'm fucking furious with you if you tell me all the details now,' Alison says, with a smile that tells me she's softening. 'What is it for?'

I tell her and she smiles broadly, excitement flashing across her face. Excitement that makes me light up momentarily. Because this is the most positive she has seemed about my job in a long time.

'Those books you always had your head buried in as a kid, right?'

'Yes,' I say, smiling at the fact that she sounds still slightly horrified by the fact that I spent so much of my time reading and so little of it doing… well, anything else.

'And who is it with?'

This isn't such an easy question to answer. Alison doesn't know much about Avi. She knows that we crossed paths but she was at university in Sheffield at the time, making friends and finding her feet. And I've never been particularly open with my sister about my love life – or anything, really. Despite her numerous attempts to set me up on dates, to try to get me to have more of a social life. I'm always scared she'll have too much to say. And usually there's nothing to tell anyway.

'Avi Kumar,' I say, after a brief pause.

'Oh, my God,' she says. 'This is huge, Lara!' She starts to freak out, which sends another flicker of joy through me. But then she frowns a little. 'Hang on. Don't you know him?'

I nod, pursing my lips a little. 'I've met him, yeah. We used to work in the pub together.'

'How are you feeling about it?' she asks.

'Losing my fucking mind, honestly,' I reply. Opening up a little.

She smiles, taking a sip of her coffee. I bite my bottom lip, clenching my hand around the handle of the coffee cup.

'Well, you can always get a real job, like mine,' she jokes — misunderstanding my comment — with a wry smile that lets me know she doesn't really mean it. Still, it's hard to avoid the twinge that comes with it, because she doesn't *not* mean it. Alison works as a junior publicist at a PR agency. And I know she thinks her career choices are much more sensible than mine. 'But it'll be a lot less fun than kissing Avi Kumar,' she jokes, softening the blow a little.

'Right, right,' I say, keeping my tone light to cover the emotions underneath. 'I'm a little worried about this one, Ally,' I admit quietly. And, in the next second, I almost start to tell her the full truth about what happened with Avi. It's on the tip of my tongue. To ask what she thinks I should do. Because she's wise. She knows how to deal with people. She'd probably have some good advice.

'Oh, stop worrying,' she says, cutting in. 'Honestly, you worry too much. Always making things into problems when they aren't.'

I find myself taking a deep breath. Because what she's saying isn't entirely true. I worry appropriately about a career she doesn't approve of or understand. And, in any case, her perspective couldn't be further from mine, because her superpower is that she doesn't worry about anything in her life. She's blue skies and sunshine, all the time. Great job, great apartment, great dating life. Everything is always great. When we were kids too – from school to school, she was fine. Always getting the best grades. Always making the most friends. She never had any issues.

But I wasn't so lucky, so blessed with her natural charm. And this was what got me through it – all the school changes and the failed attempts to make friends. All the tense late-night conversations I overheard between my parents. None of it mattered, because I had this: the idea that one day I might be able to turn my dream of acting into a reality. Might be able to take everything I secretly hoped for and finally make it come good. I wish Alison could understand what this means to me. Why I'm so scared. But, as usual, she's ignoring my negative feelings and steering me right back to the positive. To her territory, where nothing is ever wrong. Where if anything in my life is going sideways, it's my fault entirely.

'This is the opportunity of your life,' she continues. 'You've basically put your life on hold for the last five years and now all your work might finally become something viable. The least you can do is enjoy it.'

I smile, covering my feelings.

'I suppose you're right,' I concede. Because she is. I just wish she'd hear me a little more.

'Right,' she says. 'Now, can I tell you about this guy I've met at work? I think he'd be perfect for you…'

2

'Lara Francis?' A voice calls and the sound of stilettos echo in the broad, bright corridor. After I entered the building, I was ushered up to the fifth floor and settled in a surprisingly comfortable chair to wait for my screen test.

This process is a far cry from the usual audition scene. I'm usually crammed into a hot, overcrowded room full of women who look a bit like me. Who I have to make a conscious effort not to compare myself to unfavourably.

But here, there's no need to worry about any of that. There's just me and sunlight streaming through a window, a view of London in the distance. It's peaceful and the lack of distractions gives me enough time to take a few meditative breaths, my eyes fixed on the skyline as the heels approach.

I tear my eyes from the window to find a small, sharply dressed woman about my age holding a clipboard. Her expression is not unkind, but there's a steel in her gaze that tells me she means business. This industry isn't just brutal for the actors; to make it in any capacity, you have to have unshakeable nerves. Or a relative in the industry – that always helps.

She leads me down the corridor to a door marked Screen Test Room 1. I hardly have time to wonder where Room 2 might be – and who might be in it – before she opens the door and shows me through. I thought I was calm from doing meditation breaths, but I'm not. Adrenaline pulses through me as the door swings shut and I come face to face with 6ft 2 of messy dark hair, a chiselled jawline and dark brown eyes that used to crease at the edges when I told a bad joke.

Shit.

Just before the nausea hits, I manage to glimpse that he looks a little more slick than he used to. Smooth. Polished. As professional as the handshake he's now extending to me.

'Lara,' he says, his voice turning over my name as if it's alien to him. As if he hadn't called it a hundred times across the bar.

'It's a pleasure to meet you,' he continues. The nausea deepens, edged with a twinge of anger and hurt. It makes sense that he'd try to hide the fact that we've met before. He has a new life now – and he made it very clear he didn't want me in it. When he kissed me at the party, then told me it was a mistake. When he left and didn't come back. Our contact, which was a thread of light in my life, even after he moved to LA, dissipating entirely overnight.

Even still, disappointment and confusion cloud my vision at his words.

I grasp his hand, doing my best to shake it firmly.

'It's a pleasure to meet you too, Avi,' I echo. Something flashes in his gaze for a fraction of a second – something that looks like warmth. Familiarity. It throws me completely.

I blink, frozen, my hand still clutching his.

'Lara, thank you so much for coming in today,' a voice from my left says, a throat clearing gently, and I realise how stupid I'm being.

The table of producers and casting directors should've been my first port of call, but I was so distracted by Avi that I forgot they were there. I notice the director isn't present and baulk as I approach. Alessandro D'Arienzo is a huge deal in

Hollywood; he's known for his wide range, from artistic Italian-language horror films to a credit on one of the most recent DC movies. His vision is dark and often brilliant. But, before the screen test, I realised that despite knowing his name, I had no idea what he looked like. So I frantically searched for photos of him online, to avoid introducing myself to the wrong person. But he's not here. I take a breath, a light panic rippling through me. Perhaps he's in Screen Test Room 2 with another actor. But then Avi Kumar is in here, with me.

Calm down, Lara, I think to myself as I turn away from Avi and cross the room to shake their hands. A row of people who are about to decide my future, but who aren't registering at all on the Richter scale of my nervous system compared to the man behind me.

'Alessandro sends his apologies,' the producer says. 'He was held up in Italy, so we'll be handling the screen test today and he'll be reviewing the tapes.'

I swallow. This footage is all the director will have to make the decision that could impact the rest of my life. I hoped to at least be able to make a good impression in person.

A flash of nerves arrives that's so overwhelming I almost want to run. This is suddenly feeling incredibly, inescapably real.

'Right,' the casting director says, getting up from the table and moving us to our marks. My hand shakes as I take the script from him. 'We'll start with our first scene for the day, halfway through their first meeting. Could you please read from page two to page seven?'

I nod, swallowing as I look down at the script and try to focus my gaze.

'Sure,' Avi says, his tone smooth. His voice makes me jump and I look up, his eye catching mine. I look quickly back down at the script.

Channel it, Lara, I say to myself as the producer returns to his table. He is just any other actor. *You know these lines. You know this part. You are Amelia.*

You've got this.

At the book's opening, Amelia comes into some inheritance money, decides to start her own detective agency and receives her first case from one of the victim's sisters. Realising there might be a connection with the upper echelons of society, Amelia drafts in Jackson Whitfield – an American socialite who formerly courted her – to help her infiltrate the secret society without arousing suspicion. This dialogue, where she tries to persuade him to help her, is their first conversation.

'Okay, and go,' the producer says and my head snaps upwards again.

'Amelia.' Avi starts the scene.

Miraculously, a calm washes over me as I take my cue. 'Jackson, I have a proposal for you…'

For the length of a scene, I'm able to detach myself entirely from the fact that I'm currently in the room with Avi and disappear into the character. The feeling is comforting and familiar, the edges of myself blurring into the background as I sink into Amelia. This is what I've always loved about acting: its detachment from reality. The possibilities it opens up to live a thousand lives other than your own. The possibilities it's opening up, in this moment, to pretend the man in front of me doesn't make me want to run out of this room and never come back.

And there's a comfort in doing this with Avi. Our rapport is smooth, trading lines like we've been doing it for years, falling back into our old rhythm when we'd practise for auditions in the empty theatre above the pub after closing time. It's… easy.

Alarmingly easy.

The feeling comes out of nowhere and jolts me out of character briefly. Avi falters, watching as I grasp for the next line. The perfection of his performance slipping for the first time since I entered this room. His expression replaced by concern, which only serves to rattle me further.

'Sorry,' I murmur, glancing over at the table that feels suddenly like a courtroom jury, before returning my gaze to the script as a blush of mortification creeps across my cheeks.

'That's okay,' one of the casting directors says, standing up, and for one horrible second I think I might've messed it all up.

But he stays where he is, folding his arms and looking between Avi and me with some interest.

'I'd like to move on to one of our later scenes now,' he says, clearing his throat. 'The one in the pub.'

Oh, shit. Avi's eyes flash to mine and I can see he's caught the meaning too: a romantic scene, in a pub. Avi's character and mine are arguing, then they almost kiss – pressed together, lingering for a few moments. Its setting and context are so ironic it would almost be funny if I didn't already feel like I might vomit. I swallow, my throat suddenly bone dry.

The casting director's eyes flick to the clock above the door. 'If you're not comfortable—'

'I am.' I avoid Avi's gaze. 'It's fine.'

The casting director says nothing, just gestures for us to start, and we flick through our scripts to the right page, the silence almost unbearable.

Once we've oriented ourselves, we start the scene.

'You're so thick-headed,' I say, my voice breaking a little – but it works, for the scene. Amelia has reached a point of despair with Jackson, which pretty much reflects what I'm feeling right now. 'You always act before you think.'

I look up at Avi; his eyes are trained on me. There's a question in them, and I can't tell if it's the part he's playing or if it's the real him coming through (if I even know who that is any more). Checking I'm okay with this.

My heart kicks.

'You know you've always liked that about me, Amelia,' he says.

A rush of feeling warms my skin and I nod, infinitesimally.

'Fine,' I say, dropping my hand that's holding the script. Surrendering to the scene, to the moment. 'I can't deny that your impulsiveness intrigues me.' I take a breath, stemming the tide that's telling me that the man in front of me is not his character, but someone else.

He takes a tentative step towards me and a shiver runs down my spine.

Shit. This is happening. This is actually happening.

He winds his arm around my waist, my skin coming alive at his touch. His hand clenches around the fabric of my shirt and it's a struggle not to gasp aloud. Because this isn't the first time he's touched me like this. And the last time he did…

But I can't think about that right now.

He leans down and delivers his next line, his voice low.

'I know you, Amelia Blackthorn,' he says, and my breath catches in my throat.

For a moment, I almost forget myself.

The line comes out stuttering, half-garbled.

'D-do you?' I ask.

And that's his cue; he leans in. Filled suddenly with memories from before – unwanted ones, crowding my consciousness – I reflexively take a step back, then try to right myself. But my heel gets caught on something. A wire or a piece of raised carpet. I don't have time to check and panic rushes through my limbs.

I lean towards him, tilting my face upwards. Trying to hold myself at a semi-natural-looking angle. But the carpet gets the best of me and I stumble.

Fuck.

Avi catches me before I can fall any further, holding me in mid-air while embarrassment moves through my every cell. And I look up at him, our eyes meeting. Something flashing through his gaze as his hand clenches around my waist that makes my heart thud. Some sense of who he was before – the person I'm in the room with now melting from a Hollywood star down to the person I knew. Or thought I did.

'Cut!' The casting director shouts and the breath rushes out of my lungs.

Avi sets me right and his hand drops from my waist, leaving a ghost of warmth, and a sense of crashing disappointment, as he steps away.

Oh, my God. Have I lost my mind?

The casting director is standing in the same spot on the other side of the room, arms still folded, expression as unreadable as before. I hardly dare to look at Avi, my heart is beating so hard.

'Thank you very much for your time, Lara,' the casting director says, finally, after a beat of silence.

He returns to his previous position behind the desk and shuffles some papers, then sits down, looking up at me as he does so.

'We'll be in touch,' he says, by way of dismissal.

I swallow and manage to speak, thanking them for having me and saying some other things I'm not fully aware of. My focus is suddenly on getting out of this room as fast as possible.

I glance at Avi, the nausea I felt at the beginning of this audition rising up suddenly – realising the implications of this, of what just happened. I feel like I'm being pulled in two directions: half of me is desperate never to see him again, the other half already reliving how it felt to have his hand on my waist. Even now, after all this time, I still can't keep it together around him.

And faced with the opportunity of a lifetime, I might've messed it all up. There's no way that went well.

I manage a nod in his direction and burst from the room.

I'm barely into the corridor, my heart hammering. Now that I no longer have to stay professional for the audition, it's like a dam has broken. Everything from before is coming back all at once:

hurt; confusion; sadness; a headache that feels like it's going to split my skull in two. *What have I done?*

Before I can make it to the lift, a voice calls out. 'Lara!'

I whip round, my heart thudding.

The flannel shirt he usually wore might be gone, replaced instead by a sharp tailored suit, but everything else is still there: the slight hunch of his shoulders, the half-smile that used to show me he was nervous or having an off day.

He runs a hand through his hair.

'It…' He looks momentarily as unhinged as I feel. 'It's good to see you,' he finally says, then swallows, his Adam's apple bobbing.

I falter for a second, confused. Because those are the last words I ever expected him to say.

'You were great in there,' he continues.

'I don't think I was,' I say, wanting this conversation to end but feeling bound by politeness not to end it too quickly. 'But… thanks?'

'You were,' he replies, and something knots in my chest. 'I've…' He clears his throat. 'I've been thinking about you a lot. Hoping I'd see you.'

Okay, now I literally have no idea what he's talking about. And something comes out – something angry. Frustrated. Because he has had every opportunity to try to see me in the last few years and he hasn't done anything about it.

I frown. 'Where?' I ask, before I can stop myself.

'What?' he asks.

I let out a breath. 'Where were you hoping you'd see me?'

'I don't know.' He shrugs. 'Around?'

'Around,' I say. 'Right.' *Because I work in a paper company, in London. And you live in LA and spend most of your life on film sets.*

'Alright,' he says. 'Point taken. Maybe it's not that likely we'd have run into each other. But… I'm glad to see you today. How have you been?'

I close my eyes, the feelings taking over. I was willing to do this dance for a few minutes, to be polite. But it hurts now. And, especially given how the audition went, I really just need to go home and sleep.

'Fine,' I say. 'I've been fine. Look, I really have to—'

'I've missed you,' he says. And his voice sounds so sincere that it almost breaks me.

Then that pain twists into something else. Because there are a few gaps between where he is now and how we left things.

'Look,' I say, my voice shaking. Trying to keep my cool. 'Avi. I really need to get home. And I really don't want to talk about this right now. Besides, you haven't spoken to me in three years. I got the message. Loud and clear.'

You might be famous now and everyone might fall over themselves to make your life easier. But for me, nothing has changed. You're still the person who hurt me.

He lets out a long breath.

'It's not because I'm…' He starts, then stops himself. 'Look, I fucked up,' he says, putting his hands in his pockets. 'I know that. But it's true, I have missed you. I-I'm just trying to be honest. I don't know what else you want me to say.'

Indignation flames into anger. There are a million other things he could've said to repair things between us. But instead he chose to ignore me for three years. To treat our friendship like it never happened in the first place.

'Sorry I haven't spoken to you in three years? Sorry our friendship meant so little to me that as soon as I settled into my new life in LA and got famous, I decided to cut you out of it? Sorry I just stopped talking to you without warning? Any of those would've worked just fine. The ball was in your court, Avi. You're the one who dropped it. And so you don't get to come here and tell me you've missed me and expect that to fix everything.'

'I think there's been a misunderstanding—'

'You hurt me, Avi,' I say.

'Lara—'

'And it could not be less ideal that I have to read opposite you for this part, and I'm sure you'd also rather be here with literally anyone else. But,' he looks over my shoulder at something and it seems like he's about to interrupt me again, but I'm on such a roll I don't care. I need to get this out, 'this is my chance now too. And I love Amelia more than anything. I've dreamed about playing her since I was a child. Since I dreamed about acting at all. So I respect that you're here under contractual obligations. But this is it for me. There's nothing else I want more than this. Nothing else I've ever wanted more than this. And all I'm asking is that you show me the same respect. Give me some space to actually take this chance. I think I deserve that, don't you?'

He nods slowly, looking more than a little uncomfortable as I finish my speech, my voice shaking. But I feel good about it – I've said my piece. And then I see his gaze drifting up, over my shoulder again.

I turn slowly, a spike of fear running down my spine, to see that one of the producers has followed us into the corridor. *Fuck.*

'Um…' they say, looking serious. 'Sorry to interrupt. But you left your scarf in the room, Miss Francis.'

I walk over to them, a flush colouring my face, embarrassment rippling through every fibre of my being. *Oh, my God.* I catch a glimpse through the open door of a row of faces that definitely just heard at least the tail end of me losing my cool at Avi. It's the most unprofessional thing I've ever done, letting my emotions overtake me like this in front of a potential employer. Letting my personal life into the audition room – or outside of it, at least. Conversations like that aren't meant to be held in corridors right next to audition rooms. They're private, contained. You're supposed to be a blank slate at an audition. Careful, controlled – except when you're acting the part. And you're definitely not supposed to do anything that might make them think you'll be difficult to work with on-set.

Like, for example, yell at a potential co-star.

Like, for example, lay all your cards on the table about how desperate you are for a role.

Fuck.

3

I spend the next three days going back and forth from the paper company, and hiding from my flatmates in my room. I'm so embarrassed about how I acted at the audition I can't handle even thinking about it, let alone telling anyone. And so I avoid my sister's texts asking whether I've heard back and ignore my parents' calls.

And, when I'm really feeling like torturing myself, I read my Amelia Blackthorn books. Thumbing the pages I folded over as a kid, when she said something particularly brilliant. The ones I've returned to time and time again as an adult. But they don't give me the comfort they usually do. Instead, I feel sad – like I've neither done justice to myself or to my love for Amelia.

On the third day, while at work, my phone rings. I rummage as discreetly as I can through my bag to find my phone and see Nat's caller ID on the screen.

'Shit,' I exclaim, causing my colleague Peter, who sits opposite me, to pop his head over the top of the wall separating our desks, like a displeased badger. He peers at me through his glasses, frowning lightly at the disturbance.

'Spilt my tea,' I mouth, and his head pops back down.

'Nat?' I answer quietly, getting up so fast I knock a stapler off the desk, causing Peter to pop his head up again, the frown a little deeper this time.

'Sorry,' I whisper to him, holding the phone away from my ear and starting towards the doors.

'Are you somewhere quiet?' Nat asks, as I rush at breakneck speed through the office.

'I will be in approximately three, two...' I push open the glass doors of the office and spill out into the stairwell, pushing the door closed behind me and letting out a long breath.

'One,' I say.

'Okay,' she says. I frown a little at her tone – it's almost the gentle, smooth voice she deploys to deliver rejection. But there's something behind it that's causing her voice to quiver ever so slightly.

'They loved you, Lara,' she says, joy flowing down the line.

'What?' I ask, my entire body going numb. I've gone through every emotion in the last few days, except this one. Hope. I was so sure I'd messed it up.

'That's right,' she says, sounding more proud of me than ever before. And my heart soars momentarily. 'You nailed it.' *Oh, my God.*

She starts talking about the next steps in the process. Another screen test. 'Nothing's secure yet,' she says. 'But it's looking really good. As you know, they'll be on a tight schedule due to the leads dropping out. You'll basically be thrown in at the deep end, straight into filming. Learning the stunts as you go, rather than beforehand. Everything woven into the six-week shoot. But I've assured them you're a true professional, that you can handle it.'

'I'm so happy for you, Lara,' she continues. 'You've worked so hard for this.'

And this – this certainty, this praise – is what sends me over the edge.

'I don't know if I can do this, Nat,' I blurt out, my hand shaking. I feel like I have to tell her about Avi, before this goes any further. Especially given the level of trust they'll be showing in me. It seems crazy to me that they even want to see me again — that they'd be willing to cast a complete unknown on such short notice.

'What?' Nat asks, the joy in her voice grinding to a halt.

'The history between Avi and me,' I say. 'It's complicated. We…' I pause, trying to figure out how to word it.

'We were friends, for a while. Maybe more. And things didn't end well between us. I…' I hesitate, the memory coming back. The text that broke my heart. The long months of silence afterwards. 'I already lost it at him in the corridor at the first screen test. I'm honestly surprised they're even interested after that.'

Nat takes a breath, processing my words. 'Well,' she says slowly. 'I wasn't going to share this with you, but the notes they gave me were that you were very passionate and they liked your chemistry with Avi. The altercation in the corridor was mentioned as an indicator of your shared chemistry.'

Oh, my God, I think. *What?*
Were they in a different corridor?

'I just…' I let out a breath. 'I feel like I have to tell you the full story—'

'Lara,' she says, taking a deep breath. 'I understand you have some concerns. And they make sense – they do. But I don't think your history with this person is what's important right now. Honestly, I think you need to find a way to put it behind you and just focus on the role. I know how much this part means to you, and getting it could be the start of incredible things for you.'

I close my eyes, trying to imagine a reality where I can put the past with Avi firmly behind me and take a step into a new future. Where I can remain in command of my emotions and channel them into a version of Amelia that's fiery. That inspires people. Be a version of myself that I've always wanted to be. That might, now, be there for the taking.

'They want to see you again this Friday, for an on-set screen test. Just a formality, really. They're down to two: you and Sienna Marsh.'

Oh, shit. My heart slams against my chest when I hear that name. Because I've heard it before, a million times. And to hear it in this context is nothing short of insane. The daughter of director Nicholas Marsh and it-girl-of-the-90s Georgina Staves, Sienna March is the golden child of Hollywood. Famous since before she could walk, she's had a lucrative modelling career – following in her mother's footsteps – and recently displayed her talents as an actor too. Her breakout role in a Marvel movie earlier this year made enough of a splash that she was tipped for a SAG award.

In addition to her many accolades, she is also known for being Avi's on-again, off-again girlfriend. According to the tabloids, currently very much *on*. A wave of nausea moves through me at the thought.

Because it would be a PR dream to cast the two of them in this movie – a perfectly smooth solution, especially given the other leads have already dropped out and probably compromised the PR of the film. And she'd be the much clearer choice: experienced, already in possession of a profile. And yet somehow, after everything, I'm still in the running. I blink, coming back to reality. To the sound of Nat's voice.

'They need an answer asap, so could you park your concerns for a few days and go to that screen test? Can you do that for me at least?'

Fuck.

I want to hesitate, to put the brakes on this. But something stops me. Because this is, potentially, the role of a lifetime. And some fire somewhere in me is still burning, set alight even further by what she's just said. This is between me and Sienna Marsh. And she's living the life I've always dreamed of already. A life of glittering success. Part after part that I'd have dreamed of getting as a child. And something about being up against her is making it feel real – like it might be more in reach for me.

That speech I gave to Avi still holds true – that this part is everything I've ever wanted. And I'd be stupid not to give myself the chance I've worked towards for so long.

'Come on, Lara,' she says. 'Just one more screen test? Alessandro wants to talk to you about your vision for the role too. Even if it doesn't work out – and you know I'm hoping it will – just to get that far and have that conversation could be a great experience for you.'

Right, I think. *It's just one screen test.* And a conversation with the director about a role I've been preparing for my entire life. No big deal. Except it is – a huge one. I have to take this chance.

Even if the thought of seeing Avi again makes me feel like I'm on fire.

'Okay,' I reply, resolve moving through me. 'I'll do it.'

'Excellent,' she says, sounding relieved.

A week later, after spending several days reading and re-reading the script and preparing for the conversation with Alessandro like my life depends on it, I head over to the studio where my next screen test will be happening. By the time I arrive, I'm regretting my choice of transport. I booked an Uber to save time but now I'm feeling carsick, and there was so much rush hour traffic that I'm barely five minutes ahead of my call time, and I was asked to arrive at minimum fifteen minutes early. Which means, by Hollywood terms, I'm half an hour late.

We pull into the lot – a huge car park with a large grey building across from it. It feels… strangely unassuming, given what I know is happening inside. Like it could be a warehouse. Still, it's my first time at a big studio, so my heart is racing. The most I've ever done have been adverts, and this place has played host to blockbusters with bigger budgets than I can even fathom. The people who have walked across this car park before me must be some of the most well-known names in the industry, a thought that has me feeling a little weak at the knees.

I cross the car park quickly and enter through the small blue door to the right specified in Nat's email. The lot is huge, though, and I'm immediately lost, swallowed by its corridors and staircases. But I manage after a few minutes of wandering to find the right desk, and a receptionist signs me in and passes me into the care of a waiting runner, who ushers me further into the lot. As I follow her down the long corridors, pushing open doors that say *Auditions in Progress: Do Not Enter*, the reality of what's happening starts to sink in. I'm at the final stage of an audition for my dream role.

The runner leads me to a door marked *Green Room*, holding it open for me. I'm hoping for a moment alone, to centre myself. To try to get my head around what I'm about to do.

But as I walk in, I see Avi.

He looks up, his face impassive.

'Hi,' I say. He nods.

'They should be coming to call us through in a minute,' he says, his voice neutral, and then looks back down at his script.

An awkward silence falls between us and I find myself wanting to break it. Because I can't handle this tension, not when I'm about to be running lines with the man. And while I did lose my cool at him before, some remorse is coming through now. Not for how I spoke to him – if we were in any other context, I'd have stood by what I said. But because I did it in the wrong place, at the wrong time.

I might still be angry. And he might have hurt me, badly.

But that doesn't mean I can't own my actions.

'I'm...' I will myself to say it. 'I'm sorry about how I behaved. At our last audition. It was unprofessional.'

He falters for a second and my throat tightens. His expression changes and if I didn't know any better, I'd think he looked a little sad.

'Before we do this...' he says, under his breath, and my heart thuds. 'I want to apologise too. For the other day.'

But then he pauses, his face falling. Staring at his script for a second.

'For all of it.' He looks up at me, his eyes burning with remorse. His expression is so sincere, I almost want to look away. 'All of it, Lara – I was awful and stupid, and I'm sorry. For what I did back then and for not being more aware of how it would have affected you. I shouldn't have come in expecting everything to be fine.'

I nod, feeling suddenly a little light-headed.

'Thank you,' I reply.

'I mean it, Lara,' he says. 'And I hate this as much as you do. I have always – only – wanted you to succeed. You can hate me for everything else. But you have to know that.'

And my chest pinches as he says it. Because somewhere, deep down, some part of me wants to believe that what he's saying is true.

But his feelings about my success can't be relevant to me right now. Because if they are, then I have to let in everything else too. And I can't do that. It seeped through, last time, and almost ruined everything.

I hesitate for a moment. Waiting for it to pass. Waiting to know what to say next.

But before I can say anything, a runner comes to take us to set.

The runner leads us down the corridor to the sound stage. And when she pushes the door open, I have to stifle a gasp. It's beautiful, done up to look like a Victorian drawing room. The walls painted a soft blue. Green velvet chairs arranged around an old fireplace. Paintings hanging on the wall, of Avi's character Jackson's family. Most of Amelia and Jackson's meetings happen in his stately home in London – the very room they've recreated here.

I stand staring at it for a moment, speechless. It's just how I imagined it when I was reading the book. Whoever designed this set really paid attention, maybe even loves the books as much as I do. There's a sense of magic here.

A short man stands about three metres away from us, his head turned away in serious conversation with one of the camera operators. From his stature and demeanour, I gather that it's Alessandro D'Arienzo. The film's director. The man who holds my future in his hands. I falter for a second as we come to a stop in front of him. He turns around and I fight the urge to fix my appearance. We're not in costume today, but we've been asked to come in clothes as reminiscent of the time as we can, so I'm wearing a button-down blouse with a pointed collar, which I've tucked into a long silk skirt that I borrowed from Alison. I ironed them both this morning but didn't do a very good job. I look down and spot a crease.

Keep your cool, Lara, I think.

He greets Avi first with warmth, pulling him into a hug. They've done a few films together already. Must have spent a lot of time together by now. My fingers move to the edge of the crease, about to smooth it out. I'm nervous. Given I've already pretty much told them all how much I want the part, I need to seem as calm and un-desperate as I can today. *You want them to come to you*, is the advice Nat always gives me. *Go in there with respect, but as if you've already got the part – as if they're lucky to have you in the room with them too.* Alessandro looks over to me and his face brightens. It's similar to the effect that Alison has, like I'm suddenly in the middle of raging sunlight. *Oh, my God*, I think suddenly. *I can't believe I'm actually here.* I move my hand behind my back and smile – and this time, it comes naturally.

'Lara,' he says, his Italian accent bringing a musicality to my name. 'È un piacere conoscerti.' He grasps my hand and shakes it firmly. 'You will forgive my English, per favore. But, my dear…' He steps back, still holding my hand, as if to appraise me further, his face softening as he does. 'Sei una visione – you are a vision.'

Something lights up in my chest as he says it. And I'm suddenly, immensely grateful to be here. Because even if this goes no further – even if I don't get the part – meeting Alessandro will have been one of my top-ten life experiences.

'Now, are you ready?' he says. I look up at him, but my gaze flicks to Avi.

No, I think reflexively, even as the rest of my body screams *Yes*. I manage a nod.

'So then,' Alessandro says, with a flourish. 'We will begin.'

I walk towards my mark, my steps uneven. It's a little odd to be on such a beautiful set in my comparably modern clothes – I feel like I should, at the very least, be wearing a corset. But costume-fitted screen tests are unheard of, because there's no feasible way they'd have a guaranteed store of costumes that would fit a given actor. I can hear Avi behind me and I do my best to breathe, not focusing too much on his presence. When we reach our marks, I turn my eyes to Alessandro – he's busy talking to someone else. And then I look over at Avi. His gaze is trained directly on me.

'Okay,' Alessandro says, finishing his conversation. 'We will start with the scenes that we did not do in the first test. Page seventy-five to start.'

There's a script to the side in case I need it – but I don't. I know this like the back of my hand by now. Avi nods too. And Alessandro steps back.

'Lara, if you please. Could you move a little closer to him?'

Oh, God, I think. But I nod.

'Of course,' I say, taking a smooth step forwards. No carpet catching my foot this time. I have a sudden feeling as if I'm coming out of my body, watching myself from a distance. The lights overhead suddenly feel a little brighter than they did before.

But before I can say anything else, before I can truly realise what's happening, Alessandro calls, 'Action!', his voice ringing out across the set.

I find the zone, feeling my edges melt away. Locating Amelia's strength and presence even more immediately than I did in the last audition. I fall into it, letting it take over.

'You're impossible.' Avi begins and I roll my eyes reflexively, channelling some of my anger towards him from the other day.

'Really?' My tone is laced with derision. We're arguing about the case. Avi's character is defensive — one of the prime suspects is a friend of his, a member of the gentlemen's club Jackson frequents who appears to be hiding a ring of ritual killings.

'I thought you were better than this, Jackson,' I say. 'Honestly, I thought you were a man of integrity.'

And something else lights up inside me now: hurt, alongside the anger I'm channelling. Hurt that surprises me, in the moment. Because I thought that after our conversation in the green room earlier, I'd be able to put all this aside, at least for the time being. But it's still there. I ignore it, doing my best to stay present. Amelia is angry in this moment, but she isn't hurt – not yet. The hurt coming up now is mine alone.

'I am,' Avi replies. There's a flash of him beneath his character too.

'Someone with integrity wouldn't behave the way you're behaving right now,' I say. 'You're supposed to trust me. To value my opinion. I thought we were partners.'

'I thought so too,' he says. 'But you know, Amelia – trust goes both ways.'

'Only when it's earned.' I deliver the line firmly, but can't stop my voice from shaking a little. *Shit*, I think. I let some of my own emotion seep through and I'm not sure how well it came across. Amelia is supposed to be strong in this moment. Not sad, not hurt. *Come on, Lara. Get it together.*

'Cut!' Alessandro shouts, his expression hard to decipher. Avi slips out of character, his expression softening from heated into something cooler, more neutral. I breathe slowly, coming back to reality. Determination rippling through me to get it right next time.

We run through the scene a few more times, each take feeling a little more natural than the last. After the slight stumble in the first take, I manage to get a hold on the hurt that keeps surging up unexpectedly, harnessing it for the chemistry of the scene. Channeling it into Amelia's indignance, her fire. Trying not to look too closely at Avi between takes in case it throws me off again.

Alessandro gives me some notes, better than I've ever had, and it's honestly one of the coolest experiences. We talk through my tone and the spirit he wants me to get across in each take. It feels electric, exciting. Trying an angrier version, then a softer one. Avi adapting deftly to each shift – Alessandro barely acknowledging or directing him. Because he already has his part and it's clear that Alessandro trusts him. I'm the one on the line here. But, tentatively, I start to wonder if it might actually be going well. Alessandro looks pleased and the scene is developing in exactly the direction he seems to want it to.

And so when he calls a break and I finally have a moment with my thoughts, a feeling occurs to me – a sense of belonging. Of rightness. It startles me. Because I can't get ahead of myself. Because Sienna is still in the mix. Because I don't know whether this ease I'm feeling with Avi is temporary. Whether I'm even right for this part. Whether I'll decide in the end to voice my concerns about working with Avi. But even still it persists, slowly bubbling into excitement. I stay with it for a few moments while Avi grabs a drink and Alessandro talks to the first assistant director about something. His gaze passes over me a few times in a way that makes my heart thump. Whatever the next scene he's about to call is, I'm ready. In this moment, I want to do everything I can to win this man's approval.

A runner approaches us and I wait for him to tell us what we'll be doing next.

But he simply spreads his hands, his expression carefully measured. My heart kicks.

'It seems,' he says, 'that Alessandro has seen enough for today.'

And through all my earlier feelings, my heart sinks like a stone.

What?

I deflate at his words, worry stuttering through me. We've only done one scene and while I took Alessandro's direction just fine, I was hoping to show my range. To have more of a chance to prove myself. To – despite the person standing opposite me – have more of an opportunity to enjoy this experience on a giant set, which might well be my last. But it seems we're dismissed and from the look on Avi's face, it's final. He smiles at me and shrugs, turning to pick up his script off the nearby table.

'You did great,' he says quietly. 'Don't worry about Alessandro – he just likes a short audition sometimes. It doesn't mean anything.'

I freeze for a second, lost for words, but then he gestures as if he's about to go to the green room. I start to move too, ready to follow him. But before I can, the runner – who has been conversing with Alessandro for the last few moments – rushes over to me.

'Alessandro would like to talk to you, Lara,' he says. 'Before you go.'

He looks up at Avi.

'Alone,' he clarifies. A breath rushes out of me, remembering suddenly the brief. A screen test and a conversation. The conversation I've been preparing for for the last few days, but which flew out of my mind during the nerves of the last half hour. I've been making notes in a purple notebook that I didn't bring with me today because I've already memorised them. My vision for Amelia. My connection to the character. Everything scrawled in there, organised into a neat argument for how I'd want the role to look if I played her.

And if he still wants to have the conversation, that means I still have a shot.

I follow the runner down a short corridor into a small, windowless room outside the sound stage where Alessandro is waiting, sitting in a chair. I suddenly feel like I'm in a police station, about to be interrogated. I walk towards him, sitting down in the chair opposite him. A grey plastic table between us.

'Now,' he says, placing his hands on the table enthusiastically. 'I wanted to thank you for coming today. And I wanted to talk to you about your vision for this role.'

I smile, waiting for the notes I've memorised to materialise in my mind. But they don't — it's suddenly, horribly blank.

'Of course.' I try to buy myself a little time. 'It was my pleasure.' He smiles and looks at me expectantly. I knot my hands in my lap. 'And, um…' I falter. 'Amelia is…' I pause again, trying to find the right words. To express the magnitude of this role, for me. 'She's very important to me. She's a character I have loved for a long time.' And I search, again, for the speech I'd prepared. The professional vision I honed, right for the marketing of the film. Based on my knowledge of her character. But it's not there.

He nods. 'And when did you first experience this love for her?' he says simply. His tone kind.

'I'm sorry?' I ask, not sure I've heard right. Because we're not here to talk about me – we're here to talk about her. I might have a personal connection to her in my mind, but I wasn't expecting him to care about that. Only how much respect I have for the role.

'This love you have for Amelia,' he says. 'I would like to hear about it. If you wouldn't mind.'

I close my eyes, my throat drying up a little. His kindness making me emotional. But the notes I have are gone, completely, from my mind. And he's looking at me with such an open expression that I find myself wanting to answer him honestly.

'I started reading the books when I was a teenager,' I say, my voice shaking a little. 'I was…' I hesitate, unsure how vulnerable to be, but a *fuck it* instinct comes over me. 'My dad lost his job when I was a child and we had to move schools a few times. I always struggled with new people and socialising; people didn't really warm to me at school. Still don't, actually – that's more my sister's territory.' I flinch as I say the last bit, wondering if I've overshared. *Well done, Lara, tell him you're a social recluse, why don't you*. But his expression doesn't change, his eyes still kind, still fixed on me.

He nods slowly. 'Yes,' he says. 'Us creatives – I fear this is often the way. We can be... how do you say it? Lone wolves.'

I nod, surprised and touched by his words. Finding a little more confidence, I continue.

'Once I found acting, I sort of stopped caring about all that stuff. Before acting, though, I had Amelia. She was...' I pause, because this part feels all kinds of embarrassing. Like I'm a twelve-year-old again, talking about how much I love my favourite book. Not a professional actress trying for a role. But I've already said so much, I might as well go on. 'She was everything I wanted to be. When people had problems, she fixed them. When...' I blink, hardly daring to believe I'm actually saying these words out loud. 'When she walked into a room, people took notice, you know? And I've accepted that that'll probably never happen for me. That my talents lie elsewhere. But she somehow even made me feel okay about that. Like, whenever I needed a little strength, I could draw on it from her.'

I finish, folding my hands together to stop them from shaking. Alessandro is quiet for a few seconds. I feel exposed, suddenly silly, for sharing so much of my life with him.

'Thank you,' he says. 'For sharing, Lara. I appreciate your honesty.'

He looks pensive for a second and I wait for him to say something else. But he doesn't. He just smiles, then stands and walks over to the door.

'I will be in touch soon,' he says, opening the door for me to leave.

4

When I get home that evening, Alison FaceTimes me from an Uber on her way to meet some friends for drinks. She's made up, wearing her signature hoop earrings. Looking, as always, absolutely stunning. Her blonde hair framing her face perfectly on the screen. I remember as I answer that I'm wearing her cardigan and shrug it slightly off my shoulders – I stole it from her wardrobe a few years ago and have successfully hidden it until now. I wore it today as a good-luck charm; even though she's been less than supportive of my career, something in me wanted to have a piece of her with me today. To channel some of her confidence.

'Hey, bitch,' she says, clearly already a few drinks in. 'Just calling to see how your audition went today.'

I bite my lip, not sure how much to tell her. Not sure, really, if I know how well it went to begin with – I'm still a little shell-shocked by the whole thing.

'I think it was okay,' I say. 'Hard to tell, really.'

'I'm sure you did great,' she says. 'You are great.' And my heart warms. Such praise from Alison is rare.

'Of course,' she continues. 'All those years shut away in your room have to count for something, right?'

There it is, I think. I bite the inside of my lip as she says it. She squints, as if she's looking at the screen. 'Is that my cardigan?' she asks.

'No,' I say, shrugging it further down my shoulders. She looks more closely and I struggle to shove the last bit of yellow fabric off screen.

'Lara!' she snaps. 'I've been looking for that for ages.'

'I promise it's mine,' I lie.

'Liar.' She laughs, seeing through me straight away. 'It looks better on you anyway. But it had better be back in my wardrobe at Mum and Dad's next time I'm there or I'll hunt you down. Why don't you come for drinks with me and my friends tonight? We could celebrate your audition.'

'I'm okay, thanks, Al,' I say. Her offer is nice, but I'm not sure I have anything to celebrate right now – I don't want to get ahead of myself. 'You have a good time.'

'Boringggg,' she drawls. 'And I will.' She blows me a kiss. 'Love you. Tell me as soon as you hear, okay?'

'I will,' I reply, blowing her a kiss back.

Nat calls me the next morning and asks me to come in. As I climb the stairs to her office, I can feel my throat dry up. I lied to my boss about a doctor's appointment for probably the millionth time since starting my job at the paper company, and felt awful for how easily he bought it.

I have no idea if Nat's going to have feedback for me. I have no clue what I'm walking into. And I've been turning the audition over in my mind ever since I left the studio. The conversation with Alessandro went well, I thought. And the scene we ran. But I still don't know how I compared to Sienna, who seems to be the obvious choice. Besides, it would be insane to have heard back by now. Maybe Nat just wants to check in and make sure I'm not going to pull out because of my worries about Avi. Which I know I'm not. I'm determined to see this through as far as I can.

'So,' she says. 'My prodigal client. How was your screen test yesterday?'

'It went…' I pause, trying to assess exactly how it went. Because, to be honest, I don't know. The whole thing is still a huge blur.

'I'm not sure how it went. Look, Nat—' I'm caught again by a sudden impulse to tell her the full story.

'I *am* sure how it went,' she says, looking at me strangely. My heart thuds. 'Because Alessandro called me this morning.'

'What?' I feel my chest tightening. 'He did?'

'He did,' she says.

'What did he say?' I ask, trying to prompt her. Anxiety vibrates through me now. But all she does is flick through some papers on her desk.

I wait, watching. A million emotions running through me until she looks up. There's a glint in her eye that makes me hope more than I've dared to until this moment.

'Now,' she says, clasping her hands together. 'I've just had one of the greatest directors of our generation telling me he'll agree to any of your contractual demands, as long as you agree to do this film. You were up against Sienna fucking Marsh – and he chose you. You, Lara.'

I find myself struggling to understand exactly what she's saying in this moment, the words flowing over me like they're in a different language. My entire body suddenly numb.

'Now,' she continues. 'From what I've heard, Sienna's still very willing to take the part if you don't want it. So you had better really think about whether the concerns about your relationship with your potential co-star are important enough for us to even discuss right now. Because I swear to God, Lara, these opportunities only come around once in a blue moon…'

Oh, my God, I think, some feeling coming back to my limbs. *Oh, my God. Oh, my God. Oh, my God.*

I'm waiting for any sort of concern to surface – for my past with Avi to come rushing in.

But that's not what comes to my mind.

Instead, it's just pure, soaring joy.

'He loved how you spoke about the role, Lara,' she says. 'He thought you were really aligned with his vision for Amelia. He wants to bring your Amelia to life. So,' she says, sitting back. 'Is there anything we need to discuss before you accept?'

And I find myself thinking instead about everything I've done to get here. All of it rushing in: the late nights, reading scripts. The constant uncertainty. The crashing disappointment, every time I got a no. The determination to pick myself up. To keep going. Everything I've given up, leading to this. And I feel it too. I remember my hand scribbling those goals on the page. Putting them in the Amelia book. As a bookmark or a prayer, I don't know. Maybe as a hope that things would work out.

And here I am, watching them work out. Like a dream. Except, this time, I'm not imagining it. It's real.

A smile lights up Nat's face as she waits for my response.

I find myself shaking my head. Because while the feelings about Avi are still present, there's a voice inside me that's far louder.

And it's telling me Nat's right – the past doesn't matter right now.

It can't. This is my future and I have to grab it with both hands. A smile spreads across my face – one that matches hers. Because, finally, we've done it.

'Nothing to discuss. I'll take it.'

5

A few weeks later, a car arrives outside my house share at exactly 3 p.m. to take me to my first costume fitting. I worked my last day at the paper company yesterday. Daniel, my manager, took the news that I was leaving incredibly well. He told me that if acting doesn't work out for me, I have a bright future in paper – which was totally baffling, given I mostly just sit at my desk killing time, but very sweet. The job was a stopgap more than anything – something to give me financial security while I went after what I wanted. But strangely, I found myself feeling nostalgic as I left. My life has existed in bits and pieces for the last few years, people passing in and out of it at random. Which is fine by me, usually. But the paper company was familiar. Regular. I had started to get comfortable there, so much so that I didn't really realise until I was packing up my desk and saying goodbye, and found myself sad at the prospect of moving on.

Alison lost her mind over me getting the part. It was nice seeing her consternation, her worry, melt into pure joy and excitement for me. To know she no longer feared that I wasn't going to be able to get where I wanted. Because I was already there. I hated myself for it a little, but I did have a small sense of triumph at having proven her wrong, that all this grinding, all this work, was worth something. That I didn't listen to her repeated suggestions that I give up and do something else. Something more grown-up and sensible. I've been getting texts from her every day, begging me to let her tell 'just one colleague'. But it's all under wraps, apart from immediate family for right now. And it's a good feeling, having it just between us. My parents are thrilled too, and I feel like I'm in a happy little bubble.

Nat and I are still working out the details of my contract with Alessandro. I've told her she can't ask for 10 million more or make any ridiculous demands. She wanted me to be able to keep some of my wardrobe, which I've agreed to – but only so far as one outfit of my choice. I don't need a wardrobe full of period costumes. And to be honest I don't know where I'll even store the one dress, but the idea of having a memento is lovely. Everything else, I've turned down. A larger trailer, I don't need.

Despite being the lead, I didn't want Nat to fight for me to be number one on the call sheet either. It matters a lot, to some people. But I knew that Avi's profile and absolute bulldog of an agent would have combined to ensure that it was contractually agreed for him to be number one. And I'm honestly still wrapping my head around the fact that I'll be there at all. Some of Nat's other requests make sense: an intimacy coordinator is heading towards being standard practice these days, but, just in case, she's going to make absolutely sure that there's one there. A part of me is enjoying this process – it's the first time I've ever been able to ask for anything other than just agreeing to their terms and showing up on time. But the rest of me just wants to get the contract signed as quickly as possible.

I'm ready for a fresh start – for the next part of my life to begin. I've started packing up my room, all seven square feet of it, filled wall-to-wall with books and old movie posters, and some fold-out chairs I stole from my parents' garage. Now heading back to my parents' garage, along with everything else. For the next six weeks until the end of the twelve-month contract I signed, Spencer will lease out my room and I'll be moving into a fancy hotel in West London, a short drive from the studios; all the crew, including Avi, will be living there too. And after that... who knows?

I get into the car, a Tesla – a fact I learn when it takes me several minutes to figure out how to open the door, which doesn't seem to have a handle. The driver gets out to help me and spends most of the twenty-five-minute journey to the studios telling me about how much more aerodynamic the Tesla design is than cars with regular handles.

Once we arrive, I get out of the car and step onto the car park, onto the same lot where I had my audition. I take it all in, knowing that this is going to be my home for the next six weeks, along with some off-set locations around London. I honestly can't wrap my head around the fact that I'm here, so instead I just operate on autopilot, excitement coursing through me as I make my way through to Reception and sign in.

There's a flash of joy as I walk down the corridor behind yet another runner, a joy in the knowledge that this isn't just an audition. That the part of me that has been expecting another shoe to drop for the last few days might be able to start to relax.

Because I've made it here. If only teenage Lara could see me now – landing a role in a major film. The film she always dreamed of. One she didn't know would ever even exist. There was no guarantee that Amelia's story would ever be picked up. So the fact that it's going to be on screen, with me as the lead, is beyond my wildest dreams.

After I've been led to the costume department, I find a row of costumes labelled *Lara – Amelia* on a rail. My hands fly to my mouth immediately because they're beautiful. Jewel-toned silk and velvet, petticoats and corsets. Like the most incredible array of princess outfits anyone could imagine.

I was always more of a Lara Croft kind of dress-up girl. Partly because of my name, partly because Alison looked so radiant in her Cinderella costume that it was her lane more than mine. So I stuck to trousers and daggers.

But maybe this I can make an exception for. Especially since I know Amelia will have a special sheath under her skirts to keep her dagger close.

The head costume designer – Suzanne – is here, along with her assistant, Marissa. I don't have much experience with costume departments. The theatre productions I've done have been so low-key that it's pretty much just been one incredibly stressed-out person who's asked me to bring half of my own clothes because they didn't have enough of a budget to rent everything. And in advertising, the clothes are neutral, chosen specifically to avoid drawing attention away from the product.

But from the five minutes I've already been here, the rumours seem to be true: in film, the costume department is the best department. The clothes are beyond imagination and the designers seem to be some of the nicest people I've met in the business. Within seconds of my arrival, Suzanne has given me a warm hug, congratulated me on the role and started to talk me through each 'look' they've prepared for me to try on today for my fitting.

There are several rounds of costumes: a rich burgundy corseted ballgown, accessorised with emerald jewels on my ears and at my neck; a dark-blue dress buttoning up to my neck, with lace cinching the waist, and a pale-pink silk dress with a bustle, sleeves frilling out at my wrists. They're all so beautiful that I can't help it – I become overwhelmed with emotion. Because I can't believe this is actually happening, that there's any chance I might've said no to this.

From my conversation with her, I assess that Suzanne has an even deeper knowledge of Amelia than I do, from reading the books seventeen times. From the cut of the skirts to the exact colour of the silks, she's thought about every single aspect of each outfit on this rail. Which, I suppose, was to be expected – but what I wasn't expecting was for her to be so interested in what I thought. Whether it fits my vision for her character too.

We pull out dress after dress, and Marissa and Suzanne take turns helping to lace me into each corset. We try out different lengths and styles of petticoat, working out which ones I can run in and which ones are better for less action-heavy scenes. We discuss where might be best for Amelia to conceal her weapons: in a hidden pocket down the side of her corset, for easy access; in a secret sheath hidden in her skirts, like the books; in the ankle of a boot.

And even without the hair and make-up – I'll have my test for that next week, the day before we start filming – I can see it. With each look, I feel myself stepping more and more into the character of Amelia. Into her confidence, her strength of will, her sharp wit. All the qualities I used to wish I had when I read the books as a kid. All the qualities I thought would make moving through the world that little bit easier. The sensation buzzes across my skin, of transformation.

It's like magic. Everything I've only ever been able to imagine, coming to life in front of me. My hands shake as I help Suzanne do up the buttons.

By the time it comes to the last dress, I feel almost out of my mind with excitement. It's made of a thick, beautiful silk in a deep russet. The skirts drape perfectly around me, and the corset has embroidery so detailed it must have taken someone several hours by hand. I didn't know how beautiful clothing could be, never thought I'd be this moved by wearing a dress. But the fact that I'm going to get to wear it again, to play a role I only ever dreamed of, has tears running down my face. Like it's hitting me properly, for the first time. The magnitude of this. The shimmering life – of playing Amelia, of being an actor in a big-budget film – that I've only allowed myself to imagine in the last few days, coming into shape around me.

'We'll give you a few minutes, love,' Suzanne says, sensing that I'd like a moment alone. As she and Marissa leave the room to make some tea, they tell me that if I'd like to take the dress off while they're gone, and I can manage, that's fine. Otherwise they'll help me when they return.

I stand staring at myself in the mirror for a few seconds, the shimmer lingering. Then the door opens. I turn. And in the doorway is six feet of Armani suit, perfectly coiffed hair and a Rolex watch that flashes on his wrist as he steps into the room. A look of surprise and then awe passing over his face as he does.

Fuck.

'Hi,' he says. 'Sorry, my fitting's in a few minutes. I can go—'

'H-hi,' I say, apparently unable to get any words out without stammering.

An awkward silence falls. I swallow, trying to think of what to say.

'So I accepted the part,' I choke out, eventually. *Idiot, Lara.* Of course he knows that.

'Alessandro told me,' he says, an inscrutable expression on his face. 'I wanted to call, but I didn't know…' He trails off, but I get the gist: he didn't know whether I'd want to hear from him. Whether I'd even still have the same number or if I'd have blocked him.

'Congratulations,' he says, his voice shifting a little. And I wonder if I hear a sliver of disappointment.

Which makes sense, even as my heart nonsensically sinks at the thought. Because I shouldn't care what he thinks of my casting, at all. And from his perspective, he could have been doing this job with his girlfriend opposite him in the leading role. I can't have been his first choice for this, even without our past.

'Thanks,' I reply.

'You — you deserve it,' he says. And hearing him say those words kicks off a myriad of emotions in me.

But I can't engage with any of them right now. I'm already so overwhelmed — and this day has been so joyful so far. I grope for a change of subject and land on one before I can really consider what I'm saying.

'I'm sorry,' I blurt, my chest tightening. 'About Sienna.'

There's a pause. *Oh, fuck*. Now I've practically given him an opening to tell me he's disappointed.

'What?' he says, eventually. Looking... confused? But that doesn't make any sense.

'Your girlfriend,' I reply, stating the obvious. Continuing to dig myself into a hole. 'You must be upset that she didn't get the part.'

'Oh,' he says. 'Ah.' And I can almost hear him thinking of how to spin this, how to convince me he's excited about the prospect of spending six weeks with me, rather than with his supermodel girlfriend. 'You know, that's not—'

But before he can finish the sentence, the door swings open again. Marissa and Suzanne come through it, chatting and holding their cups of tea. Suzanne with one in each hand, presumably having made one for me too. When they see Avi, they stop in their tracks.

'Hi, Avi,' Suzanne says her tone familiar. They must know each other. 'I thought we weren't seeing you for another ten minutes?'

'I'm early,' he says and shoots me a glance. 'I'll wait outside.'

Suzanne nods and he heads towards the door. But before he reaches it, he turns back to look at me, a slightly strange expression on his face.

'Lara,' he says. 'You, uh… you look beautiful in that dress.' And he chokes the words out as if there's something stuck in his throat. But they still hit me like a truck.

What the ever-living fuck?

Suzanne and Marissa exchange a look and he leaves the room, the door swinging shut behind him.

I arrive back at my flat that evening, ready to pack up the last few boxes of my things. Alison and I managed most of them in one car journey, and she's lent me her car again to collect the rest. The new flatmate is moving in tomorrow, so this will be my last night in the flat. I'll be staying with my parents for the next week until filming.

I unlock the door, expecting Spencer and Hannah to be out; they said they were going for drinks this evening.

But instead I see them sitting at the table, an array of fajita accoutrements in front of them.

'Surprise!' Spencer says.

'I-I don't understand,' I start, confused.

'We couldn't let you get away without a goodbye dinner,' Hannah says. I falter – I hadn't expected this at all. 'Or without nailing down a day for you to come and give a talk at my school,' she adds, half-jokingly.

'This is so kind,' I say, putting my bags down and walking over to the table. 'But I have—'

'Packing to do,' Spencer says, with a sideways look at Hannah. 'We know. But will you at least give us a chance to hang out with you before you become so famous you don't want anything to do with us any more?'

It's a joke, but something hits me as he says it.

Because that's exactly what Avi did to me. I'd never want to make anyone else feel that way. I like Hannah and Spencer. I just never really imagined they were inviting me to their monthly dinners and pub trips through any other impulse than politeness. I've not exactly added much to the flat in my time here.

And so I put my things in my room, come back to sit beside my flatmates and start to make myself a plate. Spencer asks me about how the costume-fitting went and I leave out the detail about Avi.

Hannah talks about her school play, and how the lead was suspended for stealing a goat and bringing it into school as a prank. So now she's had to recast, and the only person both interested and available has such terrible stage fright that Hannah's worried the entire play is just going to be an hour and a half of silence.

Spencer tells us about the new lead in the musical he's currently in the chorus of on the West End, and how much of a diva they are – insisting on never interacting with the rest of the cast outside rehearsals and performances. Because they were on a few episodes of *EastEnders* and therefore apparently 'too good' for the rest of them.

And for the first time, pretty much since I moved in, I feel almost… comfortable. Maybe it's because I'm leaving tomorrow, so I feel less self-conscious.

But the thought occurs to me suddenly, out of nowhere – maybe it's because I never really gave Hannah and Spencer a chance. Because I assumed their interest in me couldn't have been genuine, so I kept to myself rather than opening up to them. *Why haven't I done more of this?* I think to myself.

'To Lara,' Hannah says, raising a glass. My chest warms. 'I know we haven't known each other that long, but I'm really thrilled for you. And I know Spence is too.'

'On that note…' Spencer says, pulling out something from under the table. It's wrapped and book-shaped. My heart thuds as he hands it to me.

I push my thumb under the paper and open it. It's a special edition of *A Murder in London*, the first book in the Amelia Blackthorn Chronicles. Leather-bound with embossing and gold-foiled edges. I run my hand over it, then open the cover. They've written a note to me on the inside wishing me luck, and signed it 'from your former flatmates'. I'm so moved, I honestly don't know what to say for a few moments.

'Thank you,' I finally manage. 'This is… wonderful.'

No one has ever done anything this kind for me.

Well, except one person.

'We wanted you to have something to remember us by,' Spencer says, dramatically clutching his chest. I laugh and Hannah does too.

And the next morning when I leave, I feel – for the second time since I accepted this role – sad to be saying goodbye.

6

The night before I'm due on-set for our first day of filming, I hardly sleep. I wake up, restless, at 3 a.m., an hour before my car is due to pull up.

I arrived at the hotel yesterday afternoon and it's lovely. Five stars. Soft towels. A view of the London skyline. I group-called my family, and gave Alison and my parents a tour of my room. They were as blown away as I was by the rain shower and clawfooted bathtub. And the robes, which Alison asked me to steal for her. After my parents said goodbye and went to bed, I tried to talk to her about my nerves for today, but I got her usual response, telling me I should just focus on the good. On the fact that I'm in the movie, that my demented commitment to this career is finally paying off and I should stop worrying. Stop finding problems.

Which upset me more than I let on at the time. Because, again, she's right – anyone would kill to be in my position. But that doesn't mean I can't be nervous too. Alison often bemoans that I don't talk to her about things enough, but whenever I do I somehow end up feeling like my emotions don't matter unless they're exclusively positive. Like there's something wrong with me for letting in anything negative at all. Like, even when I'm doing something right, I'm somehow getting it all wrong.

Thankfully, I didn't see Avi when I checked in. I'm not sure what I would've said – and I'm still incredibly nervous about seeing him on-set tomorrow. But I have to focus. Have to make the most of what could be my big break.

The book Hannah and Spencer gave me sits on a table in my room, and I can see it from my bed. I tucked the note from when I was younger into it – as a talisman, a reminder of how far I've come. And after room-service dinner (Nat insisted I make the most of the perks), my phone pinged with a message to our group chat. I click it when I open my phone, a flicker of warmth passing through me as I read it.

Hannah S: *Good luck tomorrow, Lara!*
Spencer M: *You're going to kill it. And if it helps with the nerves, in my first big-budget production I managed to knock over one of the leads and sprain*

> *their ankle during rehearsals. So whatever happens tomorrow, it'll certainly be better than that!*
>
> Lara: *Thanks, guys! You're welcome to come visit set anytime.*

I don't expect them to take me up on the invitation. In fact, I'm fully expecting that as soon as someone new moves in, they'll forget about me. But in spite of all that, a part of me lights up at the idea of them coming. Of a piece of my life lingering, for once.

I click out of the thread and open my emails, scrolling through the call sheet Nat sent me yesterday. A list of appearances on-set today. Ranked in order of importance. My name just below Avi's, at number two. A thrill passes through me as I read it again.

The highest I've ever been on a call sheet was 137, for a 'powerful non-speaking role' in a crime thriller — a role that ended up being cut from the series entirely. I still remember watching it, my heart clenching as I realised I wasn't going to get to see myself on screen. That the hope and excitement I felt was for nothing.

So to be number two is nothing less than incredible.

I scroll down, noting some of the other names on the list.

Roman Kane at number three, playing the villain: a mastermind behind the murders of several London socialites, made to look like suicides. His role is charismatic and charming, with a dangerous streak — much like what I've read about his presence on-set. He has a profile almost as significant as Avi's, but far more divisive. Known for his commitment to a method approach, hardly breaking from role on-set, he's described universally as either the best person people have ever worked with or the worst, depending on the role. Which doesn't bode well, considering his character is a sociopath.

Deborah West at number seven, playing my mother. I knew about this one from the casting announcement, and still haven't got over it. She's one of the greatest stage actresses of the last fifty years, and rarely does films. Getting to work with her will be a dream come true. Something I'd never have imagined, even a few weeks ago.

I scroll down a little further, taking in the full list for the first time. Then stop in my tracks.

Because a name is there that I didn't notice yesterday.

My eyes latch on to it, widening.

At number seventeen, there in bold letters that stand out to me so noticeably I can't believe I ever missed them.

Sienna Marsh: Socialite Number 3.

I frown as I read it.

Why would she take such a small role? Sienna's such a huge name – this can't be anything but a waste of her time. And she was up for my part, so I don't know why she'd accept anything less.

But then it hits me – Avi. She must be between jobs and want to be on-set with him. Which is nice for him, I suppose.

Possessed by a thread of curiosity now, I get up from the bed and open my laptop on the desk in the corner of the room. I type her name into Google and press enter.

What I find is impressive. Page after page of interviews. Actors on Actors. *Forbes* '30 Under 30'. Magazine shoots. The cover of *Teen Vogue* in their 'role models' issue. Because not only is she a supermodel and now an up-and-coming actress, but she's also known for her charity work and advocacy.

She's perfect. But I already knew that.

I scroll down to some paparazzi photos, taken this past week in London. She must have already flown in for the film – is probably already in this hotel, a notion that sends a sense of intimidation through me. The fame might not affect me with Avi – I knew him before, so I have some conception of him as normal – but Sienna looks… otherworldly. Blonde hair falling silkily over her shoulders. Her carefully distressed jeans. Her hand hanging artfully from Avi's as they step out of a famous sushi restaurant together.

I hate myself for it, but I zoom in – taking in every detail. Their designer clothes. Their posture: heads tilted together. Laughing.

They look so happy.

A strange feeling passes through me as I look at it, and I bite the inside of my lip hard to try to repress the emotions that rise up. Because they're perfect together. Because it would have been easy – so easy – for Alessandro to have cast Sienna in my role. The film would have practically sold itself. But a second later, that feeling hardens into determination. Because he chose me. And in this moment, it lights a fire under me – to prove him right.

I close the laptop and check the time. It's 3.45.

Fuck.
I need to get to set.

I rush downstairs, happy in the knowledge that I won't run into Avi this morning. He has a different call time and should already be on-set. The lobby is empty and it's pitch dark outside. No one else up at this ungodly hour.

I rush down the steps, the car already waiting. My driver – I learned on the drive to and from my fitting last week – will be the same throughout filming. His name is George. He is polite and funny, and has a penchant for a very specific kind of Scottish whisky and cigars. I am still both completely floored that I have an actual driver and am apparently entirely incapable of opening Tesla doors.

I spend most of the twenty-minute journey in relative silence, after some back-and-forth with George about the early hour and the route he plans to take, and decide to comfort myself by flicking through the script in my bag, turning to today's pages. The notes I've made in the margins contrasting: green pen against the black type. I've gone through the whole thing several times since signing the contract, making notes in line with my vision for Amelia's character. Ideas for emotional inflections on each line. What I perceive to be the motivations behind each scene. I do this for every script – even the smaller plays I've been in as side characters. It helps me get into the role. And in this case, the notes came as naturally as breathing. I hardly had to think about it at all.

We'll be starting with a few conversational scenes between Avi and me – no kissing until much later in the filming process, thank God. Alessandro wants to film in loosely chronological order, so we'll mostly follow the plot of the film as we go. It's an unorthodox approach – with most films shot out of sequential order – but I'm excited about it. We'll start with Amelia and Jackson meeting for the first time since she broke their engagement. Because she's starting up her own detective agency and needs his help with a case.

Having read the full script, I know there won't be any full-frontal sex scenes, so there has been no need for nudity clauses in my contract (or complete meltdowns at the thought of having to do that with him). Just a few kissing scenes – bridges I'll have to cross when I get to them. I turn to the first and wince as the memory resurfaces, of the first audition. His hand on my waist, kicking up the image of that night in the corner of the pub. Where everything changed between us, then abruptly fell apart.

Stop it, Lara.

I move quickly on to the next scene, one I'll be filming with Roman this afternoon. Amelia's first interaction with the villain, before she knows he's the man she's looking for. While I'm still worried about working with him, because his reputation precedes him, even working with a potential sociopath worries me less than filming with Avi. Which is concerning, to say the least. But I'll just have to keep my cool. There's too much at stake to let it affect me.

I get out of the car when we arrive on the lot and walk around the side of the building to a gated area, one that was empty when I did my audition but which is now completely transformed. Most of these trailers were here yesterday when I came for my make-up test. But the key difference today is people – there are about three hundred more people, and a million times more chaos. Everyone rushing around like we're in a hospital emergency department, all talking into radios. And I've seen versions of this before, sure, on advertising sets. But it was never anything on this scale.

I hardly have time to catch my breath before I am beset by five feet ten inches of curly red hair, tortoiseshell glasses, and an expression so simultaneously enthusiastic and serious that it's immediately jarring. The man looks at me expectantly. I'm about to say something, but then he holds his hand up – talking into a microphone attached to his ear. As if to tell me not to speak until he's finished. As 'talent', I might be high up on the call sheet, but as far as organisational pecking order goes I'm expected to just do as I'm told.

What kind of world have I walked into?

'Lara,' he says, finally. 'Our star! It's so delightful to meet you.' He reaches out his hand and I take it. He starts shaking my hand so aggressively I am slightly worried he's going to dislocate my elbow.

'H-hello,' I reply, so stunned by the last few seconds I can't quite find words.

'I'm David,' he says, finishing the handshake. 'The second assistant director. I'll be looking after you today.'

'Great—' I start to reply, but he's listening to something in his earpiece again.

'Are you ready to head over?' he says, and it takes me a second before I realise he's talking to me. I nod and he speaks into his microphone, placing his hand gently on my elbow and steering me towards set.

'Lara arrived,' he says, with all the gusto of a military commander. 'Lara en route to WHAM.'

Lara overwhelmed, I think.

'S-sorry,' I say, still stunned, as he starts moving me towards a giant crowd of people milling among the trailers, which have now been set up all across the car park. 'What's WHAM?'

'Oh,' he says. 'I forgot this was your first film. Wigs, Hair and Make-up. WHAM. We'll get you to Make-up first. I'm afraid we're on a bit of a time crunch this morning, so if you could keep pace that would be great.'

'Sure,' I reply, tripping over my own feet as I try to keep up with his pace. By the time we reach the make-up trailer, I'm sweating through my very thick wool jumper, which seemed like a good idea this morning but is not at all appropriate for the spring weather we're having.

'Lara at WHAM,' he says, then turns back to me. I'm really going to have to get used to this hearing-other-people-talk-about-me-in-the-third-person thing.

I've never heard my name spoken aloud so many times in such a short period.

'I've heard such great things from Alessandro,' he says in a tone so bright I can't quite tell if it's sincere. 'I'm sure you're going to be just brilliant.' And then he practically launches me towards the steps of the trailer. When I look back to say goodbye, he's already disappeared.

I open the door to the trailer. Which is, to my relief, empty both of Avi (though I know I have a later call time, I was suddenly worried he might still be in here having his sideburns attached or something) and anyone else it might be overwhelming to run into in my sleep-deprived and dazed state. I am welcomed by Sarah, my make-up artist for the course of the film. She did my test yesterday and seemed very friendly. She settles me into my chair and starts rifling through the tray next to us, pulling out some instruments that look familiar to me now, but which looked like torture instruments yesterday.

'How are you feeling this morning?' she asks, putting some cleanser on a cotton pad and starting to scrub my face.

'I'm… fine,' I say.

'I saw you were with David,' she replies, raising her eyebrows in the mirror conspiratorially. 'Quite a character, that one.'

'He's certainly… energetic,' I reply, searching for an adjective to describe the whirlwind I just experienced.

'Between you and me, I think he's on speed,' she says, spreading some primer on my face, then pausing for a second to mix my foundation shade. I frown, wondering if she's serious. 'No one has that much energy. And being second AD is no joke.'

To try to prepare myself for what it would be like on a big film set, I've been doing a bit of research over the last few weeks: part Googling, part quizzing Nat. I've read a lot of Reddit threads full of horror stories – of people being hit by cars on-set, of directors losing their minds, of actors putting up soothing posters of cornfields in their trailers to try to recover from the stress of filming between takes. Eventually I stopped reading, determined not to psych myself out. But what I did learn, which was useful, is that there's a very clear hierarchy around David's role. Runners work at the bottom of the pile, getting coffee, looking after anyone and anything that needs attention on-set. Then the second AD is basically the operations director for the runners, a role that requires your brain to be in several places at once, which perhaps explains David's slightly manic energy and sudden disappearance. And above that you have the first AD, who never leaves the director's side and has creative input. The roles are pretty much unconnected in terms of their requirements and interactions with one another, which is interesting – but it's usually understood that once you've done your time as the organisational mastermind, you'll progress to helping shape the creative vision. However, there are no guarantees; sometimes people end up stalling at David's level for years. The top of the pile is the director – in this case, Alessandro. The person running the show. The person I am more than a little nervous to see this morning.

We had a lovely phone call a week and a half ago in which we expanded on our shared vision for Amelia. He wants to position her as a fresh female character for the modern world, someone to inspire the younger audience to know their own minds. To be unafraid to express their opinions. Exactly how I have always seen her too. It felt trippy and surreal at the time – a sense passing over me while I was talking to him that it wasn't quite happening. That I might blink and find myself fourteen again, reading the book and daydreaming about playing her in a film, rather than actually doing it.

But since then, we haven't spoken.

And since then, I've had enough time to wonder if I might be in over my head.

A feeling that's bubbling up right now, try as I might to keep it at bay. I pull at a loose thread on my sleeve. Sarah notices and pauses, foundation brush halfway to my face.

'Nervous?' she asks.

I let out a breath. 'I'm… doing okay,' I lie.

She reaches into her bag and for one horrible moment I think she's about to give me a sedative or something. But instead, she pulls out a small tin and I relax. Bach's Rescue pastilles. A herbal supplement my mum used to give me when I was too nervous to go to school. The same one I took before my first audition for this part, weeks ago.

'I give these to my daughter for her GCSE exams,' she says. 'Take them, if you want.'

And the gesture is so warm and maternal, so reminiscent of home, that I find myself incredibly moved. But I manage to pull myself together enough to take them out of her hand and slip them into my pocket.

'Thank you,' I reply and she winks at me, then goes back to applying my make-up.

About half an hour later, I'm transformed. Pale foundation covering my face and neck. Blush lightly dabbed on my cheeks. Rouge on my lips. I look like myself, if I had been born three hundred years ago and had a better make-up routine. Everything enhances my features in ways I've never had the skills to do myself. But I can't enjoy the effects for too long because David is already waiting outside to take me over to Hair.

'You look stunning, my dear,' he says to me, then takes my hand and leads me with a flourish to the next trailer – literally two metres away. I could probably have managed the walk alone, but I'm beginning to learn that that's not an option here – there are eyes on me at all times. There's David and a couple of other runners now too, a few metres behind him – ready to step in, in case he has to rush off. I feel like I'm being stalked. If my stalkers were all very kind and overly attentive, and about five years younger than me.

'Now, Lara, what can we order you for breakfast?' he says, coming to a halt outside a door with the words 'HAIR' on it.

'Sorry?' I reply. I was expecting to wander over to the food table in the green room, like I usually do. Not have someone order me food. That feels like an extravagance I don't know how to respond to.

'We'll have it waiting in your trailer,' he says, ushering me towards the steps. 'Lara at Hair,' he barks, then looks at me like I'm a soldier who is about to disobey his command.

'Uh...' I say, panicking. Trying to think of an easy breakfast for them to source in the approximately three seconds I have before David launches me into this trailer. 'Just some juice?' I say. He nods to me, then clicks with his fingers to get the attention of one of the runners behind him, making me flinch and want to apologise to them.

I immediately regret my choice. Juice, at this hour of the day, is likely to give me a sugar rush that I'll crash down from later. Which, given I'm already feeling sleep-deprived and more than a little unhinged, is a terrible idea. But when I turn to ask for something else, he's pulled his disappearing act again. That man would have an excellent career as a spy.

I don't have time to think about my poor choices, though, because as soon as I step through the door to Hair, someone takes my hand and leads me to a chair. I hardly have time to say hello or settle into my seat before they get to work, pulling and blow-drying, and teasing and gently coiffing my hair into submission.

And when I look up, my breath hitches.

I like myself fine, but I've never thought of myself as beautiful. Alison was always the person people gravitated towards at school. The easy smile, the long blonde hair – she and Sienna could be related, honestly. I, on the other hand, have a face I'd hope most directors would describe as a blank slate – a feature that can be an asset, in the right setting.

And when I stare in the mirror, I see it.

My dark hair has been curled into soft ringlets, most of it secured into an up-do with a jewelled pin, and some tendrils left down to frame my face, a few curls hanging down at the back. I saw all of this yesterday, when they were doing the tests. But somehow today the effect, combined with the make-up, is stunning. I still look like myself, but enhanced. *I look like Amelia*, I think. In that second, the nerves start to fall away – because I'm here for a reason. And I'm determined to do that reason justice. I want to bring Amelia to life. And now, for the first time since the costume fitting, I can visualise myself as her. See my edges melting away, completely, into the role.

When the hairdressers are done, David – who has magically appeared outside the door, like the stealth wizard I am learning he is – leads me quickly across the set to my trailer.

'Lara at her trailer,' he says to nobody. Then, to me, 'I'll come and get you for blocking in a few minutes.'

'Thanks,' I say, but he doesn't wait around, just rushes off again.

I look up at the door and find myself frozen in place. I've never had my own trailer before.

I feel like an idiot, standing here staring at it. But every moment so far this morning has felt like a dream. And I keep thinking I'm going to blink and it'll all disappear. But my name is there, in small black letters printed on a white laminated sheet. *Lara Francis.*

'Everything okay?' a runner asks from behind me, and I nod.

Get it together, I remind myself. But then I ascend the steps and open the door. What I see inside makes me stop in my tracks.

The whole table is covered in flowers. Great bouquets of them: lilies, roses. And I think I see some yellow, too: sunflowers. My favourite. I walk over to the table and see something next to them that almost sends me over the edge.

An old, tattered teddy bear from Build-A-Bear Workshop, wearing sunglasses.

Freddie Mercury Junior. Mine and Alison's shared bear. My parents could only afford to buy us one at the time, and we begged them to go to the Build-A-Bear Workshop for so long they couldn't stave us off any more. We fought over what to call him and my dad is a big fan of Queen. Alison has custody of him at the moment; we switch every Christmas. And I have no idea how she got him in here, but I snatch him up and hold him close. Something of home. Something that tells me that – maybe, just maybe – Alison is more understanding of my nerves than she's shown me.

As I'm holding him I take in the rest of the room, my eyes snagging on my costume for today, hung up in the corner in what looks like a dry-cleaning bag. I set Freddie down gently and unzip it, taking in the silk. The intricate corset. It's the same red dress I was wearing when Avi interrupted my fitting.

But before I can examine it further, David appears outside my trailer, ready to take me to set for our blocking of the scene. Before finishing getting ready, they want us there to determine camera angles and lighting, and make sure they can follow mine and Avi's movements across the set. Then, while I'm getting into costume, the crew will have a short rehearsal to ensure everything is in place before shooting.

'Hey,' Avi says, when I reach set. He's wearing sideburns and is fully made-up for screen, but is also in jeans and a T-shirt. I must look ridiculous too, and I can't stifle the laugh that rises in me.

'Hi,' I reply. I feel slightly less nervous seeing him than I thought I would. But there's a strange thrill that runs over my skin at the sight of him. A thrill I steadfastly ignore.

'Amelia mia,' Alessandro says, his tone warm and affectionate. 'How wonderful it is to see you.' And I light up at the sound of his voice.

We run through a few different iterations of the scene for this morning, Alessandro moving us accordingly. Making sure we're in the right position for the crew, memorising our marks. It feels… nice. Relaxed. Almost normal. And I start to wonder if I've been stupid, for being so nervous.

David comes to collect us once we've finished, and walks Avi and I back to our trailers along with a few other runners. Avi looks at me like he might be about to say something, but, before he can, David is giving us both a run-through of the schedule for later and ordering us into our trailers. Still, I catch his eye and he flashes me a smile.

Once I'm safely back in my trailer, I start to take the red dress out of its cover, then realise I'm going to need help doing it up.

I move to the door of the trailer, ready to open it and find a runner. Before I can, I hear someone talking just outside.

'Did you see Sienna Marsh is here?' they say, speaking in hushed tones. I peek out of the window to see a couple of people dressed in costume. Maybe they're extras or people lower down in the call sheet. I don't recognise either of them.

'I did,' another voice responds. 'What do you think she's doing here?'

'Well,' the other says. 'It's only a rumour, but…'

There's a pause, as they look around to see if there's anyone nearby. I duck down so I'm not visible through the window.

'It's Lara Francis's first film – she's a complete unknown. And apparently, some of the production team thought they might be taking too much of a risk. Alessandro was desperate to cast her, but he had a hard time persuading them because they were worried she might not be able to handle the pressure of such a compressed shoot. So, just in case, Alessandro agreed to bring Sienna in as an understudy. Someone he's worked with before, someone he can trust. So that filming won't be halted for too long if Lara's not up to the job.'

If she's not up to the job. A chill runs through my blood, turning it cold.

'It's only a rumour,' I whisper to myself as they walk away. But it doesn't do anything to quell the spike of worry that shivers through me, making me nauseous.

I take a breath, wondering what the fuck to do with this new information. Alessandro vouched for me, at least — according to what they just said. But the nerves I thought had dissipated since the blocking return now in full force. I thought I was starting to maybe find some footing, but this — even if it isn't true — has made that footing shakier than ever. Even to have people speculating about my position here hurts.

They have taken a big risk by hiring me, I think, insecurity starting to creep in through the cracks. Sienna's beautiful face, her perfect, polished smile flashing into my mind. But I push the thought away as quickly as it comes. Because I have to focus. It will not serve my performance today. I'll just have to treat it as a rumour and leave it at the door when the time comes to perform. Alison has a saying: as within, so without. What you fear, if you worry about it for long enough, comes true. It's why she's always trying to nudge me towards positive thinking. Convinced that my tendency to worry creates more problems than it solves. Maybe it's finally time I took a leaf out of her book.

And in any case, I don't have time to worry about it – I have to get into costume. My first task is to be ready for my call time. I open the door to find a runner with blue hair approaching, hand to their earpiece. As she gets closer, I see she has piercings all across one eyebrow. She might be small, but there's a buzzing energy about her that tells me she's ready to go at any moment. Like, if David is the commander of the army, she could definitely be his deputy.

'Hi,' I say, trying to keep my voice steady. 'Would – would you be able to get someone from Costumes to help me put this on? It's just, it's a corset and—'

Before I can say anything else, a panicked look crosses her face and she's speaking into her earpiece.

A few seconds later, David appears suddenly from the right, making me jump.

'For God's sake,' he says, marching over at speed. He starts barking into his microphone. 'How did NO ONE realise that Lara was going to need a costume assistant? Hmm? Are you all STUPID?' I flinch a little at his tone, which is made all the more harsh for this hour of the morning. It's almost 6 a.m., so still not a normal time to be awake. I've really picked the wrong career for agreeable start times, considering I struggled most days to even be ready by 9 a.m. for my day job at the paper company.

'I…' I want to tell David it's not a big deal, but the blue-haired girl with the eyebrow piercings gives me a warning look and David just holds his hand up to silence me until he's finished barking instructions, then arranges his features into a calmer expression and meets my eye.

'I'm so sorry, Lara,' he says, shifting now into the placating tone he's been mostly using with me. It makes me feel like I'm in preschool again. 'If you wouldn't mind going back into your trailer, there'll be someone here shortly.' Then before I can go back into my trailer, he starts talking again. And when I hear him, my stomach sinks.

'I have half a mind to fire someone over this. Who was on costumes?'

'Harrison, I think,' the blue-haired girl says.

'Harrison, huh? Of course it was fucking Harrison. Well, Harrison,' he says back into his microphone. 'Your daddy might have got you your job here, but he's not around to help you now.'

He marches off and I walk back through the door of my trailer, feeling very sorry for Harrison, whoever he is.

I know that this is how things work – that everything on-set has to run as smoothly as possible. That it's their job to make sure I have no delays so that I can do my job properly, in as few takes as possible, and Production don't have to pay overtime on the already ridiculous cost of the project.

But I have to wonder: if a mistake as seemingly minor as this can cause such a furore, what happens if I fuck up?

And a small, insecure part of me pipes up and tells me that, given the conversation I just overheard, I already know the answer to that question – the solution is blonde and beautiful, and currently dating Avi. *Stop it, Lara*, I think.

I swallow, then head across the room to distract myself before the costume assistant arrives. I examine the rest of the contents of the table: a large, white bouquet with pink gardenias from Alessandro – a gesture that makes my heart pinch now, because the confidence he expressed to me on the phone clearly isn't shared by everyone; some orange roses from Nat, and, at the back, the sunflowers, with a card attached. I assume they're from Alison and my parents – that, somehow, she got in contact with Nat to arrange to have them and Freddie here.

I pick up the card and am about to open it when I notice something else: a small, brown shoebox in the middle of the table. I lift the lid and, as I do, a smell reaches me that turns my stomach.

What the fuck?

But I don't have time to think beyond that, because then I see what's inside.

And I start screaming.

I throw the box to one side, the contents spilling out. Freddie Mercury and the card I'm holding fall to the floor, and before I know it I'm pressed against the back wall of the trailer, climbing onto a chair.

Oh, my God, Oh, my God, Oh, my God. This is not happening. You're sleep-deprived and you're hallucinating.

The door to my trailer bursts open and I think it's going to be David, or the blue-haired girl, or another runner.

But it's not. It's Avi, breathless and half-dressed in his costume. His buttons undone, waistcoat hanging open. Chest bare and perfect for the world to see.

'Lara?' he says, taking in my position, eyes wide and confused. 'What the fuck is going on?'

I can't find words in this moment, can't even find surprise that he's here. I'm frozen in fear, shaking on the chair I'm standing on. All I can do is point in the direction of the box that's still lying open on the table. Its contents splayed next to it.

He walks over to examine it and flinches slightly, stepping backwards. But before I can tell him to stop, he approaches again. Picking it up. Holding it by the tip of its tail.

A dead rat.

'Put that down!' I say, unable to look in his direction. I can't believe what's happening right now. Avi Kumar, in my trailer, swinging around a rat corpse.

'Don't touch it, Avi,' I plead, partly so I don't have to look at it any more. 'It might be diseased.'

But he's not listening. A look has come over his face that I recognise: determination. Anger. He flips the lid of the box with his other hand and reads the card I neglected to open.

To Amelia, from your co-star, Roman. So looking forward to working with you.

Avi turns to me, the rat still swinging from his hand. Eyes blazing, so he looks more than a little deranged.

'I'm going to fucking kill him,' he says, then moves to the door of my trailer before I can stop him and kicks it open.

I scramble down from the chair and follow him blindly, grabbing at the door before it can close.

'Avi,' I say, my voice desperate. 'Avi, stop.' I'm seriously panicked now. Because I've seen him like this once before, when a guy felt me up across the bar. And it didn't end well.

The blue-haired runner has caught sight of what's happening and looks appropriately horrified.

'Avi leaving Lara's trailer. Avi holding… something.' She looks a little closer. 'Unidentified animal corpse. Repeat, Avi holding unidentified animal corpse.'

Avi stalks down the row of trailers, checking the names on each before reaching the right one. I follow him and so does the runner. 'Avi and Lara approaching Roman's trailer. Avi entering Roman's trailer, with corpse.'

'Avi,' I say again desperately, as he yanks open the door. I try to place my hand on his arm before he can enter, but he shakes it off.

'Stay outside,' he says to me firmly.

Fuck that, I think, as the door swings shut in my face. I pull it open and follow him in.

Roman's trailer is a confusing mirror of mine. He is sitting in an armchair a few metres from the door, in full costume, apparently unfazed by what's happening. His hand idly playing with one of the tassels on his waistcoat.

'Good morning,' he says, his tone light and bemused.

'What.' Avi is practically spitting now. 'The fuck. Is this?'

Roman squints at it. 'I'm not sure,' he says. 'Could you bring it a little closer?'

Avi lets out a shaky, furious breath. 'I'll do more than that in a minute if you don't tell my why the fuck this was in Lara's trailer, in a box with your name on it.'

'Avi,' I say. 'Please… let's just leave it—'

Avi throws his hand up to stop me talking. Roman peers around him, now apparently interested in my presence.

'Hello, Amelia. Wonderful to make your acquaintance. I see you received my gift.' *Amelia? Is this guy okay?* I mean, clearly not, if he's putting dead rats in my trailer. Then he laughs. And this is it – the trigger that pushes Avi over the edge.

'Listen here,' Avi says, walking slowly over to Roman. Holding the rat extremely close to his face. I've got to give it to Roman; he doesn't even flinch. Either those method-acting rumours are true or he is actually a psychopath. 'You might think it's funny to fuck with other people on-set. To scare the shit out of them so when the cameras turn on you don't have to do anything. Whatever you need, so you don't have to actually do any acting. Right?' He moves even closer now and Roman's smile widens.

'I'll tolerate it, Roman. I've done it before. Put as many dead rats in my trailer as you like, if that's what gets you through the day. If that's what convinces you you're anything other than a talentless piece of shit who seems to genuinely enjoy upsetting other people. But if you ever do anything like this to Lara again, I swear to God I will end you.'

'Ooh,' he says. 'Careful, Jackson. Anger doesn't suit you.'

Avi looks back at me, his expression so far past anger he looks almost… calm.

'Lara,' he says. 'Will you please wait outside?'

I shake my head slowly, unable to speak but also unwilling to leave. I get the sense that my presence is the only thing blocking a physical altercation right now. I take a breath, trying to find the words to defuse this. I may be new to film sets like this, but something tells me starting the day with a punch-up between co-stars isn't exactly ideal.

But, thank God, I don't have to intervene. Because a few seconds later there's a loud, impatient knock at the door.

'Everything alright in there?' David's voice sounds lightly panicked but glossed over with a soothing tone.

'Everything's fine,' Avi calls back, not moving from his position over Roman.

'Avi,' I say, recovering myself and moving over to him. I place a hand on his arm – the one not holding the rat. 'Avi, look at me.'

He turns to me, his eyes still burning.

'It's not worth it,' I say. And he lets out a breath, his shoulder dropping slightly. Seeming to recover something of his composure. But I still don't feel like he is hearing me completely.

'Please,' I say, desperately trying to de-escalate. 'Can we just focus on what's important, right now? It's my first day on a big set, and I need to get into my costume so we don't miss our call time. I really don't want to have to tell Alessandro we're late because we were in the middle of World War Three.'

He turns back to Roman with a look of disgust on his face so potent I'm surprised it doesn't wither him on the spot. And then, before I can register what's happening, or reach to stop him, he lets go of the rat, dropping it into Roman's lap. I flinch, expecting a reaction. But all that happens is Roman looks at it curiously, then – in a move that sends bile up my throat – starts caressing it, gently.

'Pretty little thing,' he says, turning to me. 'Isn't it? I've always thought rats were such misunderstood creatures.'

And despite Avi's speech, I've really got to give it to this guy – in the last five minutes he's ensured I'm not going to be able to feel anything but fear and revulsion every time I see his face. I'm beginning to understand all the articles I read about him. Why there are so many whispered warnings throughout the industry about working with him.

'Fuck you, Roman,' Avi says, walking towards the door. I follow him and he pulls it open.

'A pleasure to make your acquaintance!' Roman calls after us brightly, before the door swings shut. David is waiting halfway down the stairs, looking incredibly startled. A crowd of runners have gathered behind him, ready for instruction – like a small, stressed army.

'How are my two stars doing?' he says cheerfully, his eye twitching slightly.

Avi lets out a breath. 'Great, thanks, David.' And he moves past him down the steps, walking back towards his trailer, followed closely by a small platoon of the assembled runners. Avi's shoulders are still set like he's about to punch something; they don't drop even as he enters his trailer. I watch him as he does so, deciding not to follow.

'Lara,' David says, turning back to me once he's sure Avi is safely back in situ. 'There's someone from Costumes in your trailer. And we're a few minutes behind, so if you wouldn't mind—'

'Oh, sure,' I say, and descend the steps in a daze.

Another runner takes me back. I move as quickly as I can, but time feels like it's moving strangely. Like I'm walking through quicksand or some kind of strange soup. The world around me feels just a little less real than before. I ascend the stairs to my trailer and pull the door open. But just before I go inside, I hear David's voice from behind.

'Now will someone please tell me,' he says, speaking into his radio, his voice quietly threatening, 'what the fuck you meant by "unidentified animal corpse"?'

7

Twenty minutes later, Marissa has laced me into my corset and I've choked down some juice. Whichever runner was in charge of my breakfast got me eight different kinds. Even dragon fruit, which I hadn't realised was a fruit, let alone a juice. So much for trying to choose something that wasn't difficult to come by; I'll have to be more specific next time.

Still, none of it is enough to counteract the metric tonne of adrenaline currently pulsing through my veins.

I turn over the events of the last half-hour in my mind like a coin, trying desperately to make sense of them. But I can't. My brain has gone into some kind of survival mode, and no information is going in or out of it.

Marissa leaves and David knocks a few seconds later to tell me that there's been an issue with some of the sound equipment, so they'll be another ten minutes.

I sit down in the chair furthest from the door, struggling to fit the billows of my dress into it, and stare at the wall for a few seconds. Its blank, grey, clean slate calms me a little. And, slowly, my feelings start to come back. The haze fading. And as it dissipates, a dominant emotion rises up: anger. At Roman, because what he did was completely fucked up. And at Avi. Because he didn't stop, didn't allow me to reason with him or tell him what I wanted. Just barged into Roman's trailer, because of some instinct to look after me that is entirely misplaced and completely inappropriate now.

What the fuck was he thinking?

I step backwards and my heel slides on something. A card – the one from the sunflowers. The one that I dropped when I saw the rat.

I pick it up and read the contents. And as I do my hand clenches, crumpling the paper in my hands.

Before I know it, I'm marching across the room to grab the sunflowers from the vase a runner has clearly, kindly, put them in. And, in full period costume, exiting my trailer and heading towards Avi's.

'Lara leaving her trailer.' I hear a runner in the background. 'Lara entering Avi's trailer.' But I'm not listening – I'm all anger in this moment. All fire. I push open the door to his trailer and find him sitting in the corner reading his script.

'What are these?' I ask, my breath coming heavily.

He looks up and places the script slowly down on the arm of his chair.

'Sunflowers,' he says, his tone level and clear.

'You can't do this, Avi,' I say, the emotions I've been holding in all bursting out in this moment. It's the worst timing ever, but I can't help it. I don't want him to think we're friends – that everything is fine now. Because it's not. And maybe I haven't been clear enough about that, because at our second audition I was so focused on figuring out how I was going to work with him, if at all, that I didn't say more. But I can now.

'I appreciate that you apologised, before the second audition. I accept your apology. But you can't just barrel back into my life, beat people up and give me these. None of that is going to make everything okay.'

'I didn't beat him up…'

I sigh, pinching the bridge of my nose. 'It's a turn of phrase. Either way, you had no right to go after him like that.'

And at this, he goes silent.

'Fine,' he says. 'But you don't know Roman, Lara. He's a prick.'

'You're right,' I say. 'Probably on both fronts. But I don't need you to fight my battles for me, Avi. I can handle myself—'

'Okay,' he says, throwing his hands up, suddenly animated. 'Fine. I'm sorry I caused a scene. But why are you so upset about the sunflowers? They're just flowers.'

'They're not just flowers, Avi,' I say, tears in my eyes now. 'They're my favourite flowers. And you know that. And it's not fair, because you were the one who hurt me. Who put our friendship on the line and then abandoned it completely—'

'Lara,' he says.

'No,' I say. 'No. You don't get to do this.'

'Do what?'

'Make me like you again.' A tear escapes down my cheek. I take a breath, my composure dropping. 'Because I'm never going to know if it's real or if you're just doing it because I'm here now. You've had three years, Avi. Three years with my phone number. Three years in which you could've sent me flowers, or called me, or done anything to tell me you wanted me back in your life. But you didn't. And I don't want to be let back in now just because I turned up in it.'

And he looks at me for a few seconds, silent. Lost for words, apparently – and a little confused, which I find strange. Because clearly he knows what he did. But I don't want to hear any platitudes from him, not right now. And so I drop the sunflowers on the table next to me, walk towards the door and push it open, stepping through it into the air outside.

I get back to my trailer and hardly have time to catch my breath – or process what I've just done – before David arrives again to take me to set. It's just as beautiful as it was before, when I auditioned – the drawing room as ornate, with a few new additions. A gilded mirror in one corner, a red velvet armchair near me. And beyond: groups of people milling around, talking to each other. Glancing at me with great interest. I suddenly feel very self-conscious. Not to mention the fact that Avi will be arriving in a few minutes and I basically just told him where to go.

Keep it together, Lara, I think.

I walk through the crowds of people and my body relaxes a little when I see Alessandro, whose face lights up like a Christmas tree when he sees me. While I can't forget what I heard outside my trailer earlier – about the other person that's here on-set, ready to replace me at any second – I'm trying not let myself focus on it. Alison would be proud.

'Amelia mia,' he says, his tone warm and affectionate. 'How wonderful it is to see you. Are you ready for rehearsal?'

I nod, my chest still a little tight. But he looks confident and calm, and some of it is rubbing off on me. *I'll just have to show everyone here why he chose me*, I think.

Avi appears a minute later, in full costume now. An embroidered waistcoat and jacket with tails. A cane in one hand. I take it in – the sight is so strange and unexpectedly cool that the reality of me being on a film set hits me all over again.

'Hi,' he says to me, in a tone that has me crashing back to reality. Alessandro moves back behind the camera, distracted by something the first AD is saying, and silence falls between us for a few seconds. I pray he won't say anything else. But he steps closer and my heart kicks.

'Look, Lara—'

'I don't want to talk about it,' I say, looking up at him. 'Please. Not right now.'

He lets out a breath and steps back. But mercifully, he doesn't say anything else and I start trying to focus on the task at hand. I'll have the next ten minutes or so to get into character – the rehearsal Alessandro just mentioned will be a short run-through, to make sure we're clear on lines and to allow him a chance to give us notes before we start shooting. Avi and I stand opposite each other and I close my eyes momentarily, feeling into Amelia's presence. To me she is as real as I am, existing in space and time. *I am the conduit for her*, I think to myself.

Thankfully, Avi seems to be a consummate professional – in this area, at least. He doesn't break character, doesn't lapse in energy. He runs lines as if nothing just happened. As if we're just colleagues. Which is what I wanted. But still, I'm on edge. Alessandro makes a few suggestions, including one for me to lift my chin a little when delivering my lines, to convey Amelia's defiance; she's asking for something she needs from Jackson and doesn't want to appear weak. It's the one flaw in Amelia's character: she feels like she can't let her guard down, even for a second, or people might stop taking her seriously. Even with Jackson, the person she trusts most. Who sees her the clearest.

We rerun our lines. When we have it how Alessandro wants it, we take a moment before one final run-through.

'Jackson,' I say, curtseying. 'I need your help.'

'Never one for pleasantries, were you, Amelia?' Avi replies, a slight smirk at the edge of his lips that makes my heart thud.

'Not when it comes to murder,' I respond.

'If you will, let us look at the facts here, Amelia.' he says. 'You leave me heartbroken, turn down my proposal. Tell me in no uncertain terms that you never want to see me again. And now you appear on my doorstep, asking for my help to solve this case?'

Something sparks in me. I've read these lines, but they seem suddenly so strangely applicable to my own situation that I'm struggling to keep my emotions in check, to level out and find the right line. But it comes out, eventually.

I nod, trying to keep Amelia's expression firm and unyielding. 'There will be payment, of course.'

He raises his eyebrows, pouring himself a glass of whisky — which for these purposes, I've learned, is water simply dyed brown. I'm glad I'm not the one drinking it. 'Always the businesswoman.'

I smile.

'Okay,' he says. 'If I were to consider your proposal, we both know I have no need of financial remuneration. So why should I do this for you?'

I roll my eyes. 'Entertainment, Jackson. Your life must be so dull, drifting from card table to card table. Aren't you looking for a little excitement? I will retain you as an assistant and you'll have the opportunity to actually do something of use for once. And you'll have the satisfaction of finding justice for the young woman who was savagely murdered last night.'

'An assistant?' he asks.

'Of course that's the only aspect of my speech you retain.'

He picks up his glass and takes a sip. 'I suppose I knew this when I met you,' he says carefully. 'That I'd always be in your shadow.'

'If you don't want to help me, Jackson, I'll be on my way,' I say, turning. Ready to leave.

'Wait, Amelia.' I turn around. 'I didn't say I had a problem with that.'

And the way he says it is so slow, so unbelievably sexy, that for a second I forget we're acting. An image appears in my mind of Avi – bursting into my trailer. Almost shirtless. *Oh, my God. Where did that come from?*

'And cut!' Alessandro shouts, rushing over to us.

I look at Avi, a little panic rippling through me.

'This was excellent, estella mia,' Alesandro says, grabbing my hands. He looks from me to Avi, delighted. 'So, bambina,' he says. 'Shall we get this show on the road?'

'Sure,' I reply, feeling more confident now than I did before. *Maybe, just maybe, I can do this,* I think. Something pulls me to look up, just as Alessandro is walking back over to his screen. And I catch something in Avi's eyes – something that looks like nerves, or fear. Which doesn't make any sense at all. Because he's done this a million times.

I'm the one who should be scared.

But, strangely, in this moment – I don't feel it.

I feel determined.

My senses narrow to a point, waiting for my call. Through 'rolling, set, camera, lights', each team is called to their respective duties one by one. And so when Alessandro calls 'Action!', my cue, I'm ready for it.

Avi and I start trading lines – the chemistry just as it was before. The rapport emerging again. And I feel it. Like a warmth permeating my whole body, spreading across my limbs.

But then something happens. I look at Avi for a second too long between lines. And some of the hurt from our confrontation earlier spills out. The edges of Jackson fading away – until he's Avi. Who put that stupid bunch of sunflowers in my trailer and reminded me how much he hurt me.

And I go cold.

I become suddenly aware of the room around me. The cameras, the people. And after a few seconds I come back to my body to find that it's just me. Lara. In a room full of people who are relying on me to do a good job.

And I can't remember my next line.

Fuck.

I'm corpsing. I have no idea what I'm supposed to say. An appropriate term because I would probably rather be dead than doing this on my first day on-set, in front of all these people.

But I'm choking, silence falling while I try to remember the line I memorised. That I recited in the car this morning. In my trailer. During rehearsal just now.

I stare at Avi while I falter helplessly for a few more seconds, groping for words. His expression turns concerned, which sends another flash of heat across my skin.

Shit. Shit. Shit.

I look out in Alessandro's direction to a sea of faces, their expressions frozen as they wait for me to speak.

But I can't speak. My voice is gone. Amelia is gone. The line is gone.

Everything is gone.

Oh, God.

'Cut!' Alessandro calls from my right and a boulder the size of a car lands on my chest.

'Lara,' Avi says quickly, as Alessandro approaches. 'Lara, it's fine. It's just first day nerves—'

'Stop talking.' I choke, placing my hands on my hips and bending over. 'Please.'

He obeys, but still looks at me with a level of concern that makes something twist in my chest. Because he's not allowed to look at me like that.

'Amelia mia,' Alessandro says, his expression still calm – though I think I see a hint of something underneath it that turns my stomach. He's worried. And why wouldn't he be? I've been on-set for five minutes and I'm already failing. 'Shall we try the scene again?'

'Y-yes,' I manage to say. 'Let's.'

Eventually, after a couple more failed takes, Alessandro calls a break – for us to go to the green room and regroup while they see to the sound issue from earlier. I wonder if he's just making up an excuse to avoid embarrassing me, but dismiss the thought. Their time is far too precious, far too expensive, for that. I hope.

David leads us to the green room and I can hear Avi breathing a few paces away from me. I move quickly, heading straight over to the coffee table. Pouring myself a cup, my hand shaking.

'Lara…' Avi's gaze is drawn to my hand. 'Can we talk?'

I take a breath, ready to say something – anything – that will make him leave me alone. That will allow me to regroup before we're called back to set in a few minutes. But before he can say anything, someone else walks in.

Sienna Marsh, in the flesh.

I almost drop my coffee.

Somehow – even in her costume of a torn-to-pieces dress, with dirt smeared on her face – she's still the most beautiful person I've ever seen.

Fuck.

'Oh my goodness,' she says, in her mellow Californian accent. It's like honey and sunlight all at once, bright and smooth and perfectly toned. 'Lara, right? It's so wonderful to meet you. I've heard so much about you.'

You have? I think. And then I can't help it – I gape for a few seconds. Because until now, the most up-close I've come to her face was when it was plastered over the wall in a perfume advert at Piccadilly Circus Tube station. Seeing her in person is surreal.

'It's… nice to meet you too, Sienna,' I choke out eventually, trying to sound like I really mean it. Because she's being perfectly nice, but her sudden appearance – after my complete and utter failure just now – is making me feel like I might have swallowed a few wasps.

'I heard about Roman putting a rat in your trailer this morning,' she says, her expression sympathetic. I glance at Avi sharply and he looks a little sheepish.

'What an asshole,' Sienna says. I turn back to her and she looks genuinely annoyed. I hesitate for a second, surprised by this response. 'I'm so sorry he did that.'

'Uh… thanks,' I reply.

'Of course,' she says, placing a hand on my arm and looking at me conspiratorially. 'You have any trouble with him, you let me know, okay? We used to summer together as kids, in the Hamptons. I know things about that man that would make your toes curl. I can handle him if you need.'

The use of the word 'summer' as a verb startles me and for a second I'm thrown. The offer is kind – kinder than it needed to be, given we've just met. But as she looks at me, some resolve moves through me. I've felt out of my depth since I arrived here this morning and this is one thing I want to do for myself. Besides, I've already watched Avi 'handle' Roman for me and I want him to hear this.

'I think I'd like to handle him myself,' I say. 'But thank you.'

And despite my friendly demeanour, I expect her to falter at this – to find it offensive, even. That I'm turning down her offer of help so decisively. But she just steps back, looking a little impressed. 'A woman of her own mind,' she says. 'I like it.'

'Anyway,' she adds. 'I have to get to the other set.' By which she means a separate sound stage, where she'll presumably be filming today. 'I just wanted to say hi. But I'll see you around, okay?'

I nod and she wafts away in a cloud of what smells like a floral perfume – a little incongruous, given her current get-up – squeezing Avi's arm as she passes. I watch her go, a million feelings rippling through me, unable to think of much more than how she moves with such grace and ease.

I arrived today determined to prove that Alessandro had made the right choice casting me over Sienna.

And instead, I've done the opposite.

Then Avi locks eyes with me. And my heart starts hammering against my chest.

Shit.

'Right!' David appears so suddenly it makes me jump out of my skin. That man is stealthy. But in this case, it's incredibly welcome. 'I'm afraid I have some bad news. The sound issue from earlier is persisting, so we can't film again until tomorrow. You're going to have to go home.'

I get back to the hotel by lunchtime and find myself with absolutely no idea what to do with myself. I expected to be on-set all day. I planned for it. So being stuck in a hotel room feels wrong. I have this pent-up adrenaline, this intense desire to prove myself after my terrible start, and nowhere to put it. I spend an hour re-reading my script, and fight the urge to leave my hotel room and go for a walk to burn this off. I might run into Avi and I don't want to talk to him right now.

I pull out my phone to find a text from Alison. *Have a great day, movie star!* And I smile in spite of everything.

Thanks, I text back. *Hope you're having a great day too. Love you.*

She doesn't need to know about this fiasco.

After I hit send, someone knocks on the door.

I tense up, thinking it will be Avi, but when I open it I find someone else.

Sienna.

Oh, God.

'Hi,' she says warmly. She's no longer in her tattered rags from earlier; now she's in an impossibly chic pink two-piece outfit. 'I just wrapped and wanted to stop by.'

'Hi,' I reply. Fighting a sudden urge to adjust my dress, which I got at a charity shop for £5 a few weeks ago, and which has a rip in the hem that I've been meaning to try to sew up.

'Can I come in?' she asks. And I am not sure how I feel about company right now but I step aside to let her in, still more than a little starstruck by her presence. I'm struggling to wrap my mind around the fact that she's actually in my room right now. Not to mention the fact that she might be coming for my job, if I can't get my shit together.

'I'd offer you a cup of tea or something,' I say lamely, for lack of anything else to say. 'But I'm not sure I have a kettle.'

'Oh, don't worry. I've never understood you Brits and your obsession with tea. It just tastes like dishwater to me,' she says flippantly. 'Though I did have an Earl Grey at the Savoy once that was just about bearable.'

And at that I can't help but wonder if Avi still drinks his tea with two sugars – or if he's left that behind too.

'So,' I say, once she's sitting down. And before I can say anything embarrassing and stupid like 'To what do I owe this pleasure?', she starts talking.

'I wanted to say hi properly,' she says. 'See how you're doing. If you wanted any advice. This being such a strange experience and all.'

I blink, not sure what to make of her words.

'What do you mean?' I ask. Wondering suddenly if she might be referring to Avi, or even the fact that she's here as my understudy. *Might be here as my understudy*, I remind myself. Because there's nothing to prove that that rumour is true yet.

'You know, your first time on a big set,' she says, her hair — so glossy it catches the light from the window — falling over her shoulder.

Oh, I think, relieved. The way she says 'big set' reminds me of a conversation I had with my mum once about going to secondary school. *Big girl school*, she called it.

'That's so kind,' I say, determining to keep my cards close to my chest. 'It's all quite new.'

She nods, tucking a strand of hair behind her ear. 'I remember my first time; I was working with this great director. He was a little insane, though. Terrified of oranges — we couldn't have any near set. I'm talking a complete orange ban. And he was so demanding to work with. It was such a crazy experience and I'd been on sets before, obviously, because of my parents, so it wasn't totally new…' She pauses, looking like she might've just lost her train of thought, then recalibrates, switching her 100-watt smile on. *Are those veneers?* I think. 'Anyway. I get it, kind of.'

'Thanks,' I reply. This woman might live in a totally different world to me. But her making the effort to come here and try to relate to me – impossible as that might be – is nice.

'Sure,' she says, getting up. 'Well, if you need anything I'm just down the hall. Next to Avi.'

I frown, slightly confused. I assumed they'd be sharing a room.

'Number 34,' she says. 'Drop by anytime.'

'I will,' I say – which is probably a lie, because she ever so slightly scares the shit out of me. And there's no way I'm venturing that close to Avi's room. She picks up the book on my table, the special edition that Spencer and Hannah gave me.

'This is beautiful,' she says, running her hand over the gold edges. 'I've been meaning to buy a copy – I haven't read it. Which I know is crazy, being in the film and all. But I figured the script is basically the same, right?'

Oh, God. A flicker of indignation flares up and I push it aside. *This is normal, Lara. You know it's normal. It's just how things work with films.*

'Right,' I reply, struggling to keep it together. A wave of anger passing over me.

Because Sienna has no ill intentions. I know it's common for actors not to want to read the books for the films they're in. Much as it frustrates me in this case – perhaps irrationally, especially given I'm so protective of Amelia and probably blinded by that. I'm not naive. I have to be realistic and rational. I know this is how it works. Your agent puts you up for parts and you go for them, whether you've read the book or not.

But this only serves to strengthen my resolve. I cannot in a million years let myself screw this up.

Because otherwise, I'll be replaced by someone who doesn't know Amelia at all. And she deserves better than that.

Once Sienna has left, I make the most of the clawfooted bathtub, sinking into it in an attempt to reset ahead of tomorrow. And after about an hour, I'm feeling better. The resolve from earlier, with Sienna, still burning. I get out and wrap myself in the fluffiest dressing gown I've ever seen and hear my phone ringing across the room. Spencer's caller ID flashes up on the screen.

'Hey,' I say, surprised he's calling me.

'Hello, stranger,' he says, his tone bright. I light up at the sound of it – a memory flashing up of hearing it around the house that makes me realise how much I've missed it. Even if we didn't interact much, it sounds familiar. Comforting, among all the new experiences I've had in the last twenty-four hours. 'How's filming going?'

'Oh, fine,' I say, keeping my tone light. Because I don't really feel like discussing any of it. If nothing else, I don't need to psych myself out of the relative calm I'm feeling right now. 'A lot of new stuff. But it's fun, being on such a huge set.'

'I bet,' he replies. 'Must be nice to have breakfast brought to you and runners at your every whim. The best I've ever had from the West End was someone who bought too many coffees for the stars by accident and gave me one by default. But that's what I get for choosing stage work and not big budgets.'

I falter for a second, wanting to tell him that I'm not here for all that. But I can tell from his tone that he doesn't mean it. It's just my own insecurities coming up. Wanting to be clear that I'm not just here for the money – I'm here because I love it. Because the idea of reaching people is exciting to me.

'Anyway,' he says. 'I wanted to ask about something. Two things, actually.'

'Shoot.'

'Well, the first is that Hannah and I are going for drinks next Thursday – and we wondered if you wanted to come?'

'That's so kind,' I reply. 'I think I'll be too busy with filming, though.'

'Of course,' he says. 'That's what we expected. I'll keep you posted though – we're trying out pubs in West London over the next few weeks, so Hannah can check them off her list. I'll let you know where we go next.'

'Please do,' I say, and my heart sinks a little – because I do feel bad. But I'm expecting to be on-set all hours. And I don't want to say yes and let them down.

'The second thing,' he says, 'is that we found a box under your bed. It was a bit of a fiasco, actually. The guy moving in is French, and for some reason thought he had to bring his own bed. So he insisted we dismantle yours and put his up instead. It's been a fucking nightmare with the landlord. But in the process, we found a box. I found the new guy rifling through it, but managed to get it off him. It looks like it has some postcards in it. I was wondering if you wanted to pick it up or whether you'd like me to store it for you?'

Oh, God, I think, a sinking feeling dropping in my chest. Because I know exactly what box he's talking about. The one I stored Avi's postcards in. The one I almost opened a few weeks ago, before my first audition. The one I must have completely – or intentionally – forgotten about when packing up.

'Um…'

'It's no issue if you want me to keep it for a bit,' he says. 'I know you're busy – and I'm assuming they're probably precious if you kept hold of them.'

'They aren't,' I say quickly – too quickly. He pauses on the other end of the line. 'Sorry,' I say. 'It's just… some correspondence. From an old friend.'

'That's nice,' he says. 'Are you sure you don't want me to keep hold of them?'

No, I think. Because there is a reason I kept hold of them for all these years – a reason I don't really want to go into right now. Because it involves the person I have to see on-set tomorrow. The person who sent me those postcards regularly for six months. Who flew home for the pub Christmas party that year.

Who kissed me, then freaked out and disappeared. Who texted me the next morning and broke my heart.

Who left after that and stopped talking to me at all.

I bite my lip, the pain coming back all at once. The memory of receiving that text: *Last night was a mistake*.

'You can throw them away,' I say, letting out a breath. Because that person isn't here any more. I can't keep holding on to relics of a friendship that no longer exists. I have to let them go. To see him as my colleague. Not anything else.

And maybe, if I do, I'll be able to get through the next six weeks in one piece. And actually do a good job of this film.

'Okay,' Spencer says. 'If you're sure…'

8

The next morning I arrive on-set full of determination to do a better job, with an unexpected lightness to my step – as if my interaction with Sienna and telling Spencer to throw away those postcards have strengthened my determination to persevere. To make something of this opportunity. Unfortunately, though, within the first ten minutes on-set, I find out that the sound system is still causing issues and that the schedule for this morning has changed from filming to stunt training. A ripple of disappointment runs through me – that I won't have a chance to prove myself just yet.

But I can't dwell on it for too long. This is just as important and I've been genuinely excited for this part of the process too. I'll have a stunt double, but not for the fight scenes where my face will be visible – some sparring with Avi's character, as he helps me with my physical combat skills, and one actual fight with Roman's character, which given our previous meeting will be interesting to film. These scenes will be shot in slow motion and then sped up in post-production.

The stunt coordinator's name is Lucy. She's a friendly and impressive woman who is a full foot taller than me and looks like she could definitely handle herself in a fight. I'm in the middle of talking to her about her career — how she got here, coming up through being a professional boxer — when Avi arrives. My throat instantly dries up.

I worry he's going to try to talk about what happened yesterday. But he doesn't. Just greets Lucy warmly, by name — in the short time I've observed him on-set, he seems to have a propensity for learning and remembering everyone's names — and flashes me an inscrutable smile. She runs us through a few of the moves, then steps back to allow us to rehearse them. At full speed, first, then slowing them down once we have the moves right.

Avi and I make it through the first few sequences without speaking. Left jab, right hook. Avi blocking with alternate hands. Stepping backwards as we go. Lucy slows us down and speeds us up as necessary. And I start to feel... comfortable, almost. Like he could be any other actor.

'Wow,' Avi says, as I throw a kick and he dodges it. 'You're good at this. How come I never knew you could throw a punch?'

Spoke too soon, I think. I take a breath, because, after the fiasco yesterday I'm determined to keep our relationship as professional as possible. Not to lose my cool again. To just focus on doing a good job.

'I used to do karate,' I reply, throwing another punch to try to avoid engaging further in conversation.

He dodges and then says, 'Interesting,' as if he's waiting for me to say more. But this isn't a topic I'm willing to elaborate on. So I ignore it, throwing a left hook instead. We get back into a rhythm and are silent for a few moments.

'So… I was wondering if maybe you wanted to run some lines later?' he asks, blocking another jab.

Oh, I think. And my first instinct is to say no, obviously – because the last thing I want to do is spend time with Avi one-on-one. But I'm on-set now. Committed to the role. And this definitely falls under 'Things I Should Do To Make Sure I Don't Fuck Up This Job'.

'I think it would be helpful,' he says. 'You know, after what happened yesterday…'

And I can't help it – this sends some frustration surging up. I can't blame him for yesterday; it's not his fault I forgot my line. But I don't need him to tell me I fucked up – I already know.

Keep your cool, I think, as I spin him and pin his arm behind his back. But apparently I'm not keeping my cool, because I pull his arm so he's actually pinned. Our bodies pressed against each other. I can hear his breath, heaving.

'That's great, Lara,' the stunt coordinator says – and at the sound of her voice I come to my senses. 'Now release him.'

I let go of his arm and take a step back, my heart hammering.

He brushes himself off. 'Look, I'm sure yesterday wasn't the start to filming you wanted. And it's fine, because it's your first time on a set. But I know you, Lara. I know you want better than that. And I know Alessandro too. He's a patient man, but if you push him too far this isn't going to be the experience you want it to be.'

We reset ourselves at our marks.

'Why do you care about my experience?' I ask, some of my confusion bursting out of me. Because on one level, I understand. We have a shared goal: to make this film a success. I have to accept that.

But what he said at the audition and here on-set is so at odds with the way he's acted over the last few years – like he doesn't care about me at all – that I can't get my head around it.

The stunt coordinator gives the signal and I lunge forwards a little quicker than intended; I catch him by surprise, twisting his arm behind his back and kicking his legs out, throwing him to the mat.

We crash down onto it and I land on top of him.

'I don't think you want to hear it,' he says.

'Try me,' I reply. Our faces are inches apart, our bodies flush against each other.

'Because I care about you, Lara,' he says, his voice full of emotion. His expression shifts, a little frustration underlying it. Frustration I share – because he's right. I didn't want to hear that. He doesn't get to just tell me that now, after ignoring me for three years. 'If you want to believe that I'm an arsehole and I hate you, then fine. But I want this film to be a success, for both our sakes. And I know that you do too.'

The stunt coordinator calls over and tells us we're done for the day. We get up, an awkward tangle of limbs that makes me blush as he reluctantly reaches out his hand and pulls me to my feet, avoiding eye contact.

But as he does, there's a pull in my stomach. Like there's a hook there, attached to him. And an image flashes through my mind: of Alessandro's face, yesterday. So disappointed in me. I might not like this, but I promised myself my personal relationship with Avi wouldn't get in the way of my work and here I am, letting it. *The postcards are gone, Lara*, I think to myself. *You've committed to a fresh start.*

'Avi,' I say, my heart clenching. 'Wait.'

'What?' he says, seeming a little irritated. I fight a bristle of anger at his tone, taking a breath.

Because I have to do a good job. Want to. And whether or not Avi cares about me is beside the point. The point is Amelia, and what's best for her. I exhale slowly. 'I think running lines is a good idea. Can I come to your trailer this afternoon?'

And some of the frustration melts from his expression, his face brightening into a smile that makes me almost want to look away.

'Straight after filming?' he asks. I nod. 'Looking forward to it,' he says. 'I promise you won't regret it.'

I hope not, I think, as I watch him walk away.

David informs me when I arrive back on-set that the sound issue is fixed, meaning we're safe to film again. And so I'm put through hair and make-up. Sarah, the same woman who did my make-up yesterday, asks how my first day went and I avoid the question by saying instead how relieved I am that the sound issue has been resolved. Then I thank her for the calming pastilles she always has on hand – one of which I take before reaching set.

My stomach knots when I think about what I've just agreed to with Avi, because a) I don't want to believe that I need his help and b) I feel strangely vulnerable about spending time alone with him in his trailer. But I also know that I can't afford to let anything get in the way of doing a good job. Especially after Sienna came and found us after our stunt training, her presence reminding me of what might happen if I screw this all up. They invited me to have lunch with them, but I elected to eat alone in my trailer instead.

I arrive on-set to find Avi already waiting on his mark. Alessandro greets me briefly and I do my best not to overanalyse his tone and read too much disappointment into it; at the very least, he seems frustrated by the delays and keen to get moving and start getting some useable footage filmed. But I know he'd be a little less anxious had I not completely screwed up my first take.

Come on, Lara, I think as I approach my mark. *This is your chance.*

After we've prepped and blocked everything, Alessandro goes back to his place and calls 'Action!', and Avi and I start the scene. The same scene we were doing yesterday – directly back into the fire. Into the spot where I messed up.

At first, it's going well, I think. I remember my lines, hit my marks. I feel calm, collected. In control of myself and the scene. Avi is electric – right in the moment. His talent shining through so brightly that for a second I forget I was ever annoyed with him.

This feels good.

'Cut!' Alessandro calls. I falter, slightly concerned – because we haven't yet finished the scene. Alessandro approaches us slowly, his expression carefully measured.

'Avi,' he says. 'You were excellent. No notes.'

I hold my breath.

Oh, shit, I think. *So the problem is me.*

'Now Lara,' he says, grasping my hands. My heart thuds. 'Carina mia. Amelia mia. How can I say this? You look a little… constipated. Do you think you could look less constipated?'

Oh. My. God.

This might be up there with the worst feedback I've ever received, second only to an acting teacher who told me a boulder would have more charisma on stage than me. My face flushes under my make-up and I avoid Avi's gaze.

'Uh, sure, Alessandro,' I say.

And so I set my shoulders, breathing into the scene. Embodying Amelia. Trying to forget that there are cameras on me and a thousand people watching me.

The next take is – somehow – even worse.

And so we try again.

And again.

But no matter how many notes Alessandro gives me, I can't seem to get it right. First it's my posture, then it's the tone of my voice. Then it's – everything, apparently. And the more I try to implement the notes, the more wooden I become. With every failed take, I want the ground to swallow me up even more. My frustration – with myself, with Alessandro, with Avi, with this whole situation – is rising, making it more and more difficult to get out of my body and into the scene. And I see Alessandro trying to rein himself in, the delivery of his feedback increasingly sharp. Like he might be about to blow. The knot of nerves twists tighter each time.

I can feel the seconds ticking away, each one worth more than I've ever earned in my life. Budget is everything – and if we go into overtime, the production team are going to be out of pocket and probably furious. And still, I can't seem to get it together.

'Lara,' Avi says in a low voice to me after a particularly awful attempt where I almost tripped over a table. I see Alessandro discussing something with the first AD, a look of despair crossing his features. I feel horribly out of control, like I'm about to lose this role. 'Remember the play we did, a few years ago?'

'What are you talking about?' I ask, unsure why he's bringing this up now.

'Beatrice and Benedick,' he says. '*Much Ado About Nothing.*'

And my heart clenches – because that's the last play we did together before he left.

'I do,' I say, letting out a breath.

'Well,' he says. 'Let's pretend we're doing that. Remember that rehearsal where we couldn't make it work?'

The memory surfaces in my mind. We were struggling with an overzealous director. No matter how many notes they gave us, they weren't happy. And I was about to give up, honestly. But Avi taught me a breathing exercise – convinced me to try it. For one more take.

I don't want to go there, though. Because about halfway through that rehearsal was when I realised for the first time that I liked him as more than a friend.

But now I look up at him and his expression is pleading. And I glance towards Alessandro, looking like he might be on the verge of an aneurysm.

'Okay,' I say, returning to my mark. 'Let's try it.'

He takes my hands, gently, while Alessandro gets the next take set up. I look at Avi and follow his breath. In, out. His hands, his presence, grounding me for a second. Alessandro finishes his conversation and Avi lets go. And for a second I feel the absence of his touch. But then Alessandro is counting down and I'm stepping into the scene. All my anxious thoughts suddenly gone.

I'm back on that stage, twenty-four again. My life stretching out ahead of me like a great long carpet. Avi across from me, the electricity pulsing between us. His eyes locking on mine.

'Action!' Alessandro says for about the fifth time.

And, miraculously, this time, something flows.

It's fun. And I don't have time to worry about the fact that I'm enjoying it, because I'm so in the moment nothing else seeps in. The feeling from the audition is back – of ease. A naturalness to what we're doing that erases the rest of the room until it's just us. Amelia and Jackson, finding a way to work together after all their history.

And when Alessandro calls 'Cut!' at the end of the scene, I hold my breath.

But then his hand is on my arm, and Avi's, his expression lit up like the sun.

'My children,' he says. 'We have got it.'

And my eyes lock with Avi's, a soaring sensation cutting through everything else.

We did it.

Once we're wrapped for the day – after filming a few more great takes, to the point where I might actually be starting to feel competent on-set for the first time since I arrived – I grab some food from craft services and start making my way to Avi's trailer to rehearse. I'm walking through set, flanked by a few runners, when Roman jumps out at me from nowhere.

'What the fuck?' I say impulsively. I place my hand to my chest, my heart hammering against it.

'No sidekick today, Amelia?' he asks. *Amelia, again?* This man is insane.

'My name is Lara,' I say. 'And if you're talking about Avi…' His face darkens at the mention of his name.

'I have to say,' he says. 'I was a little… offended that you didn't seem to like my gift. I was under the impression that ladies tended to appreciate such gestures.' He places his hands behind his back.

'I'm not sure how ladies generally feel about it, but I'd wager they're not usually grateful when people put dead animals in their trailers, no,' I reply.

'I'm terribly sorry to hear that,' he says. 'I thought perhaps we would have an understanding. That perhaps there was a darkness in you that matched mine. But I see abundantly now that I was mistaken.'

I fight the urge to roll my eyes. *Does he really get off on this method-acting bullshit or is he just trying to freak me out for fun?*

'I have to go,' I say. 'I've got to rehearse with—'

'Jackson?' he says, his face brightening. 'I have to say, you two seemed to be familiar with one another. Almost as if… this wasn't the first time you'd become acquainted. Have you met before, perhaps?'

'No,' I say quickly. I don't know if he's still play-acting or what, but in any case I don't need Roman knowing anything about our history together. Clearly, he's dangerous.

'Interesting,' he says, almost to himself, looking at me carefully. 'A nervous liar.' Then he steps to one side, bowing deeply. 'Well, don't let me get in your way.'

'I…' I'm ready to defend myself. To say something, anything, to make him stop looking at me with such an infuriatingly knowing expression. But nothing comes up. Instead, I watch him straighten up, so I move to walk past him. But before I can go, he calls me back.

'Amelia, wait,' he says. And despite my better instincts, I turn. He produces a flower from his pocket and hands it to me with a flourish.

'A flower for a lady,' he says. I get the sense that he's not going to leave me alone unless I take it, so I snatch it from his hand and walk away.

What, I think to myself, *the fuck was that?*

I arrive at Avi's trailer and knock on the door, hearing two voices. His, and the musical lilt I now recognise as Sienna's.

She's laughing at something he said. And out of nowhere, a memory surges up. Me, doubled over behind the bar, snorting lemonade out of my nose. Avi, doing an impression of Tom the bar manager that was so accurate I couldn't breathe from laughter.

'Hi,' he says, pulling open the door. 'What's with the flower?'

'Roman,' I say and immediately regret it. His face darkens.

'Was he messing with you again?'

'No,' I say. 'He's a perfectly normal, very balanced man. I think we're going to be great friends.'

'Hi, Lara,' Sienna calls out from the other side of the room. My stomach drops slightly. Extra practice time with Avi was making me nervous enough. But revealing just how vulnerable I am in the role of Amelia to the woman who's competing with me for it? That's definitely more than I thought I was signing up for.

'Hi,' I say brightly. Because she does seem nice and I don't want to be rude. I sit down across from her.

'Would you like some herbal tea?' she asks, dropping the 'h', such that it takes me a second to understand what she's saying. 'I found this stuff in Dubai and it's honestly magical. So many healing properties. Great for your digestion, your cholesterol. A shaman I work with told me it has spiritual benefits too – connects you to the divine.'

'Oh,' I say, a little lost for words. 'Uh, no, thank you.'

'Diet Coke?' Avi says instead and I nod. He used to tease me about my caffeine consumption; I'd drink at least three a day, most days, including at the pub. I wonder if he remembers. He pulls one from his fridge and tosses it to me.

'Lara's always been a caffeine addict,' he says casually to Sienna as he sits down. I frown a little, remembering what she said when I met her. *I've heard so much about you.* I wonder what he's told her.

'Well,' she says. 'I'd better get going. But have a great time, you guys!'

She leans over and kisses Avi on the cheek.

'See you later,' he says and watches her leave, a curious expression on his face.

There's something about this exchange that has me almost uncomfortable to witness it. Not, though, because I feel like a third wheel. Because – though I can't quite put my finger on exactly what it is – there's a strange vibe between them. Stilted, almost performative. But maybe they're just a more private couple.

'So,' he says. 'Shall we get started?'

★ ★ ★

About an hour later, we've tried a few different approaches to the scene we're rehearsing: an argument between Jackson and Amelia. She's persuaded him to join the case, but when she tells him her theory — that there's a secret cult running from one of the gentlemen's clubs in Pall Mall that is behind the series of ritual murders of London socialites and courtesans — Jackson is a little more than sceptical. Avi gives me a few notes on my delivery, suggesting different tones of voice, different gestures. They're very good notes and while my fragile actor ego wants me not to need his help, I know it's for the best that I take them. And he takes some notes from me too. That was our superpower when we performed together before — we were always in tune with one another. Always able to see what the other needed, to push them that one step further. But I brush that thought aside — much like the postcards, it belongs in another time.

When we're done rehearsing, he gets me another Diet Coke from the fridge and we sit down to discuss some character notes. Making sure we're on the same page regarding their motivations.

'I see Jackson as basically an idiot,' Avi says, which makes me laugh unexpectedly. I take a sip of my drink to cover it. 'At first, at least. You know, he has this determination to do the right thing, but he's also blind to the stuff Amelia sees. Too comfortable in his own world.'

'That's how I see him too,' I say, excited by the insight. 'He's like – well-intentioned, but a bit thick-headed. He lets his rationality cloud his judgement sometimes.'

'Agreed,' he says. 'Though he's a good foil to Amelia – she's impulsive sometimes. Needs someone to hold her back from making decisions too quickly.'

'And obviously, he's obsessed with her,' I say.

'Why wouldn't he be?' He smiles. 'She's great. So fearless and sharp. Unafraid to be herself. To say what she thinks. I love Amelia.'

My heart thuds a little. Because those are all the reasons I love her too.

'So do I,' I say quietly.

'What is it about her?' he asks, leaning in. 'I know you love the books.' *Of course you do – you tried to buy me a first edition of the first book for my birthday.* But we don't need to talk about that right now. 'But I'd love to hear more about why you like her so much, as a character.'

'I...' I think of my teenage self, hiding my book under the desk at school. Reading, to escape, to become someone else. And I almost say it, almost start telling him. But we never talked about it before. Because that version of me is vulnerable – too vulnerable to tell him about, even when we were close. We always stayed in the present – it was what I loved about our relationship. And so we never really touched on my past, not even when he told me he'd lost the eBay auction for that book – the most thoughtful almost-gift I've ever received, just because he saw me reading the books during my lunch breaks. Because we didn't need to. He saw things and remembered them. Seemed to get me – my drive, my ambition – in a way I'd never really felt understood before. So much so that the past didn't seem to matter when I was with him. It was like I could be someone entirely new. And with that thought, suddenly it's like the air clears and I wake up to where I am. Sitting in his trailer. A million miles away from that feeling.

I smile, putting my drink down. 'I should probably go.' Because this conversation is getting dangerously close to intimate. And while I want to do whatever it takes with Avi to make this film a success, I don't want to blur any lines.

'Lara, wait…' he says, before I reach the door. 'Did I say something wrong?'

I care about you, Lara.
My chest pinches and I shake my head.
'I'll see you tomorrow,' I say, opening the door and closing it behind me.

9

The next couple of weeks pass in a blur. We've filmed all of the opening scenes of the film now and I'm really starting to find my feet. I've nailed my breakfast order – a croissant and a flat white – and have managed to talk the runner down from sourcing it from a French bakery, convincing him that Pret was fine. Alison has been texting me trying to convince me to come out with her friends – because they want to quiz me about what it's like to be in a movie – but I've been able to fob her off with a promise that I'll meet her friends at her birthday party in a few weeks.

And I've been in touch with Spencer and Hannah too – the new flatmate is driving them insane, apparently. He keeps shutting himself in his room and blasting electropop music. And he doesn't really speak English, but likes to resort to yelling when they try to have conversations with him. Hannah has jokingly begged me to come back, a few times. And I've been updating them on what it's like to be on-set, sending requested selfies from my trailer. Photos of the spread at craft services, which they were both absolutely stunned by. (I was too, honestly – there's enough food there that I could probably survive on one table's worth for weeks, if the apocalypse happened and set was shut down.) Nat calls for check-ins every couple of days and there's little to report except that things are actually going well, which is a huge relief.

At 6 p.m. every evening after filming, I head over to Avi's trailer and we run lines for the next day together. After our conversation on that first day, he doesn't really press for personal stuff. I think he finally understands what I want: a professional relationship that isn't going to cause me any problems on-set but which means I'm comfortable enough around him, and with our dynamic, to start to find my stride.

I'm receiving praise from Alessandro most days and only some notes, which are manageable. And Avi starts to blur into Jackson. As if – if I think about him as his character, rather than who he is, even when we're not filming – I can get through this. And I feel myself slipping into Amelia more easily every day. Like she's a familiar, favourite pair of shoes. It's a great feeling.

Sienna comes by my trailer every so often. I'm still not over having one of the most famous women in the world stop by for a chat, but she's mainly just giving me tips on the latest crystals she's keeping in her trailer to ward off negative energies. Or telling me about a new form of Pilates she's trying. Sienna and Avi's relationship is still a little strange to me. I know it's none of my business, but they don't seem to spend that much time together on-set. And when they are together, the most I ever see them do is kiss each other on the cheek. *Maybe that's just what Hollywood relationships are like*, I think – you probably don't want to be too affectionate in front of other people, to protect yourself from unwanted attention.

Every evening, after Avi and I have run our lines, I go back to my hotel room for room service and he goes out with Sienna – and we're not each other's concern any more. It's good. It might even be great. I haven't worried too much about Sienna being my understudy, though the thought does flicker frighteningly into my mind sometimes if I have a brief falter on-set. But, on the whole, I feel like I'm finding my feet. Settling in. And I'm definitely not thinking about the fact that the further we get through the film, the closer we get to shooting our romantic scenes together.

So far, Amelia and Jackson have been so focused on their investigation that their scenes are charged with a different type of energy. But we're approaching the halfway point and in about a week's time we'll start to see a shift in their relationship. Then there's the kiss.

And I have literally no idea how I'm going to feel about that.

The first day of our third week, I arrive at our first off-set filming location: the Maughan Library at King's College London near Blackfriars.

When I arrive, I do a double take. This set-up is compact – they've closed the street down and fenced it off at each end, runners stationed with radios to let pedestrians through between scenes. There are a few tents, for sound and lighting equipment. Our trailers are still across town, on the regular set. And as opposed to the fifty to a hundred people who are usually milling around, for today there are only about twenty. It feels intimate, and exhilarating. To be out in the open, filming like this. I'm reminded of when I walked across a set of a hospital drama once, as they were filming a car crash scene. I was ushered by a runner because I was passing through on my usual route to the paper company. Craning my neck as I passed, in awe of it. So to watch people doing it now, and be on the other side of it, is insane. The building is also breathtakingly beautiful, like a giant cathedral, all arched windows and spires. There's a horse-drawn carriage in front of me and several supporting actors milling around dressed in full costume. I feel, for an instant, as if I have truly stepped back in time.

Amelia and Jackson are there to investigate, looking at old records of satanic cults in the city. The police believe that the murder they're investigating was a suicide – that the woman was interested in witchcraft, and her connection to the devil overwhelmed her and caused her to take her own life. But Amelia recognised that the markings were not drawn by her own hand. According to the victim's relative, she was left-handed. So once she's managed to persuade Jackson that the case might involve some of his friends, they head to the library. After filming some dialogue outside, we head inside the building. Which is almost as stunning as the outside: a great rotunda filled floor-to-ceiling with books, rising up to a glass dome ceiling. Jackson and Amelia rifle through some of the books, poring over archives.

Once we've taped the B-roll of us examining the records, Alessandro gives us the signal to move to our marks for the next scene, one of my favourites. The dialogue is sharp and full of life. Setting up Amelia and Jackson's chemistry with one another. The central tension of his initial scepticism about her theories conflicting with his feelings for her, his desire to trust her instincts.

Avi and I exchange a glance to check we're both ready. A nod, to show we are.

'Action!' Alessandro calls, and I step forwards to deliver my line.

'Don't be an idiot, Jackson,' I say. They have found records of a cult run out of Jackson's own club, members tracing back years. Though the records stopped ten years previously – a fact that Jackson has latched on to.

'I'm just trying to be rational, Amelia,' he says. 'There could be other explanations.'

'Yes, well – maybe if you weren't so invested in ignoring the flaws of everyone around you in pursuit of being liked by them, you might actually be able to see the truth.'

'That's not fair,' he says. 'And besides, we don't know if it's the truth. You're jumping to conclusions straight off the bat.'

'And when,' I say, stepping closer, 'have I ever been wrong?'

Avi looks down. 'Rarely,' he admits. 'But you have to understand, Amelia – if you're right, these men are serious. You don't want to mess with them.'

'If it's in the pursuit of justice,' I say, 'I don't care.'

'I just don't want you to get too caught up in all this,' he says. 'I could never forgive myself, if something happened to you…'

And he reaches out, his hand brushing mine.

As he does, a thrill rushes across my skin that has my pulse surging. I look up at him, my throat tightening.

Fuck.

I stand for a second, choking. Desperately searching for my line. Seeing Alessandro in my periphery, tensing up, ready to call 'Cut!' But before he can, before I can either jerk myself back into the scene or be overcome by panic, there's a creaking sound from somewhere overhead. The light fitting they had rushed to set up earlier, because we were behind schedule.

I look up, my heart pounding, to see it above me, swinging dangerously in its bracket.

People around me start to move, to panic. And just before I realise it's going to fall, I am forced to the ground.

I hear shards of glass clinking around us as my senses come back one at a time.

Alessandro's voice, shouting in the distance. The sounds of blind panic, from several members of the crew. Footsteps rushing towards us.

Blinking my eyes open, I see carpet in front of me. A few small shards glittering.

And I feel someone's body on top of mine.

'Lara?' Avi's voice asks. His weight shifts off me, and I feel him lift me to my feet. 'Are you okay?'

What the fuck just happened?

'Please tell me you are still alive and in possession of all your limbs,' Nat says on the phone, once I'm safely back in my trailer having had a once-over by a medic and been rushed back to set while the crew deal with the fallout. I still haven't processed what happened – my breath catching at the memory of Avi's body covering mine. The shattered glass all around me.

'I am fine,' I reply. 'I promise.' But it does nothing to put out the fire of Nat's rage.

I have repeated the words 'I am fine' to so many people since the light fitting fell. To the on-set medic, who checked the bruises on my knees. To Avi. To Alessandro, who ran over in a hurricane of apologies, my stalling apparently completely forgotten. He was furious with the lighting department, absolutely losing his shit at them. Shouting in Italian. Some quite expressive hand gestures. And a lot of swearing. It's the first time I've seen him like that; I guess he reached the limits of his patience, as Avi alluded to on our second day here. It makes me incredibly glad that we've – somehow – found a way to get our shit together and I haven't been on the receiving end of it.

'I can't believe this happened,' Nat continues, her tone incredulous. 'You would think that with the amount they're spending on this film, they'd manage not to kill one of the leads.'

'Nat,' I say, as she rants about insurance and contractual agreements.

But I'm not worried about any of that right now.

And it's crazy, because I should be. I should be thanking my lucky stars that I wasn't injured, that I was fine. That Avi pulled me out of the way. And somewhere, under all of this, I am.

But my primary concern is what was happening before the light fell.

'Nat,' I say again, my tone so serious this time she stops mid-rant.

'What, Lara?' She sounds like she's ready to go on the warpath for whatever I'm about to say. Nat might not be one of the more experienced agents in the business, but she is all fire when it comes to looking after her clients. It's one of the things I love about her. But I don't want to discuss all of this right now. I need a second – alone. To process.

'I am fine,' I repeat. I want to get her off the phone.

'Promise?' she asks. And my heart thuds.

'Yes,' I reply.

Almost as soon as I hang up, there's a knock at my door.

I open it, ready to tell the runner for the millionth time that I am okay, that I don't need anything, and that I'm not going to sue the production company.

But it's not the runner. It's Avi.

'Hey,' he says, his voice low.

He's wearing jeans and a burgundy sweatshirt, his hands in his pockets. It's the most casual I've seen him since we arrived on-set, because he's usually back in his suit straight after filming, and the image startles me a little. He almost looks like the Avi I knew before.

'Hi,' I reply. I suddenly have no idea what to say to him. But he did save my life earlier and I find, for the first time since we started filming, that I don't want to turn him away. 'Do you want to come in?' I ask.

'Yeah,' he says. 'Thanks.'

He looks – now I see it – pretty shaken. He sits down in the chair next to the door, under the shelf where I've stacked the few books I brought to set with me. My old copy of *A Murder in London*, some notebooks where I've been recording the notes Alessandro has given me on-set. Plus some of my old acting manuals, detailing various techniques and exercises – the presence of which is a little embarrassing and I find myself hoping he doesn't look at them too closely. I offer him tea and he asks for two sugars. And I hate myself for it, but something lights up inside me. At the idea that he might not have changed as much as I thought.

Stop it, Lara, I think.

I move to the kitchenette and put the kettle on, pulling a mug from the small cupboard above. Moving almost instinctively, automatically.

'Are you okay?' I ask, when he's taken the cup of tea from my hands. He hasn't really spoken since he entered the trailer.

'I think so,' he says. 'The medic said that I might be in shock. But I feel like I should be asking you that question.'

'I...' I pause, an unwanted memory of how his body felt against mine for a moment, throwing me out of the way of the falling light. 'I'm fine,' I say, clenching my hand around the mug handle.

'Are you sure?' he asks.

'No,' I reply. 'But mostly because I've been asked if I'm okay so many times in the last hour that words aren't really words any more.'

He laughs. And I am reminded that Avi – no matter whether what I said was actually funny – always used to make me feel like I was the funniest person in the room.

'I hope I didn't hurt you,' he says.

'I think a few bruises are better than being crushed to death by a light fitting,' I say. He laughs again and a thrill runs across my skin. *Fuck*.

'I have to confess, I actually came here with an agenda,' he says, taking a sip of his tea. I tense up, not sure what he's going to say next.

'What is it?' I ask.

'Well,' he says. 'I did want to ask you anyway but I thought you'd say no. Then Alessandro...' He pauses. 'Well, he said he noticed that there was a bit of weirdness between us, before the light fitting fell. He thinks I'm throwing you off your game.'

Oh, fuck, I think. That's the last thing I wanted – and I suppose he didn't feel like he could say it to me. Given I nearly died. But still, it hits me like a punch in the gut. Sienna's face, beautiful and perfect, and ready to step in, appears in my mind.

'And given we've lost a day today, he's worried about anything else that might cause delays. So he wants me to take you to the Olivier Awards next week. Partly to promote the film – he thinks it'll be good for us to make a shared public appearance. But also because he thinks we should spend some time together, outside work. Get to know each other a bit. In case it's my, uh... profile that's bothering you.' He looks like he wants to vomit at that last sentence and I can't help it – I almost laugh at his expression.

'So he thinks I'm starstruck by you?' I ask, the words slipping out of my mouth, betraying the shock and – to be honest – hilarity of the situation. *I wish that was what was happening*, I think.

That would be much easier to deal with than... whatever's going on here.

He nods, a smile passing across his face, dispelling some of the embarrassment. My heart kicks. 'Pretty ridiculous, right?'

'Well, you are one of the most famous people on the planet and I think a lot of people would probably sell their mother just to be in the same room as you,' I say. 'So I can see his point.'

'Very funny,' he replies. But he doesn't laugh this time, a discomfort etched on his face that gives me pause. 'So what do you think?'

And my first instinct is to hesitate. Because a) I'm not thrilled by the idea of a public appearance, so soon. I'm not an idiot – I know I'll have to do it at some point. But I'm enjoying being in our filming bubble for now. And b) it'll be a whole evening. Alone. With Avi. Who I might be getting along reasonably well with, professionally. But who I don't really feel comfortable going any further than that with. 'When is it?' I ask.

'Thursday,' he says. The day before we're scheduled to film our kissing scene. Which makes me feel all kinds of weird. Between the light fitting and this offer, the prospect of kissing him – something

I've successfully been able to keep out of my mind for the last two weeks – has my head spinning.

'If you don't want to go,' he says, 'it's fine. I can lie to Alessandro and tell him I'm taking you out to dinner or something.'

'I…' I pause. Because there's another half of this. That maybe there's something in what Alessandro is saying. That maybe, if I spend some time with Avi, off-set, I'll be able to not lose my composure around him over something as simple and stupid as him touching my hand. I promised myself I'd do whatever it takes to get this role. To keep it.

'Okay,' I say, nodding before I really realise what I'm doing.

'Great,' he replies. 'I should probably go – but make sure you tell someone if you start to feel weird, okay? There's no sense being a martyr.'

I blink, unsure what he's talking about. Because it sounds like he's referring to us – to what I've just agreed to – and that would be insane.

'Your fall,' he says. 'It was pretty major. We don't want one of the lead stars ending up with a concussion and not telling anyone about it.'

'Oh,' I say. 'Y-yeah. I will.' He gets up and carefully puts his cup down. 'Shall we meet in the hotel lobby on Thursday, then? We can sort timings later.'

'Perfect,' I reply.

'I was beginning to think you were too famous for me now,' Alison jokes that afternoon when I call her.

Filming is done for the rest of the day so I'm in bed in my hotel room, bored of running lines and having thoroughly exhausted the TV that's on offer. I'm so sharpened to my own performance that whenever I switch the TV on I find myself taking notes, analysing what the actors are doing. Their line deliveries, their gestures. How far they disappear into each role. It's a trait I've found useful in the past. But right now it's affecting my ability to have any downtime. So I decide to check in with Al instead.

'How is it all going?' she asks. But I deflect, insisting on hearing about what's been going on with her. She tells me she's good but tired, out three of the five nights this past week. She's dating someone new: a French poet she met a few weeks ago at an open-mic beat poetry evening. It's going well, apparently – despite the language barrier. She tells me she understands about half of the words he says, but it doesn't matter because their connection is 'beyond words'.

'So,' she says eventually. 'Will you stop stalling now and tell me what's happening with you?'

I pause for a second, wondering how much to share with her. The alarm bells going off like they usually do. Because if I admit that I'm struggling, even a little, she'll just tell me everything I'm doing wrong, and how to fix it. 'It's going… okay.'

'Come on,' she says. 'I want details.'

'Well,' I say. 'The work is fun. Avi and I are doing well, I think – though we did have a bit of a nightmare on-set yesterday.'

'What happened?' she asks. I tell her about the light fitting.

'Oh, my God,' she says. 'Are you okay?'

'Yeah. A few bruises, but otherwise fine.'

'Swoon that he saved you,' she says, moving swiftly on from the near-death experience, and my heart thumps a little. 'Is he as hot in person as he looks in photos?'

'Al—'

'Come on, Lara,' she says. 'Give me something, at least. I need some gossip for my colleagues. They're already finding it hard to believe I'm telling the truth about your job. I showed them the announcement and everything.'

'Fine.' I breathe out. 'Yes, he is good-looking. But I already knew that.'

'Did you ever fancy him when you worked together?'

'Okay,' I say. 'End of conversation. He's my colleague, Al.'

'You are so boring,' she complains. 'But fine. Can you tell me about any cool perks yet, at least? Will you be doing any red carpets anytime soon?'

'Mm,' I say.

'What does that mean? Mm?'

I sigh. 'It means Alessandro has asked me to go to the Olivier Awards with Avi next week. But I'm feeling a little weird about going, honestly.' Since this morning, I've been turning over my answer to Avi's proposal in my mind, wondering if I answered too quickly. If I made the right decision. I'm still not sure if it'll be the positive move I think it will.

'Oh come on, Lara—'

'See, this is why I never want to tell you anything—' but she's already off.

'You have to fucking go, Lara. If you want to stay at home with your scripts on a normal day, ignoring the rest of the world, I can't stop you. But there's a difference between reclusive and stupid. And this is stupid. You wanted this career – you went after it, at the cost of literally everything else. If you don't go to events like this, then you're just getting in your own way.'

Something pinches in my chest. Because I'm nervous – that I'm going to mess up, if I go. It's a scary, new environment. All of this is. And, as usual, she's not listening.

'You don't understand,' I say, feeling suddenly emotional. 'This stuff comes easily to you...' She doesn't know that staying at home started out as a survival tactic, that my relentless pursuit of this career might seem weird, but it's the only thing that makes me feel normal. Doesn't know what it's like to stand in a room of people, not having any idea what to say. To go from school to school knowing there's no way you're going to make any friends, so you may as well stop trying. Coming home to a household full of anxiety, and not being able to stop yourself from absorbing it. Alison was always impervious to that stuff – I never was. Acting was the only thing I could do to escape it all.

'It might come easily to you too,' she says. 'If you actually tried.'

This hits me like a punch in the gut. 'I do try,' I say, but even as I say them I can hear that the words ring hollow.

'Do you?' she asks, her tone searching. I don't answer – I'm still wrapping my head around the turn this conversation has taken. Regretting saying anything to her in the first place. 'You never hung out with any of your flatmates. You say no to literally every event I invite you to. You've kept your life so small, Lara. And it could be so much bigger, if you let it.'

I did let it, I think. When I worked in the pub with Avi. When I was around him, everything made sense. I felt funnier, more interesting. Like something about him brought out everything I was never able to express unless I was on a stage.

And, in the end, it didn't get me anywhere. And I realised what I've known the whole time. That this – my career – is the only thing I've ever been able to rely on.

'Look,' she says, her tone softening slightly. 'All I'm saying is that getting out of your comfort zone isn't always a bad thing. You never know what might happen.'

'I have to go,' I say. I can't face hearing anything else from her.

'Lara,' she says.

'It's fine, Ally,' I say. 'I'll talk to you soon, okay?'

I hang up and put the phone down. My eyes landing on the book Spencer and Hannah got me, sitting across the room. 'We wanted you to have something to remember us by.' Spencer's words appear in my mind. This is everything my life has been so far. Moving on from one role to the next. One job to the next. One flat to the next. Picking up mementoes, but not people. Never stopping for too long. Never putting down roots, anywhere. Because I assumed I couldn't. And I'm still not sure that I can, or want to. I like my life small. It's safe, and manageable.

But some of Alison's words stand out to me: *you're just getting in your own way*. Because there's some truth in them. As much as I hate to admit it. Because if my career is the only thing I can rely on – and attending this event is going to help it – then I need to go.

10

The following morning, I reach WHAM a little later than usual thanks to a later call time, but Sarah is just as bright and pleased to see me as she always is. I'm still feeling a little off-kilter after how I left things with Avi last night, but I'm determined to put that aside for today. I need to focus on the role, on what's best for the film. And if that's the Olivier Awards, then fine. I just need to keep going – for the good of Amelia.

'You seem more confident these past couple of weeks,' Sarah says as she draws a brush across my face. 'Filming going well?'

'I think so,' I reply tentatively.

'I take it Mr Kumar is making you feel welcome?' she asks, and the way she says his name implies familiarity.

'Do you know him well?' I ask, surprised.

'Oh, yes,' she says, with a bit of a knowing look. 'Alessandro hires me for most of his films, so I've worked with Avi quite a few times in the last few years. Has a bad habit of fidgeting in the chair. I had to glue his sideburns on three times the other day.'

'What was he like when you first met him?' I ask before I can stop myself. Curiosity about his life when he left the pub getting the better of me in this moment, erasing some of the anger I'm feeling towards him after last night.

'Well,' she says. 'You'll know more than me what he's like.' *I don't know about that*, I think. 'Most of what I do is paint peoples' faces,' she continues. 'But you can get quite a good idea of a person from doing that, I suppose. Sometimes they spill their secrets.' She pauses, leaning in and gently blushing my cheeks.

'He was very green, his first film,' she continues. 'Polite, always on time. Not demanding, like some others. You know, asking me to source make-up from some natural mineral in Timbuktu because it's the only thing they'll wear on their face.'

She finishes putting on the blush and reaches for some lipstick, painting it across my lips with the small brush she's been using for precision.

'But there was something there,' she says when she's done. 'Something that I'm not sure has gone away since. It might be that girlfriend of his – goodness knows they've been on and off more times than I can count in the last few years. But he's always struck me as…' She pauses as she leans over the counter to reach for the setting spray.

'What?' I ask, my attention rapt.

'Well,' she says as she spritzes my face. 'I suppose he's always struck me as… a little bit sad.'

I frown as she steps back.

'Right,' she says. 'You're all done.'

I'm out of WHAM an hour ahead of my call time, and bored, so I end up wandering around set a little. I've grown tired of sitting in my trailer alone these last couple of weeks.

I walk across the lot to an echo of 'Lara to craft services'. I'm almost used to it now, but not quite.

I stop at the breakfast area first to pick up some food. I still have breakfast in my trailer, most days. But that can always be supplemented by the huge spread they have for cast and crew. There's pretty much every kind of fruit you can imagine, pastries, sandwiches, vegan muffins, which look pretty disgusting to me but which I've seen Sienna eating pretty much every day, and a large array of different cheeses. I pick up a plate and load it with some fruit and cheese, then make my way over to where they'll be shooting. I don't know who is filming this morning, but it's an open set so I'm allowed near the sound stage. Crew members rush past me every few seconds. The energy buzzing and exciting.

It's cool to view it from this angle, as an observer, and not the one in the hot seat.

I stand at a safe distance from where they're filming, craning my neck to see who it is. My breath catches a little when I realise it's Avi. Jackson and Amelia have their history, but she's said she'll never marry him. So he sleeps around with most of London's high-society courtesans. One of whom — I realise with a rush of recognition — is Sienna. I forgot that that was her role. It's part of the reason why Jackson becomes so invested in the case. About halfway through the film, Sienna's character is murdered by the satanic cult they've been researching and Jackson's motivations change. He becomes obsessed with bringing the killers to justice, dropping all of his previous scepticism and worry about Amelia and throwing himself into the case entirely.

But her character isn't dead yet.

Sienna is wearing a scanty nightdress and Avi's shirt is discarded on the ground next to him, his abs on show for all to see. I hate myself for how much I'm enjoying the view. He was always toned, back at the pub. But he was leaner back then. He's definitely been spending some time in the gym. *Stop it, Lara*, I think, embarrassed by my own thoughts. *Why are you even thinking about this? He has a girlfriend. Stop being a creep.* As I watch, they press their bodies close to one another, kissing. I want to look away; it almost feels too intimate for me to be watching.

That'll be you, in a week's time. I ignore the anxiety that flickers through me at the thought and spear a piece of fruit on my plate.

Avi is dressing now; apparently their encounter has just ended and Jackson is leaving for his club. He smiles and delivers his lines – which I can't hear from here – with a sparkle in his eye that I've not been conscious of enough to truly notice when we've been working together. Even from here, without headphones to hear the dialogue, I can see how effortlessly he embodies Jackson. Embodiment techniques he's been helping me with, during our rehearsals some evenings: gestural vocabulary, sense memory, somatic acting. He's a very physical actor, excellent at commanding space. I've often leaned more subtle, but I've been learning from him – and I realise here, watching him move, just how much he's rubbed off on me.

'Cut!' Alessandro shouts. Avi and Sienna both look up at him. Avi lets out a breath. And I see something else too, something I haven't been able to notice from up close either. Because I've been so in my head, in my own thoughts. It's like the light going out of his eyes. Like the spark was turned on just for Jackson and now that he's no longer in the scene, something has darkened.

It's so subtle I could dismiss it for tiredness. But Sarah's words from earlier ring through my mind. *He's always struck me as a bit sad*.

Before I can dwell on it any further though, his eyes wander across the room. And fix on me. And something flickers through me – something that feels like caring about him, something that scares me more than I'd like to admit.

Once I'm finished with filming for the day, George picks me up, ready to take me back to the hotel. But as I get in the car, a text pings on my phone. It's Spencer. *On the off chance you're out of filming early, we're meeting at the Queen's Head in Hammersmith*, it reads. *8 p.m.*

A lump forms in my throat. And for a second, I almost type out my usual response. But I'm still feeling a little weird after watching Avi on-set this morning. Alison's words ring through my head again too. *Your life could be so much bigger, Lara.* And it's irritating, how piercing they are. How quickly she's able to identify my weaknesses and expose them to me. And I don't know if it's this film or the fact that being on-set does have me feeling a little isolated from the world, but they hit harder than they should. I check my watch: 7.30. I have time to get there and I only have to stay for a few hours. Before I can really consider what I'm doing, I ask George to take me there instead of the hotel.

I arrive within twenty minutes; it's a quick journey, since the studio is in West London.

'Thank you,' I say to George as I get out of the car. 'I'll see you later.'

'No problem, miss,' he says. 'Just text me when you need picking up. And let me know if they have a good Islay selection, will you?'

I frown for a second, not sure what he's talking about, then remember abruptly – he's a whisky fan. 'Of course,' I reply, smiling as I close the door.

I uselessly brush non-existent dust off my jeans before entering the pub, feeling suddenly nervous. This will be the first time I'm seeing Hannah and Spencer since leaving the flat, and the first time ever in a social setting – if you don't count our goodbye dinner, which feels like ages ago now.

I pull open the door and step through, scanning the room, then find them sitting in a corner. Spencer looks up and sees me, his face lighting up in a way that makes me instinctively smile. He waves me over and I sit down, then he abruptly gets up to order me wine. Hannah jumps immediately into telling me about a theatre workshop she's running, which is pulling some kids who haven't historically been interested in theatre into acting. Asks whether I might be interested in helping her run another one, at some point. I tell her I'll consider it and before either of us can say anything else, Spencer places a glass of wine in front of me.

'So glad you could make it, Lara,' he says. 'We've missed you.'

'We have.' Hannah nods and my heart clenches. Because I'm realising now just how much I've missed them too.

'So tell us everything,' Spencer says. 'What's it like?'

I sip my wine and try to paint a picture. The chaos of the set. The runners everywhere. Never being able to have a moment's peace, but honestly not minding because I'm part of such a big operation. Because it feels good, to be a part of it. To fulfil my role.

'That sounds honestly great,' Hannah says. 'I mean, I could never. But it must feel good to be pursuing your dreams.'

'It does,' I say. But something catches a little, as the words settle. The fear, still there, that I might mess up and have it all taken away in a moment. The beautiful, blonde potential understudy who is waiting in the wings if I do. The emotions I experienced looking at Avi this morning. Emotions that felt a lot deeper than they should, for someone who is just my colleague. Emotions that made me almost feel like I might still care about him as a friend.

'Is everything okay?' Spencer asks.

I nod. Because it feels too scary to say it out loud: to admit there's a problem. And there's no way I can get into it all right now – everything with Avi. But then it occurs to me: maybe I don't have to share exactly who it is. Maybe I can ask for their advice without needing to reveal everything.

'It's just…' I try to find the right way to phrase it. 'There's someone on-set — someone I have a bit of a history with.'

'What kind of history?' Hannah asks.

'We were friends,' I say, taking a sip of my wine. 'We — we worked together. And then he moved away, but we still kept in touch. But then…' I pause, the details of what happened coming back. The postcards and texts gradually tapering off. His return, for the Christmas party. Our kiss, the surge of feeling I had when he pulled me in. The sense of something clicking into place between us. Then his abrupt departure. The flurry of regretful texts the next day.

'He came back and we kissed, and I guess he regretted it. Sent me a load of texts the next day telling me it had been a mistake. And I was hurt, so I lashed out. Told him he was wrong, to put our friendship on the line like that. And we haven't really spoken since. I kept waiting for him to reach out — thought that maybe after some space, we could fix things. But he never did. And…'

I take another sip of my wine, trying to shrug off the pain that's resurging at the memory of it. 'Well, I guess we're not friends any more. And now I have to see him on-set every day. And I'm worried

I'm going to do something stupid that might ruin everything.'

Spencer and Hannah are both silent for a few seconds. I wonder whether this was a bad idea, whether I've shared too much.

'It sounds,' Hannah says, 'like you're more in control of this than you think.' Spencer nods, as if he agrees.

'What do you mean?' I ask.

'I mean,' she says. 'This obviously isn't an ideal situation – I'd hate to work with any of my exes. But you just said it yourself: you're worried about your own actions, not his. You can't control what he does and you can't control how you feel about him. But you're a true professional – Spence and I know that. We've watched you run those lines like a machine, night after night. Going after what you want with everything you have. I don't think the person you are is going to let anything get in the way of that.'

Spencer nods. 'I think you can trust yourself a bit more, Lara,' he says. 'I mean, look how far you've come. Look where you are. I really don't think this is going to mess that up. You just have to show up and do your job, and be professional. Nothing else is really under your control anyway.'

I nod, something fluttering in my chest. Because I've been trying to deal with this, alone, for the last few weeks. And I might not have told them everything, but even sharing this feels like a huge weight off my shoulders. And I know they're right, that I need to just keep my head up and do everything I can. But there's something about feeling understood, about having the qualities that make me feel lonely, sometimes, reflected back to me in such a positive way, that gives me renewed confidence. Confidence I desperately need, ahead of going to the Olivier Awards in a few days.

'Thanks, guys,' I say, a warmth passing through my chest.

11

A few days later, I'm in my hotel room trying dresses on for the awards show. I've been turning over the conversation with Spencer and Hannah in my mind, and the confidence I took from it is definitely lingering. I'm ready to take on this evening, whatever it brings. To try to keep control of my own actions and let the universe do the rest. As far as spending time with Avi, at least. For everything else, I'm still feeling pretty nervous.

And from a clothing perspective, I feel completely lost. Alison brought over a few of her favourite outfits last night, though she was pretty fierce about not wanting me to steal them like I did her cardigan, and stayed to watch a film and take advantage of my room-service bill. It was nice, and she only slightly rubbed in my face the fact that I was taking her advice and going to the awards show. All of the options she brought seemed good at the time: a light-blue satin slip, a beaded gown she wore to her senior prom at school and a long, draping dark-red option. But now that I'm trying them on, none of them feel quite right on me.

They're beautiful, they all look beautiful. On Alison. Because they're all her: her sparkle, her shine, her ability to enter a room and command the attention of everyone in there instantly. And on me, they look wrong.

I pull the blue satin one on again and assess myself in the mirror. I have an hour until I'm supposed to be meeting Avi downstairs and I just finished my hair and make-up, hoping it would improve the overall effect — bring it together, maybe. But the dress still doesn't look right on me.

A knock sounds at the door and I open it to find Sienna.

'Oh,' I say, stepping backwards. A little surprised she's here. I've barely seen her recently; her visits to my trailer have been fewer and further apart since she's been filming, which, honestly, has made my job on-set easier. I like her, but every time I see her I get slightly derailed by the anxiety that she might be waiting in the wings to replace me at any second. Though we're far enough through filming now that hopefully that shouldn't be a concern any more – at the very least, reshooting my scenes would be a huge cost. Still, I can't help but feel it lingering slightly: the feeling that I shouldn't be here.

'Hey,' she says. 'Is this a bad time?'

'No,' I say, stepping aside to let her through. 'I'm just getting ready for—'

'The Olivier Awards,' she says, smiling.

And in this moment, I realise how insane this all is. I can't believe I haven't thought of it before – this woman must feel really weird that her boyfriend is taking me as a date to the awards ceremony instead of her. Honestly, it's actually completely ridiculous now I think about it. But I've been so selfishly caught up in my own stuff the last few weeks that I've barely stopped to even consider how it must feel for her. I mentally add self-obsessed to the list of things Alison would probably chastise me for if she were here.

'Yeah,' I reply. Suddenly not sure what to say.

'I just came to say bye,' she says. 'I'm heading off to a modelling contract tomorrow. I wrapped yesterday, so I won't see you again on-set.'

'Oh,' I reply, her words hitting me with a wave of shock. Because if she's leaving, that means…

There's no need to worry about her replacing me any more.

The tension I've been holding on to for the last few weeks suddenly dissipates from my limbs. I didn't realise how much it was weighing me down – the fear that my big break, that Amelia, might be taken away from me. Especially since things have been going well and I've been enjoying it more than ever. And maybe I was stupid to even believe it in the first place. But now, I don't have to worry about it at all. *Oh, thank fuck for that.*

I do my best to not let my emotions show on my face, because whether she knew about it or not, it would be pretty rude to look so pleased that she is leaving, especially given I'm about to steal her boyfriend for the evening. And I'm not pleased, I realise with a jolt. She's been kind to me when she didn't need to be and I'm suddenly sad that I won't get to see her again for a while.

'Well… it was really nice to meet you,' I say, recovering some of my composure. I feel bad that I misjudged her when we first met, that my insecurities probably got in the way of us spending more time together. 'I guess I'll see you on the press tour?'

'I guess so,' she says, smiling. She hitches her handbag over her shoulder, as if she's about to leave. 'Have a great time this evening,' she says before she does. 'The Oliviers are always a hoot.'

'Thanks,' I reply, adjusting the dress again.

'Is everything okay?' she asks, turning back towards me.

'Oh… Yeah,' I say, ready to brush it off. But something about the way she's looking at me compels me to be honest. 'I just… I borrowed this dress from my sister and I don't feel like it looks right on me.'

She assesses my dress and frowns. 'I think you look great,' she says. 'What's wrong with what you're wearing?'

'I don't know,' I say. 'Besides, don't they always ask you who you're wearing at these things? I'm not sure "I stole this from my sister" works as an answer.'

'I think you're overthinking it,' she replies. 'But if you want some help—'

'Oh, no,' I say. 'I couldn't ask you to do that.'

'Honestly, it's no trouble. I'm not packed yet. And I've got some pieces in my room you could borrow.'

And I hesitate for a second. But truly, I don't have time to overthink this in the way I usually would.

'That would be great,' I reply.

★ ★ ★

A few minutes later, I'm in Sienna's hotel room. It smells just how she looks, like fresh-cut grass, flowers, summer. There are a few outfits laid out across the bed that I assume are for her travels – all carefully coordinated and presumably designer. Her make-up counter looks straight out of a *Vogue* GRWM video. Clarins and Chanel. I can't see a single drugstore brand on there. *No wonder her skin always looks so beautiful*, I think. I have a flash of the current chaos of my hotel room: clothes splattered across the floor. The probably expired E45 cream I stole from my mum, which is the single product in my one-step skincare routine.

'Sorry about the mess,' she says, wrinkling her nose a little, and I stifle a laugh. Because she looks serious and I can't see a single thing out of place.

She rifles delicately through a few dresses hanging in her wardrobe. 'I had my stylist set some things aside for tonight,' she says as she goes. 'In case you didn't want to go, Avi asked me as his back-up.' *What the fuck?* I think, registering how calm her tone is. The ridiculousness of this situation hitting me all over again. How is she okay with her own boyfriend treating her as back-up to his co-star? Hollywood is so weird.

'Sienna…' I say, about to apologise.

'Boy, am I glad you said yes, though. I kind of hate these things,' she says. 'And I'm flying to Paris early tomorrow. So you've saved me. I have a date with some room service.'

'Oh,' I say, surprised. She must mistake my surprise for nerves, because she turns back from the wardrobe and looks at me apologetically.

'I mean,' she says. 'They're always pretty fun. I'm sure you'll have a great time. It's just… it all gets a little tiresome, you know? The same people. The same questions, over and over. Once you've done them a few times, it's all quite…' She trails off, and returns to the wardrobe.

I falter for a moment, surprised again. I've always assumed that someone like Sienna, born and raised Hollywood, would enjoy these events. That everyone enjoyed it. But it appears I was wrong about that. Perhaps she and I aren't as different as I thought.

'Got it,' she says, pulling out a navy silk dress. It's stunning. 'I think this will look great on you.'

'Are you sure?' I ask, touching it. The silk feels like water.

'Of course,' she replies. 'It's Prada, in case they ask. I'm pretty sure we're the same size, but try it on just in case.'

I take the dress from her hands carefully since it's probably worth more than anything I've ever worn, and she turns away to allow me to change. I pull it on, the zip sliding up to just above my tailbone. It's riskier than anything I'd usually wear: backless and impossible to wear a bra.

'Done,' I say, and she turns.

'Perfect,' she says, touching up my hair a little. Tossing it over my shoulder. And something happens – I feel a spark, the same joy I get around Alison sometimes when we're getting along. The kinship I feel with her – not, usually, with anyone else.

I step aside to look in the mirror.

The material clings to my body like it was made for it, hugging my form so masterfully it has created shape where there is usually none.

I feel the same as I did in Alison's dresses, like I'm wearing something not meant for me. But the longer I look, the more I feel like I could be the person who wears this dress. Who attends the awards shows. Who has a big part in a major movie. I could be the person who's made it.

Just for one evening.

'Thank you,' I say, a little overwhelmed.

★ ★ ★

I walk down the corridor to the hotel stairs, my steps slightly impeded by the dress, which fits tightly around my legs. I'm wearing a pair of Alison's heels, the ones she wore to her prom: low stilettos with nude straps criss-crossing up my ankles. They feel secure enough, but I'm not a big heels person so I still don't feel totally confident. I grip the banister as I descend, concentrating so hard on not falling that I don't really look up until I'm halfway down. And when I do, I see him, waiting in the lobby in full black tie, looking every inch the incredibly famous person that he is. A few people look over at him as they pass, trying to figure out whether who they're looking at is actually Avi Kumar or someone else. My breath catches as he looks up, his eyes locking on mine.

He's seen me dressed up before, but nothing like this. We'd go to concerts, sometimes, with other people from the bar. Plays, occasionally. But I've always been a black-top-and-jeans kind of person.

'Hey,' he says, when I reach the bottom of the stairs. 'You look… incredible.'

'Thanks,' I say, feeling more than a little awkward about the fact that I'm wearing his girlfriend's dress.

As he offers his arm, I find myself taking it. At least partly for the stability it provides.

We descend the steps and get into the waiting car, a thrill passing across my skin as he takes my hand to help me in.

'I'd usually attend this event with Sam, my publicist,' Avi says. 'And maybe even some security. But Sam's on holiday and I thought it might be a bit less weird for you without men in black suits following you everywhere. So, no security tonight.'

I blink. I didn't even think about this. Had no idea having security for something like this was normal, let alone expected.

'Thanks,' I say. Because he's right – though it might've been comforting to have a barrier between us and everyone else, I don't need anything else adding to how strange this experience is about to be for me.

For the first few minutes of the car journey, I sit in silence. But then the apprehension of what we're about to do overwhelms me to the point where I need to talk. Need to say something – anything – to distract myself.

'So,' I say, clearing my throat. 'Is an Olivier on your list?'

'What do you mean?' he replies, frowning a little.

'You know,' I say. 'The list. I thought everyone had one.' Mine is in a notebook in my parents' garage somewhere – written in glitter gel pen as part of a manifestation exercise Alison had me do when I was fourteen. She wrote down what kind of house and family she wanted; I wrote down all the awards I wanted to win. When she saw it, she rolled her eyes and told me I was probably going to end up living alone with several cats. Which, to be honest, as long as I made it in the meantime – didn't sound like a bad proposition. I like cats.

'Lara,' he says. 'I have literally no idea what you're talking about.'

'The list of awards you want to be up for, at some point in your career.'

'Oh,' he says, frowning a little. 'No, I don't think so.'

'Why not?' I press, confused. Avi was always amazing on the stage.

'I don't know,' he says, and something about his tone has me looking up. Catching his eyes, which suddenly betray a level of vulnerability I didn't expect. 'I think that kind of stuff – stage stuff – is probably out of my range now.'

'What do you mean?' I ask.

'The films I've done,' he says, an expression crossing his face that I can't quite decipher. It looks… sad. Which is strange, considering we're talking about his glittering career of blockbuster film after blockbuster film. 'That's what people expect from me now. I have to keep up an image. And it's all I really get sent any more. Honestly, Jackson is the most interesting role I've had in ages and I had to fight with my agent to take it over an action film he wanted me to do instead. So I don't think those kind of opportunities will come my way and if they do, I shouldn't really take too many of them.'

He pauses for second. 'Sometimes you just have to stay in your lane, you know?' And he says it confidently, like it's a script he's rehearsed. But I can see beyond it – to the emotion underneath.

'I think you're great on stage,' I say quietly. 'And I think you can get in whatever lane you want to.'

He's silent for a few seconds.

'Thank you,' he says.

But when I look up, I can see from his expression that he's only saying it, that he doesn't believe me. But before I can say anything else – before I can find a single word – the car slides to a halt.

We're here.

The awards are being held at the Royal Albert Hall, but I can't see any of the building right now.

My senses are assaulted by a million camera flashes going off in my face, all at once. Voices shouting, asking me to look at them. Asking me what my name is, why I'm here. I can't get my bearings for a second – my nervous system is entirely unable to process what's happening. I tense up, freezing in place. I hadn't expected it to be so instant, so overwhelming. *Fuck*, I think. The first pictures of Avi and I together – instead of me gracefully emerging from a car and smiling towards the cameras – are going to be of me looking like a deer in headlights. Trying desperately not to trip on my way up the carpet. But before I can panic completely, before I can start to wonder what I'm doing here and climb back into the car, Avi's hand finds mine.

And normally I'd feel strange about this, might even pull away. Because it's too friendly, too close. Because his girlfriend lent me the dress I'm wearing and she's been impossibly gracious about the fact that I'm here instead of her. But in this moment, something inside me relaxes.

'Avi!' They start shouting. 'Who's this? Your new co-star? What happened to Sienna?'

He ignores all of their questions, steering me masterfully up the carpet, beyond the barriers to the main press line of interviewers and official photographers. Stopping to smile warmly and wave to a few of them as we pass.

'Okay,' he says, when we reach the edge of the press line. A fresh wave of *Oh, my God* rearing up as I look at them. 'The move for this is: as short an answer as you can give, as big a smile as you can manage, then on to the next. Okay?'

'Okay,' I say, but my voice shakes and betrays my concern, because he stops for a second instead of moving me forwards.

'I can take the lead for the first few, if you want,' he says. 'Introduce you. Answer their questions. Then you can follow me.'

And I almost nod. But then a new strength surges up, a determination to show what I'm made of. Sienna might be gone, but I still have something to prove – to Alessandro, to myself. I want to do this right and not lean too much on Avi. I want to stand on my own two feet.

'Thanks,' I say. 'But let's just take it as it comes. I'll be fine.'

'If you're sure...' he says, still sounding apprehensive.

'I am,' I reply, quickly, before I can change my mind.

We make it through the first couple of interviewers, my throat drying up with each new person we approach. But it goes fine and the questions are short – about who we want to win tonight and how excited we are to be here. I manage to get out a few names and Avi moves us on. I start to become a little more confident in my answers. Start to relax.

But as we reach the third reporter, my heart rate starts to increase. She's a representative from *Teen Vogue*, about twenty-two years old with butterfly clips in her hair. She's smiling, but I'm immediately intimidated by the gaze she levels at us, a warning that she means business. There's something about her that feels more intense than the people we've spoken to so far. Like she might, without warning, go for the jugular. And then I realise where this is coming from: I watched a video recently where she brought up a musician's dating life on the red carpet, forcing them into a corner of answering it and admitting that they were seeing the person there had been rumours about, before their publicist intervened and pulled them away. She addresses us both, and I nod and smile, trying to keep it together.

She has nothing on you, Lara, I think. *You have about thirty Instagram followers.* And it gives me some momentary comfort. She talks to Avi first, which gives me a few seconds. But then she turns to me and starts asking questions, and I find myself suddenly feeling like I'm staring down the barrel of a gun.

'Sorry?' I ask, my throat closing up.

'I said, could you tell us a little bit about why you're here?'

'Uh…' I say, my mind completely blank. Silence falls for a few seconds and her expression starts to turn confused. *Shit*. 'My name is Lara Francis,' I manage to choke out. 'I'm in a film.'

Oh, my God. You sound like you're introducing yourself on the first day of school.

'Um, okay…' she says, her tone a little sarcastic, and my stomach drops through the floor.

'It's a brilliant film.' Avi cuts in before my panic can truly take hold. *Thank God*. I kick myself for needing to rely on him, like I just vowed not to. But I do, in this moment – I'm way out of my depth. Like, fathoms away. In the centre of the ocean, with no boat.

'Really great,' I agree, stupidly.

'Directed by none other than Alessandro D'Arienzo,' Avi chimes in again.

And he talks for a few moments about the film while she gives me side glances, still clearly more than a little confused about how incompetent and entirely unprepared I seem. Then she turns back to me.

'Sounds like you might be one to watch,' she says and, if I'm not mistaken, it still sounds a little bored, like she's already tired of talking to me and wants to move on to the next more interesting person. And to be honest, I can't blame her. I'd be bored of me right now too. 'Could you tell us a bit more about your look?'

'I'm not sure I can, actually,' I say, without thinking. I can't remember the designer Sienna told me about. The reporter laughs, as if she can't quite believe how terrible at interviews I am. I scramble to say something, fast, so she doesn't think I'm a complete idiot. 'I can tell you that my shoes are my sister's prom shoes.'

She laughs again, and this time it sounds more genuine. Like I might be in on the joke.

'True couture, then,' she says. I nod, feeling a little more confident now.

'And the dress, I remember – it's Prada. Sienna Marsh lent it to me.'

And I'm proud of myself, for a half-second. For getting a full sentence out, for answering the question. For remembering the designer. But then I see Avi's face and realise what I've just said. Something sparks in the interviewer's eye as I mention that name. And my stomach drops. That was probably the worst possible thing I could have said.

'Sienna Marsh,' she says. 'Interesting.' She turns to Avi, who tenses up infinitesimally at my side. 'And what does Sienna think about the fact that you're here this evening with Lara instead of her?'

Shit, shit, shit.

I hardly dare to look at him, worry spilling through me.

But Avi just shifts slightly, as if stepping into professional mode. A smooth glaze coming over his eyes, which is a little terrifying.

'Sienna couldn't make it tonight,' he says. 'And I'm very happy to be here with Lara. She's my co-star and we're here to promote our new film. Nothing more than that.' He looks at me and the interviewer opens her mouth, as if she's about to press further. But he shuts her down immediately. 'Now if you'll excuse us, we have a few more interviews to do.' He moves away and I follow.

'I'm so sorry, Avi,' I mutter under my breath as we walk down the carpet. 'I bet you wish you'd come with Sienna now instead.' But he just places his hand gently on the small of my back, sending a ripple of sensation across my bare skin.

'Lara,' he says. 'Sienna didn't even want to come. And besides, I'm glad you're here with me.' And something in my chest flutters as he says it.

We do a few more interviews, which thankfully pass with no huge disasters, apart from one slightly unfortunate moment where the interviewer asks me about my favourite part about being on-set. After saying the obvious – about it being a pleasure and a privilege to work with Alessandro and Avi – I somehow get it into my head that I need to say something innocuous to avoid any further questions about Avi, so I end up talking at length about the fact that they have a great array of fruits at catering. The interviewer's polite smile definitely starts to falter halfway through: I'm not sure he's ever heard anyone being so effusive about melon.

Eventually, we make it to the final interviewer, a well-dressed man reporting for a TikTok channel who asks me what my three favourite films are. *This is my wheelhouse*, I think, and I reel off three films by some of my favourite directors, getting overexcited talking about them. He's a huge film buff too, so we have a really interesting discussion. And when I look up at Avi, waiting for him to answer, I think I catch him smiling. And I think I know why – I used to have those kinds of conversations with him. Used to watch films with him, even. We'd set up a projector in the bar and hang out after Saturday shifts sometimes, locking up a couple of hours after closing. Analysing the line delivery together. Thinking that could be us one day. *And it is us, now*, I realise with a jolt. Just not in the way I would've expected.

I watch him answer too, calling on some of the directors I mentioned. But also talking about some action films. I wonder if that's part of his branding, if his agent has told him to show an interest in action movies so he keeps getting those roles.

Before I know it, we're through the press line and I start to relax. But then I see we've actually reached the worst part.

The photographs.

A line of cameras not unlike the one that greeted us when we got out of the car stretches ahead of us. Photographers crowding behind metal barriers. Shouting names, calling for people to pose differently. My heart migrates to my throat.

'I'll go first,' Avi whispers. 'Just follow my lead.'

And he steps forwards, for a few photos alone. Smiling at the cameras easily, angling his body to most accurately show off his suit. I realise for the first time this evening that we match; the blue detailing on his lapels is the exact same as the one on Sienna's dress.

After a few more photos, he turns and moves to the side, beckoning me over. I stumble over my dress as I'm walking towards him and freeze. Waiting for the cameras to flash in my face.

'Breathe,' he says to me quietly, apparently noting my nerves. Turning his face away from the camera as he does so, so they won't pick it up.

I look into his eyes, their intensity burning into mine, and do as he says – a deep breath in through my nose, out through my mouth. It helps. As does the hand he places gently on the small of my back. His contact a grounding force as he steers me to the middle of the carpet and we turn towards the cameras.

They flash and I blink a few times, adjusting. Avi's hand stays in place as he poses. The flashes becoming slightly less terrifying the more they go off. Responding to the calls of 'Over here!' and 'Look this way!', my body in sync with Avi's as we look in each direction in turn.

We do it again and again on several different markers down the carpet and then it's done.

He walks towards the edge of the carpet, reaching back to take my hand.

'You did great,' he says, his voice low – and a few weeks ago, it would have made me feel strange to hear that from him. I might have found it patronising, even. Told him I didn't need it. That I could do this on my own. But right now, it just makes my heart thump a little harder against my chest. I'm proud of myself.

Once we're inside the hall, my panic subsides a little. There's less shouting in here. Fewer cameras. The chaos dulled down to a low hum. Just people – a lot of people – milling around. Avi moves quickly through the crowd and heads straight for the bar, grabbing two glasses of champagne.

I take a sip, the liquid fizzing against my tongue.

'Don't stop – we've got work to do,' Avi says as I think about leaning against the bar. And the next twenty minutes are a blur of faces as he introduces me to everyone he recognises: the director of his most recent film; a producer who owns a company that exclusively funds scripts written by women, who says she'll let me know if there are any projects coming up; a few actors whose faces I recognise from films. And all of it trips me up initially. But then I see how familiarly everyone interacts with Avi and the sheen dissipates – they're all normal people too. Like me. Like he was, once. But I'm definitely not going to think about that right now.

The call to take our seats sounds and we wind our way down the aisle. Avi whispers to me, his voice low as the lights dim. 'After the show, do you want to get out of here? We could skip the afterparties. I've got an idea for something more fun we can do.'

I lean in, my heart pounding. A part of me still wondering how – exactly – I ended up in this situation: next to Avi Kumar, at an awards ceremony.

'Sure,' I reply.

The awards pass quickly, the joy as each honouree gets up on-stage apparent on their faces, their speeches clearly carefully rehearsed. I glance at Avi a few times as they step up, his expression inscrutable. Once the last person has collected their award and we're invited to head over to a nearby hotel bar, Avi meets my eye before declining politely. 'We have an early call time tomorrow,' he says, before taking my hand and heading over to the bar to sneak a half-empty bottle of champagne when the waiter's back is turned. I baulk slightly as he takes my hand, my skin reacting to his touch as his fingers close around mine. No one notices his theft and we slip out of a side exit, out of sight of the cameras.

We walk down the street and cross the road, heading for Hyde Park, the entrance opposite, with the Albert Memorial rising up above us. All intricate arches, the golden statue reflecting the streetlights. As I look up at it, a wave of sobriety hits me and I start to wonder whether it might be better for me to go home. This evening has already been a success. But he hands me the champagne bottle and I take it, unthinking. And then – before I can really realise what he's doing – he starts climbing the fence to the park.

'What the fuck are you doing?' I ask as he climbs it easily – it's only waist-high, so it's not a huge feat, but it's still definitely trespassing.

'Pass me that, will you?' He gestures for the bottle through the fence.

'Avi, I'm not doing this. This is illegal. And besides, it's getting late,' I say, having huge second thoughts about what I might have agreed to. His excuse from earlier reminding me that we actually *do* have an early call time tomorrow. 'I should probably go home and get an early night—'

'Come on, Lara,' he says, a challenge in his tone. 'What's life without a little risk?'

His tone sets something off in me — the challenge hitting its mark, as little as all the reasonable parts of me want it to. Lighting into a flame. I look back over my shoulder. Crowds of people starting to emerge from the hall onto the street. If I'm going to follow him, I'd better do it now, otherwise I'm at high risk of exposing my underwear to some of the most famous people in London.

'Fine,' I say, surprising myself with how quickly I respond. I take off my heels and throw them to him, then hitch up my dress and climb over. Somehow — miraculously — managing not to rip the dress. 'But if we get arrested, this was your idea.'

'You were great tonight,' he says, ignoring my comment and reaching out to steady me as I land on the ground next to him.

'If that's great, I'm not sure you have your scale right,' I reply, deflecting his praise. Because I'm not sure I deserve it. I made it through the evening, sure. But I almost caused a press catastrophe and will definitely look terrified in all the photos.

'Really,' he says, as we start walking, heading behind the memorial and away from the crowd. Into the vast expanse of green beyond. 'You were. My first awards, I almost threw up from nerves about the press interviews and accidentally spilled a glass of champagne on Jack Nicholson's shoulder.'

'You did not,' I say, laughter bubbling up despite myself.

'God's honest truth,' he replies, putting his hand to his chest. 'He did not take it well.'

I smile, something happening as I look at him. Some part of me opening up in a way it hasn't so far. An alien feeling emerging, one I haven't experienced in a while. I feel… safe, here. Even trespassing in a park. Even after doing the scariest event of my life. Something about being here, with him, feels like it did before. This realisation terrifies me. But it feels good too.

We walk for a few more moments in silence and I grab the champagne bottle from him.

'Can I ask you something?' Avi says, breaking into my thoughts.

'Sure,' I reply.

'The karate,' he says. 'I never knew that about you. How come you're so good?'

I frown a little, then remember our stunt training – what feels like ages ago now.

'Oh,' I say, heat curling in my chest. Because this is a piece of information that, usually, I'd prefer to keep private. But something – the champagne, or the fact that I've come so far this evening that I'm starting to adopt a 'fuck it' attitude to the whole thing – has me answering him. 'My parents enrolled me when I was younger. I had some trouble at school.' I take a sip of the champagne and pass the bottle back to him.

'What kind of trouble?' he asks. *I should've expected that,* I think. He's never been one to leave things well enough alone. It's partly how he got through my walls back at the pub in the first place. Always asking the right questions, seeing through whatever defences I put up. Until, eventually, they came down.

'My mum and dad moved around a lot, so I went to about six different schools.'

He nods. 'I remember you telling me.'

My chest pinches. 'Well,' I continue. 'I was under the radar, mostly – never out there enough to catch anyone's attention in a bad way. But in the last school I was at, I was bullied. So they enrolled me in karate. I think it was a self-confidence thing.'

'Did it work?' he asks.

'Sort of,' I reply. 'But then I started doing school plays. And it was like… I felt like I could breathe for the first time.' I take the champagne back from him, feeling a little vulnerable here. Because this is the closest we've come to talking like we did before.

'I get that feeling,' he says. 'I used to feel that way too. Like… you're the most yourself when you're up there being someone else.'

Used to feel that way, I think. I wonder if he means that he doesn't feel that way any more. I recall the look on his face when he wrapped the scene with Sienna the other day. Because usually he's so bright, so put together – so, seemingly, happy with this life he's chosen. But Sarah's words have burrowed into my mind. *He's always struck me as a little sad.*

'Exactly,' I reply. And in the next second, I almost take a step towards him. Almost ask him what's been going on, why he's been silent for the last three years. Why it seems like some of his spark might have gone out. What's going on underneath the polished exterior, the exterior that I'm starting to see is a bit of an act.

'Can I ask you something?' I ask, suddenly emboldened by this conversation.

'That seems fair,' he says. 'Go ahead.'

'Why won't you really do theatre?'

'Ah,' he says, glancing sideways at me. Looking away, back ahead to the path in front of us. 'I guess I should've expected that.'

I look at him, waiting for an answer. But it doesn't come quickly.

'It's a complicated thing,' he says. 'Being someone in my position. A British-Indian actor who has made it good. People… people like to put me in boxes. To hold me up as a standard. When the press isn't tearing me down, that is. And I don't mind it, mostly – I can inspire people who want to make it in an industry that has historically not made room for us. To be in a position where I've made it – it feels big, you know? Like I can't take it for granted. Can't do anything to mess it up. But it's a lot of pressure and my agent has strong opinions about my career direction. As a result, so do I. I can't really afford to disagree with him or I might lose all this. So sometimes that means I don't get to go after the roles I want to. Have to consider all that.'

I nod, his words hitting me hard. A rush of anger surging up at what he has to deal with – because I have seen the articles. Hateful segments questioning whether he's been cast as a 'diversity' hire, peppered through the other articles holding him up as one of the up-and-coming actors of our generation. But there's always someone questioning his talent. And they've made me furious on his behalf in the last few years. But I hadn't thought about the other side of it either. The pressure he might feel, being in his position. How people might try to pigeonhole him. How he might feel like his position is more fragile than other people's. How that pressure might make him feel out of control of his career, dictated by what other people think is best. Sadness and anger ripples through me as he speaks. Because it's not fair for him to be limited like this. To feel like he can't go after the roles he wants. To feel stuck between being held up as an idol and being torn down from a pedestal for no reason other than blind hatred.

'It is hard, though,' he says. 'Sometimes I feel like more of a brand than a person, as far as my agent is concerned.'

'I'm really sorry, Avi,' I say, looking over at him. 'That sounds really hard.'

He shrugs, a smile passing over his face that doesn't quite reach his eyes.

'I have a good life,' he says. 'A life most people would kill for.'

And I can't help it – he looks so sad as he says it, that the words tumble out of me before I can stop them. 'But are you happy?'

He stops in his tracks, his expression shifting a little. And I almost want to take it back. But I don't. Because I want to know. Because I've seen enough in the last few days to make me question if he really is. Because, despite everything, there's still a part of me that I've been lying to myself about for the last few days, but which is coming up now in full force. A part that cares about him.

'Uh…' he says, faltering. 'That's a difficult question.'

'Is it?' I ask.

He looks down at the floor, the champagne bottle swinging by his side, forgotten.

'Is happiness really the goal?' he says, finally. 'I'm grateful for everything I have. Grateful to be alive. Grateful to be in a position to help my family. To inspire people.' And again, I can see that his smile doesn't quite reach his eyes. And it makes me so sad. Because he shouldn't have to feel grateful, shouldn't have to push down his own wants and needs, accepting something less because of how other people react. And I want him to know that he'd inspire people by going after what he wants too.

'I will say this,' he says, looking at me. 'This film… it's the closest I've felt to happiness in a long time.'

Oh, fuck.

And it's a complicated statement. Because there's so much behind it. So many different ways it could be interpreted. But as I look at him for a long beat, I see something softening in his eyes. Something that is real. A light that I've only really seen so far when we've been acting together. When we've been running lines. A light I attributed to the joy of the performance.

'Avi…' And without thinking about it, I'm taking a step towards him. He lets out a breath, unmoving. I take another step. *Oh, my God, what am I doing?* I think. But I don't stop. Something has taken hold of me that I don't quite understand. I'm all fire, drawn in by his gaze, his eyes that aren't leaving mine. His hand reaches up, tracing gently down the side of my arm. My skin in flames at his touch.

I could kiss him now, I think. And I realise I want to. The line that this would cross between us and everything it would mean hovers in the background, waiting to slow me to a halt. But in this moment, I just see him.

'Lara…' he whispers. He leans in towards me, his fingers still dragging against my bare skin. I can hear his breath, almost feel his heartbeat. We're so close now. It would just take one tiny step forwards. I tilt my face towards him, my chest hammering.

But then I open my eyes and see him, and realise what I'm doing. *Oh, my God*, I think. I take a startled step backwards.

And before Avi can react and I can move another inch, a voice sounds from a couple of hundred metres behind Avi, the glare of a torch shining in our faces.

And just like that, everything comes crashing down.

Sienna. The dress I'm wearing – which is hers. The fact that I almost did something so stupid. Something that would have been more destructive than I could've ever imagined.

What the fuck is wrong with you?

'Oi!' a man in a high-vis jacket shouts, marching towards us at speed. 'What do you think you're doing?'

And there's no time to think about this further. We have to get out of here.

'Shit. We should go,' Avi says. I nod, swallowing down the emotions that are crashing over me in this moment.

And we run.

12

The following morning I arrive at the studio for our kissing scene feeling like I might burst into flames. Avi and I managed to avoid arrest, splitting up and getting separate Ubers home to avoid being caught together and causing an actual press catastrophe. My stomach twists at the idea of what Sienna would have thought, seeing those photos. But nothing happened. It was just two people, in a park. At least, that's what I'm telling myself. To stave off the crashing guilt and horror about what I might've done, had I not come to my senses before the park police arrived.

I am not this person – I am not impulsive. I do not step over the line into other people's relationships. Especially not the relationships of people who seem to be genuinely nice human beings, who have done nothing but welcome me to an unfamiliar environment and lend me dresses and give me tips on crystals (which, while misguided, were genuinely well-intentioned). And yet, yesterday, I almost did. *I must be losing my mind*, I think, as I make my way to set.

Not to mention the fact that I'm about to actually kiss him today. On camera. In front of a whole room of people. How I'm going to get through that, I have no idea. It's so ironic, too, because the Olivier Awards actually went well – were a success, even. I should be feeling good about this. But I don't.

Roman passes me on my way to set. Waves, with a slightly malevolent smile. But even his usual weird behaviour doesn't register today. Because I have other – much bigger – things to worry about.

'Hi,' Avi says when I reach him. 'How are you feeling about today—'

'Fine,' I say, keeping my expression level. Determined not to talk about it. Because if I do, I'll freak out. And I can't afford to freak out right now. I'll have to park my mental breakdown – as Nat would say – and have it later on, in my trailer.

This scene that we're about to film is the culmination of everything Avi and I have been working towards for the last few weeks. Everything we've been trying to do together. It's a rewritten version of the scene we ran in our audition – now no longer in a pub. Now a full kiss scene. And a million times more terrifying. I need to stay focused, to keep my cool – I can't let anything get in the way of this film.

The intimacy coordinator waits for us to hit our marks, then introduces himself. His name is Harold, and he's dressed in a vibrant pink shirt and a pair of chinos. A pair of bright blue glasses frames his face. I've never worked with an intimacy coordinator before, but from my understanding he'll break the scene down into mechanics, clearing our consent for each aspect of it. I close my eyes momentarily, preparing myself.

'Right,' he says. 'The first thing to establish is that we're all comfortable with the run of play. Lara, is it okay if Avi takes hold of your waist?' I nod and Avi gently places his hand on my waist. My pulse immediately increases.

'Now. Would you be comfortable with him pulling you in?' Harold asks.

'Y-yes,' I say and Avi's grip tightens. He pulls me towards him in one movement, our bodies flush against one another.

'Right, now if you could look up, Lara,' Harold says, 'that would be great.' I tilt my chin upwards.

'Would you be happy for Avi to take hold of your face?'

And as much as I'm trying to keep control of myself in this scene, as much as I'm aware he has a girlfriend – whose dress is currently hanging in my room like a symbol of my treachery – I find myself back in the park last night. Thinking about how he looked at me right before we almost... Avi places his hand on my cheek, his fingers grazing my jaw. Sending electric pulses across my skin.

'And then, you will kiss,' Harold says, with all the excitement of my old manager at the paper factory. It pulls me out of the moment for a second and I almost laugh. *I'm going insane*, I think to myself. Because I honestly feel unhinged in this moment. Avi looks at me inquisitively and I bite my lip.

'Are you happy with that?' Harold asks, looking at us both.

Yes, I think. The word slipping into my consciousness quicker than it should. *Oh, God*.

'O-okay,' I breathe.

'Sure,' Avi says, his voice low. He gently removes his hands from me and steps backwards. I stumble on my feet slightly before I straighten up.

'I'll just check in with Alessandro. The safe word is "hold" – if you need to pull out of the scene, say that and we'll cut, no questions asked. Does that work?'

We both nod, my heart hammering.

'Great,' Harold says. He moves over towards the monitors, and I see both Alessandro and the first AD leaning in to hear his report. I pull at the folds of my dress, willing myself into character. Waiting for the cue to begin.

'Right, my wonderful stars,' Alessandro says, looking at us with pride and expectation. 'Now is the time to dig deep. This is the big scene, okay? I need big feeling.'

I avoid looking at Avi and nod, a swirl of nausea curling in my chest. 'Action!' Alessandro calls, after a few seconds. And I straighten my shoulders, delivering my line.

'Jackson, this isn't right…' I pause. 'You're a detective now. Or at least an assistant. You need to behave more professionally.'

Amelia is telling Jackson off for getting drunk and compromising a witness by getting in a bar fight. Their conversation is heated, which helps – I channel some of my apprehension into tension, anger.

'I know,' Avi says. 'But you're avoiding my question, Amelia.'

'Your question doesn't matter,' I say. 'What matters is that you compromised the integrity of our case. Compromised a witness, Jackson. You're letting your personal feelings cloud your judgement.'

'I am,' he says. 'In more ways than one. Now, let me ask you again. Do you remember what I said to you the other night?'

'No,' I say. He takes a step towards me.

'I think you do,' he says. 'And I think you love me too, Amelia. And I think you're scared to admit it.'

'The case is the only thing that matters,' I say, my heart pounding. 'Nothing else.'

'You matter,' he says. And then he takes the cue. Placing his hand on my waist. 'You matter to me, Amelia.' My heart is practically in my throat at this point. Avi pulls me towards him, his grip tightening. My lips parting slightly as I look up at him.

And then, just like that, he's kissing me.

His lips press against mine – gently at first, then more firm. His hand gripping my dress as he strengthens his hold, pulling me towards him until our bodies are pressed against one another. And somewhere I'm aware that this is a film set, that there are more than a few people watching us in this moment. But the rest of me is here, the room shrinking down to just me and him. The warmth of his body, his soft lips. The way his hand cups my face, his fingers grazing my jaw and setting me on fire.

It's good – *too* good. So many things spilling through in this moment. His face, in the park. The kiss, from years ago. Everything I've been keeping at bay for the last few weeks – for the sake of the film. Unlocked now.

'Cut!' Alessandro calls.

I step back, my world feeling like it's tilting on its axis. My body thrumming with desire for him. A want, a need, to step forwards and kiss him again. And then everything else: crashing guilt about having these feelings at all. The emotions I had last night. Seeing him clearly for the first time since we've been thrown into each other's lives again. Everything I felt, the first time he kissed me. Before he disappeared. Like everything we experienced up to that point led to that moment. Like he and I were on a collision course for something. And it's how I feel again now. But it can't be. Because he's not mine any more. Never was. Avi looks a little shell-shocked too – he runs his hand through his hair, an expression on his face that I can't quite pinpoint and am not sure if I even want to. Alessandro comes over, enthusing about the take. Letting us know that he thinks we got it on the first try, which is pretty much unheard of for a kiss. Though he'd like to do a few more takes, just to be sure.

But I'm only capable of one thought. The ghost of a feeling that has been following me since last night, since Avi placed his hand on the small of my back during the photographs. Since I almost kissed him in the park, and ruined everything. That — even with the best of intentions — if I got too close to him, if I let the distance between us start to melt away like I have in the past few days in order to do a better job on-set, there might be consequences. Pandora's box might open and all my unresolved feelings for him might spill out.

And I'm pretty sure that's what just happened when we kissed.

'Still on for my birthday party next week?' Alison asks over FaceTime a few hours later. I've been sitting in my trailer since we finished filming the scene, pretty much staring into space and trying to figure out what the hell I'm going to do about all these emotions that have suddenly surged up. I have my first and only scene with Deborah

West this afternoon – a living legend and pretty much my idol since I was twelve – which I'm determined to nail, but I find myself unable to focus on anything but Avi. So I was relieved to see Alison's name flash up on my phone screen. She's been telling me about the under-the-sea theme for her party and putting the final plans in place. Including a lobster costume I have begrudgingly agreed to wear.

'Of course,' I reply.

'Well, considering how difficult you are to pin down at the moment…' she says. 'I thought I'd just double check.'

I try to avoid rolling my eyes. Because she's referring to the fact that for the last few weeks I haven't been able to have lunch with her, or see her beyond her visit to my hotel room last week when she brought by the dresses. But I have planned everything down to a tee for this – I know I'll be done with filming on that day by 6 p.m., and my plan is to travel straight to the venue so I'm there on time. I've promised. It's Alison's party, her day. Of course I want to be there.

'Al,' I say. 'I'm on a film set. I'm under contract—'

'I'm just joking,' she says. 'Anyway, I saw those pictures of you at the Olivier Awards last night. You looked hot. That's definitely not my dress, though. Aren't you glad I made you go?'

'Yes,' I say vaguely. Because, honestly, my presence at that event might have caused more problems for me than it solved. But Alison doesn't need to know that. Despite the fact that a part of me wants to tell her all about me and Avi — to get it off my chest — I can't be sure that she'll understand.

'I miss you,' she says, out of nowhere. I smile, a warmth and a little surprise surging through me.

'I miss you too, Ally,' I say. 'But you saw me just last week.'

'Yeah,' she says. 'I know. It's just… I feel like since you started doing this film you've disappeared. Even when we're together, you're not really there.'

I blink, not sure how to respond. Because that's what it takes to make a film like this. I have to commit myself entirely. Especially given everything with Avi, though that thought makes me feel a little unwell.

'Just…' She pauses, her tone shifting a little. 'Just make sure you don't drown, okay? Make sure there's still some room for Lara in there.'

'I will,' I promise. There's something in her words that hits me harder than I think she intended. Because right now drowning does feel a little closer than I'd like it to. But not entirely because of the film.

'Great,' she says. 'Love you. See you next week.'

'See you then,' I reply.

I put my phone away and try to focus, picking up the script in front of me, running my eyes over the lines one more time for my scene with Deborah. I'm excited about it, the excitement bursting through even the confusion and anxiety I've been experiencing for the last few hours. If I'm honest with myself, it's been the day I was looking forward to the most out of filming. Hardly allowing myself to even think about it for fear of psyching myself out and getting starstruck. Because Deborah is one of the icons of 1990s and early 2000s cinema and theatre, in possession of an OBE for her contribution to British arts. And a determination surges up through me as I read the lines again. I need to be on my game. I can't process any of my emotions about Avi right now. This has to come first.

And before I know it, David knocks on my door. It's time.

He marches me to the set. I do my best to keep up, but struggle in the heels I'm wearing.

'Sorry,' he says, looking back at me. 'We're in a rush today. We only have half an hour with Deborah.'

Half an hour? I think. Though I guess her appearance is essentially a cameo, a favour to Alessandro whose career she has staunchly supported for the last ten years.

En route to set, I almost run straight into Avi. *Oh God,* I think. Because it's the first time I've seen him since our scene this morning. And I was half-hoping the weirdness I felt after our kiss was going to be a blip. But apparently, given the massive increase in my pulse, it wasn't.

'Hey,' he says. 'Good luck out there.' Thankfully, David pulls me away before I can formulate a response. I just nod at Avi and allow myself to be dragged along. But when I turn around to look back, I find him still looking at me. An unreadable expression passing across his face.

I reach set and find Deborah there already waiting. Seated in a wing-back armchair, a cane next to her that I presume she needs to walk. They must have included it in the set as part of her character, for her convenience – it's decorated wood and looks antique. I wonder if she owns this one or whether it's a prop.

'Good morning,' she says, a little dismissively. My stomach sinks an inch because she's looking at me like I'm a piece of dirt on the bottom of her shoe. And I don't know what I expected, but it wasn't this. *Maybe she's just tired*, I think, hopeful that I'll be able to prove myself to her in the scene, in any case. Holding on to the fact that – even if she's looking at me like I'm a piece of gum stuck to the bottom of her shoe – I'm still in the room with one of my idols.

We run through the lines a few times. The scene is a conversation between Amelia and her mother about the case and her arrangement with Jackson. It eventually ends up with her mother telling her she's a disappointment and Amelia telling her she doesn't care – that she's going to forge her own way, no matter the cost.

Deborah is commanding. Exciting. The whole room seeming to bend to her presence. It's more than a little intimidating. But I do everything I can to keep up. Elevating my concentration. Keeping myself in the moment, in the scene. Shelving any thoughts about Avi firmly somewhere else.

'That boy,' she says, 'has always been beneath you, Amelia. He gets you into trouble.' Her character is dismissive – thinks little of Jackson because he's American and comes from new money. Wants Amelia to marry someone aristocratic. 'You'd be better off associating with people of your own class. Giving up all this silly investigation business he's got you into.'

'The investigation was not Jackson's idea,' I say. 'And he's more than you think. More of a man than any of the idiots you'd have me marry, Mother.'

'Oh, Amelia,' she says. 'What am I going to do with you?'

We run through the rest of the scene and I'm feeling good – great, even. Like Deborah has me raising my game, higher even than I do with Avi. Deborah is on fire and I feel like – by proximity to her blaze – I'm lighting up too. Really getting a chance to show what I'm made of. And then we're done with rehearsal and moving into our first take.

'Cut!' Alessandro calls after our first run, rushing over to both of us. Giving Deborah feedback, delivered as delicately as he can. Telling me to give it some more oomph. And by the time Alessandro calls 'Cut' after what will hopefully be the final take – especially considering we only have five minutes left of Deborah's time – I feel incredible. Like there will definitely be some takes in there that are some of my best work. I wait for Alessandro to approach and officially release us, deciding not to initiate conversation with Deborah again; after her reaction to me greeting her, she doesn't seem to be one for small talk.

'So,' Deborah says, interrupting my reverie while Alessandro reviews the footage to make sure we can wrap in time. 'How long have you been in the game for, dear?'

'Oh,' I say, both flattered and surprised that she's talking to me. 'Just a few years. But this is my first feature.'

'Mm,' she says, with a slight flick of her eyes.

'Why do you ask?' I say.

'I mean, dear,' she says, grasping her cane and getting up out of the chair she's been sitting in. 'That I can tell.'

I baulk for a second, so shocked by her blatant rudeness that I can't formulate a response.

'Don't take it personally,' she says, taking my silence as an invitation to further explain. 'Some people have the je ne sais quoi to make it in this industry. The gumption. And some,' she looks at me, dragging her gaze slowly down my form, 'don't.' I swallow, my throat suddenly dry.

Before I can say anything else, Alessandro makes the call and she's turned and started making her way across the set.

When I'm back in my trailer and ready to head to my hotel room, I find myself at a complete loss. Turning Deborah's words over in my mind, each one like a knife. This is a woman whose poster was on the wall of my childhood bedroom. Who I've watched, studied – old performances on YouTube, on stage, every single film she's ever been in. And so her negative opinion hurts more than I'd like it to. Hurts catastrophically, even.

But while I'm circling the edge of sinking into a complete depression, I hear Avi's voice outside my trailer, talking to one of the runners. Before he can knock, I reach the door and open it.

'Hey,' he says, his voice soft. My stomach knots at the sight of him. I forgot we said we'd run lines. 'Is this a bad time?' he asks.

I contemplate saying yes. I've only momentarily distracted myself from my feelings about him with the disappointment of my scene with Deborah. And right now both are threatening to crash through all at once. But I don't. Because something else surges up: a desire not to be alone. I need a friend. And he's about the closest thing I have, on-set, as alien as that thought feels.

'Is everything okay?' he asks quietly, stepping inside.

No, I think. And it's not just because of Deborah. It's because the lines around him are blurring. Because I feel awful about the fact that I almost kissed him. Because something about that on-set kiss has unlocked a myriad of emotions I can't even begin to deal with right now. And I wouldn't know how to deal with it if I tried.

'I just finished my scene with Deborah,' I say, because that – at least – is something I can share with him. His expression shifts immediately.

'Ah,' he says. 'What did she say this time?'

'What do you mean, this time?' I ask, confused.

'Just that she has a bit of a habit of terrorising people on-set. Go on,' he says.

'Oh,' I say, letting out a breath. Almost wanting to laugh now. But there's a tiny part of me that doesn't find it funny – at all. 'Well, she effectively said that I'm talentless and will never make it, and might as well give up now.'

He barks out a laugh, and I look at him, shocked.

'Sorry,' he says. 'It's just – obviously you know that's ridiculous, right?'

'Yes,' I say. 'But also no.' And I feel so small in the moment, needing his reassurance.

'Lara,' he says, leaning forwards with a serious and kind expression. 'That woman once told me her pet corgi had more charisma than I was demonstrating in a scene with her.' I let out a bit of a laugh at this and he takes a step towards me. 'And trust me, that was even worse an insult than you think – I've met the dog. He's horrible.' I laugh at his joke and his face lights up. A brief silence falls.

'I've got a poster of her up in my childhood bedroom,' I say to fill it, closing my eyes at the thought of it. When she was about my age. The film that launched her career.

'Take that shit down,' he says, his tone firm. 'Or don't. But either way, what she said wasn't about you. If I let in half the stuff people said about me it would destroy me completely. It almost did, actually.' His face darkens a little and I want to ask about it, but he speaks before I can.

'Look,' he says, leaning in. 'She's a tough old girl who's spent her whole life having to prove her worth in an industry that didn't want her to succeed. If you want my professional opinion, I think she sees young actors at the beginning of their career, feels jealous of the attention they're getting over her and puts them down to compensate for the fear that one day she'll become irrelevant.'

'Wow,' I say, after a few seconds. 'Quite harsh, but very insightful. Thank you.'

'I have my moments,' he says. And then his expression changes, becoming more serious.

'And for what it's worth,' he says, taking a step towards me. Crouching down. Placing his hand gently on my arm. 'Lara, I think you're really talented.'

'Thank you,' I say quietly.

I find myself suddenly more aware of his proximity. The feeling I had earlier, after we kissed, surging up again. Of the years we were apart collapsing into one another. Until it's just us, again. Back in that pub. At the Christmas party where he kissed me. Right before he left, again, disappearing for ever.

He has a girlfriend, I think to myself. Chastising myself for the thought. The emotions I can't seem to get away from. But the way he's looking at me, right now, is kicking them into full throttle.

'Do you want to maybe get a drink, instead of running lines?' he asks. And I let out a breath, the words coming to my lips before I can stop them.

'Sure,' I reply.

'Okay,' he says. 'Let me just get out of costume and I'll meet you in five?'

I nod, not trusting myself to speak.

We meet outside Avi's trailer about ten minutes later and he calls his driver to pick us up. I watch as we wind down a few side streets, my heart in my throat. *What am I doing?* I think to myself as the car journey goes on. Trying to convince myself that the decision to get drinks with him wasn't incredibly stupid, given my current state – that this is fine. Even while the knot in my stomach tells me it's not. That I should get out of this car right now.

'We're here,' Avi says, and I get out of the car and follow him to the entrance of a bar – a doorway, with some steps downwards. It looks… dodgy, to say the least.

'Have you brought me here to kill me?' I ask, making an attempt at humour to mask my anxiety. He laughs.

'No,' he says. 'Unless you have an allergy to dive bars. In which case, we should probably go somewhere else.'

I'm not sure what I was expecting – some fancy rooftop bar, perhaps. But as we walk down the steps, I realise how far off my expectations were.

This place looks old, in a sort of crusty well-lived-in way. I get the sense that if I touched the wall my hand might stick to it. There are beer mats stuck along the wall behind the bar, and a man with a huge beard who could be anywhere from his thirties to his sixties standing behind it. He greets Avi as if they know each other and slides two beers across the table, along with some tokens.

'What is this place?' I ask, but Avi just hands me the beer and gestures for me to follow him to the other side of the room. There are a few pool tables in the corner. A couple of people playing at the one next to us, who barely look up as we approach.

'This is where I come to hide out when I'm in London,' he says, putting a token in the table. Handing me a cue. 'When I want to feel normal for a few hours. Everyone in this bar is here for two reasons and two reasons only: beer and pool. Nothing else registers.'

'That's nice,' I say uselessly, taking hold of the cue. I imagine there aren't many places Avi can go to where he doesn't get recognised. I wonder what that must be like, feeling exposed wherever you go. Kind of like being on-set, I suppose, but followed by fans and paparazzi rather than runners. A life, observed. *It must be lonely*, I think, suddenly.

I watch as he sets up the table, placing the triangle in the middle.

'Do you want to break?' he asks, rolling up his shirtsleeves. His forearms flexing as he does. *Fuck,* I think, at the flash of heat in my chest at the sight. I shake my head to hide my reaction and he breaks first. But that was a mistake. Because the way he looks playing pool – with masterful, smooth strokes that allow him to pot three balls in a row – does things to me that it shouldn't.

'So… how's Sienna's Paris trip going?' I say, to remind myself both of her existence and the fact that I am a horrible person for having these feelings about her boyfriend.

He looks up at me, as if he's confused by the question. But then seems to remember himself. 'Uh, good. I think she's at a modelling gig right now.' His dismissive tone gives me pause and I frown momentarily. But then he clears his throat awkwardly and starts speaking again. 'You know, about her… There's something I need to—'

'It's okay,' I say quickly. Because I can't risk hearing him telling me it was a mistake for the second time. 'It was my fault, the other night. And it didn't mean anything. I mean, nothing happened, right? It was nothing. I just got caught up in the moment and…' I trail off, embarrassment and shame coursing through me.

He nods slowly, an expression passing across his face that makes my heart jump. Because it looks almost like disappointment. But that wouldn't make any sense at all.

'Say no more,' he says. 'Your play.'

We exchange shots for a few minutes, the tension rising as we do. Like something has suddenly shifted in the air between us. And it's setting me on edge, so much so that my hand slips off the cue as I'm playing my next shot.

'May I?' Avi asks, coming up behind me. Placing his hand gently on my elbow. His fingers brushing across my skin in a way that drives me insane. That feels like a drug in this moment. I nod slowly. He leans over me, helping to steady my hand. To aim the cue. Our bodies pressed up against each other. His breath tickling the side of my ear. I inhale, struggling to remember where I am – what I'm even doing.

'That's great,' he says. 'And now…' And he gently, slowly, helps me pull my arm back, releasing the cue. The cue ball shoots off clear, sending the target into the pocket. And I wait for him to move. But he doesn't, not right away. His hand still on my elbow. The heat of his body against mine sending me insane. I close my eyes and breathe into it for a moment, and find myself imagining a million other things we could be doing right now. That involve fewer clothes, and my hotel room.

Oh, my God. I need to get out of here.

'Lara—' he says. And I don't know what he's about to say. But I do know that I need to leave.

'I'm sorry,' I say, stepping back. 'I shouldn't have come tonight. I'm not feeling well. I…' I grab my coat from the hook where I left it and start to make my way towards the door.

'Did I say something wrong?' Avi asks and I shake my head. 'If it's about Sienna, Lara, I can explain—'

'No,' I say, my throat tightening. 'It's nothing like that. You're great. She's great. I'm just… I need to go home. Get an early night, ready for tomorrow. I'll see you on-set, okay?'

He nods, his shoulders slumping a little. 'Okay,' he replies. And I practically run up the steps into the fresh air outside.

Oh, fuck, I think. *I'm in trouble.*

13

The next few days, the feeling that there's something horribly wrong continues growing and growing. I feel like I'm on eggshells around Avi, even more so than I did when we first arrived at the studio. And the more I try to stave it off, the worse it gets. We're approaching the last week of filming now and I have another kissing scene this morning. One I'm dreading, because I keep having completely inappropriate thoughts about my scene partner. I've been hardly sleeping, showing up most days so sleep-deprived that Sarah has to put more concealer under my eyes than before. Pouring coffee over myself at craft services – thankfully when I wasn't in costume – but so visibly that the runners are now hovering around me intensely, scared I'm going to throw water down my skirt and ruin continuity.

'Everything okay, love?' Sarah asks one morning. 'You seem a little off, these last few days.'

No, I want to say. But I can't in a million years articulate why. Because I feel ashamed of it. Like the past is encroaching on me every second. Things I thought and hoped I'd be able to put behind me, or at least compartmentalise for the purposes of this film. And I thought I had. Things were going so well.

Then we went to the Olivier Awards. And I nearly kissed him. And now I'm somehow a complete mess.

'I'm fine,' I say instead. 'Just… a little tired. Long hours on-set.'

'It's a hard job, love,' she says. 'You have to look after yourself.'

'Thanks,' I say.

I just don't know how. Especially with everything else that's crowding in at the moment. It's all I can do to just show up and try to do a good job. She smiles at me kindly, and I find myself feeling suddenly and strangely close to tears. Probably because I've only slept for a couple of hours and Sarah is being so kind.

'All done,' she says, stepping back.

'Thank you, Sarah,' I say. And I mean it, for more than this.

'It's nothing, love,' she says. 'Just doing my job.' And then she steps back and David arrives to take me over to Hair.

Once I'm finished with prep and fully in costume, I am taken in a car to the location for the day: the College of Arms in Central London, near St. Paul's Cathedral. It's a beautiful Victorian building, with sash windows and gilded iron gates.

But I'm distracted by thoughts of Alison; her birthday party is in a few days' time and my parents are coming to set the following day. I had a missed call from her last night, so I need to call her back. I also need to reply to Spencer and Hannah – they've been messaging me to check in after drinks the other night. And I've been so overwhelmed with everything going on, and ashamed of my own stupid actions – which were those of an erratic person rather than the self-controlled, cool and calm Lara they described – that I've not really known how to answer. Right now, I don't really feel in control of anything at all. And it terrifies me.

Our scene today is breathless and exciting. The peak of the film: of Amelia and Jackson's romance, and their pursuit of Roman's character. And I'm freaking out. But I can't afford to be. We're so nearly there.

'Hey,' Avi says, approaching me. Looking impossibly attractive in a dark-green waistcoat under his usual jacket, slightly unbuttoned, which offsets his brown eyes. My pulse surges in his presence. *Jesus fucking Christ, Lara*, I think.

'Hi,' I breathe.

'Hello, lovely people,' Harold calls. He's wearing a powder-blue suit this time. A shock of colour among the crowd.

'Hi,' I reply.

'Ready to go through the scene?'

No, I think. But I nod. Avoiding Avi's gaze. Suddenly and incredibly aware of my limbs — of the distance between us. Distance we'll soon be closing.

Harold runs us through a few movements. Me putting my hand on Avi's waist. Leaning in. It all feels suddenly awkward, like he's my prom date. Like I'm a teenager again, no coordination whatsoever.

'Okay,' Harold says, clapping his hands together. Avi pulls away and I catch my breath. 'Remember your safe word, same as before. Let me know if either of you want to pull out of the scene and we'll take a break and regroup.'

But that's not what I'm worried about. Unlike before, when all I wanted to do was run – this time, my worry is how little I'm feeling that. *Oh, God*, I think, doing my best to swallow those feelings. I'm actually excited about this.

'Ready?' Avi asks, and I nod again, a lump in my throat.

We make our way over to our marks, pausing to greet Alessandro, who is in a good mood today, the weather better than he was expecting it to be.

'A beautiful day for a beautiful couple,' Alessandro says, and I baulk. Because I know he means Jackson and Amelia. But something in my consciousness jumps at the word and I kick myself internally.

We stand in our places, waiting for our cue. As Alessandro is mobilising the other teams – 'rolling, lights, sound' – I look up, my eyes snapping onto Avi's. There is an intensity in his gaze that sets me on fire.

'Action,' Alessandro calls and I step forwards.

'You let him get away,' I say, breathless, delivering my first line. My blood seeming to heat as Avi walks towards me. This is a scene where Roman has just narrowly escaped, because Jackson was so focused on Amelia's safety. And she's furious with him for not putting the case over her. But, really, she's furious with herself too. Because she could've stopped Roman and she didn't – she was as worried about Jackson as he was about her.

'It is my duty to protect you,' he says. 'Amelia, if something had happened to you…' He cuts himself off. 'Besides, I told you, I have formulated a plan. I need you to trust me.'

'It's not you I cannot trust,' I reply, the line falling off my tongue easily. 'It's myself.' And I register as I say it how present this particular line feels. So much so I almost slip out of the scene. But I hold on for dear life, keeping my eyes locked on his.

'Why not?' he asks.

'Because…' I start. 'Because you awaken emotions in me, Jackson. Emotions that are compromising my ability to handle this case professionally.'

'What kind of emotions?' he says, his jaw set. I don't reply.

'Look,' he says. 'I'll hunt him down until the end of my days, if that's what it takes. But I need you to be honest with me in order to do that. Otherwise, I'm not sure what we're doing here.'

I take a step closer.

'I don't know how to put it into words,' I say, my heart hammering as I deliver the line and wait for his response.

'Perhaps you don't have to,' he says, breathless. I put my hands on his waist, gripping the fabric of his jacket. Pulling him towards me.

He reaches up and pushes a strand of hair from my face. And leans in – time seeming to slow down as he does.

Then, before I know it, he's kissing me – for the second time in a week. And a million flames rush across my skin. My body reacting before I realise what's happening, pressing against his. His abs against my corset, his hands in my hair. The chemistry I felt the first time, multiplied by a thousand. His form curving down to meet me, so we're entwined. His lips melting into mine. A fire burning up between us.

I'm slightly aware of some sounds around me. But I ignore them. Focused only on how much we're nailing this.

How breathless it feels.

But then a hand lands on my arm. A sound, like someone is clearing their throat. I step backwards, like I'm coming up for air.

'Bambini, what is this?' Alessandro says, a light hint of amusement in his voice.

Oh, God. My stomach drops as I come back to the present, remembering the brief of the scene. That we were supposed to break away mid-kiss. That I was supposed to spot Roman running past over Avi's shoulder. To chase him.

'You missed your cue,' he continues, frowning.

Which means…

I look at Avi and see him realising the same thing.

That we've not only fucked up this take.

But we've just made out, in front of everyone.

A deep blush moves across my cheeks. More embarrassment than I've ever felt in my life crashing through me. In my periphery, Avi looks similarly chastened.

'Let's go again, Alessandro,' he mutters under his breath.

When I look up, one pair of eyes stands out through the crowd. Watching us.

Roman.

And as my eyes meet his, he smiles. A look of barely disguised, self-congratulatory glee passing across his face.

Oh, shit.

The next day, I arrive on-set still feeling absolutely mortified. We had to redo the scene five times yesterday, each more excruciating than the last, until we got a take Alessandro was happy with. Then I pretty much ran straight back to my trailer and hid out there until I was dismissed from set. Thank goodness that was the only scene we were filming.

I'm shooting with Roman today. And I'm one hundred per cent sure he's going to try to taunt me about it in some way. At least this evening I'll be able to distract myself – Alison's birthday party is happening straight after filming, and, surprisingly, given the fact that I am basically a hermit, I find myself looking forward to a social occasion. Beyond the fact that it's her birthday and her joy will be so wonderful to see, it'll be nice to be outside the increasingly claustrophobic environment of set. My lobster costume is waiting in my trailer, so I can get changed into it straight after we wrap today – I just have to get through this morning first.

The scene we're filming is a street scene, Roman chasing Amelia out of his flat after he catches her looking for evidence. They've cordoned off a cobbled street in Central London with street lamps at intervals along it. It's a beautiful street. And unseasonably cold this morning. Amelia is wearing her usual: a corseted silk dress with a small shawl. No coat. A runner comes and drapes me with a blanket while Alessandro discusses camera angles with the first AD.

'Thank you…' I say, turning to offer them thanks. But they've been called away before I can address them.

Roman is standing in their place. 'Hello, Amelia,' he says.

Just his voice is enough to set me on edge this morning. After yesterday, I'm jumpier than usual – I'd have given anything for a schedule change today.

'Hi,' I say, keeping my voice level. Turning to face him, trying to erase any tension from my tone. Because Amelia isn't bothered by him, so I can't be or it'll filter into the scene.

'I've been watching you, Amelia,' he says, under his breath. So low Alessandro can't hear. Sending an involuntary shiver down my spine. He reaches out and traces the back of his hand down my arm, almost touching it but not quite. 'I see how you look at him.'

'Roman, please don't touch me—' Before I can say anything more – before I can land on a combination of words that might get him to back off – a hand lands firmly on my other arm. I jump, startled. It's Alessandro.

'So jittery today, Amelia mia,' he says, looking concerned. 'Is everything okay?'

Roman fixes his eyes on mine, a sinister expression passing over his face. But a second later, when Alessandro looks over to him, it's gone.

'I believe so,' Roman says lightly, looking at me. 'Don't you agree?'

I exhale through my nose and narrowly avoid rolling my eyes. Because his words aren't true – but I don't have the energy or inclination to correct them right now. So instead, I nod. Wanting this interaction to be over as quickly as possible.

'Shall we get to the filming, then, while it is still fresh?' Alessandro asks.

'Great,' I reply, trying to muster some enthusiasm.

We move over to our marks, Roman a few feet behind me. I can hear his breathing.

'You look scared, Amelia. What exactly are you so afraid of?' Roman asks as we wait for Alessandro to take his place behind the monitors. I don't answer.

A few seconds later, Alessandro calls 'Action!'

We manage to get through the first take, Roman catching me leaving his character's apartment with a bag full of evidence and chasing me for a few metres. Me looking back over my shoulder, some of the fear and apprehension I'm channelling real. Because this man really has me on edge today. And Alessandro seems happy enough, but asks for another angle. We set up, ready for the scene, and Roman leans in to start taunting me again.

'Roman,' I say, under my breath. 'I've really had enough of this whole method-acting thing.'

'Oh, Amelia,' he says. 'Don't be a spoilsport. We're just having some fun. Aren't we?' He tilts his head to one side like a snake and I glance over my shoulder to see Alessandro still talking to the first AD. *Fuck*. The sight of it sends a shiver of determination through me.

'I'm not,' I say firmly, snapping my gaze back to his. 'I'm not having any fun at all, actually. So if you could back the fuck off that would be great.' I've dealt with bullies before. Sometimes taking the high road doesn't work. In fact, I'm not sure it ever did. And this time, I've had enough.

He steps back and for a second I wonder if I've got through. But then he smiles again and my heart drops.

'Ooh,' he says. 'A little fire. I like it. I can see why he likes you so much.'

What the fuck? I falter, a little concern coming up and replacing the anger. Because I can feel what's coming.

'What did you just say?'

He puts his hand over his mouth. 'Whoops,' he says. 'Have I got it the wrong way around? Perhaps it's you that has a little crush on him, hmm?'

'Roman, stop,' I say.

'I *have* got it the wrong way around,' he says, his voice full of elation. 'What happened, Amelia?' he asks, enunciating his words. As if he knows he's not really talking about Amelia any more. As if this is just him coming out – the chaos agent that Avi spoke about, way at the beginning of filming. Enjoying my discomfort. I glance over to Alessandro again, but he's still deep in conversation. 'Did he break your little heart?'

'Roman,' I say, my voice full of warning. Because I can feel anger flickering through me now, about to rage into a flame. And if he pushes me a step further, I won't be responsible for what happens next.

'He did,' he says, looking positively delighted now.

Roman takes a step forwards. I glance over my shoulder – everyone behind the cameras is still focused on the monitor. He reaches out to touch my face again and everything in me recoils at his touch.

And this time, something in me snaps.

Before he – or I – can realise what I'm doing, I grab his arm in the same adapted karate move I used in the stunt training with Avi and twist it behind his back, pulling him into a hold. One I know is painless – I might be fucking furious with him right now but I don't want to hurt him – but it has the desired effect nonetheless. He exhales in shock.

I tighten my hold, lean forwards and whisper in his ear.

'Touch me again,' I say, 'and I'll leak the stories Sienna told me about the summers you spent together as kids.'

'I don't know what you're talking about,' he says as I let him free of the hold, hearing a commotion from behind the cameras. Some runners come rushing over, with Alessandro in tow. But just before they reach us, I see a glimpse of fear in Roman's eyes.

'Bambina,' Alessandro says, his tone apoplectic. 'Could you please tell me what the fuck is going on here?'

'Sorry, Alessandro,' I say mildly, stepping backwards. 'Roman was just offering to take me through some of our stunt moves for tomorrow while we waited.'

Roman sets his jaw, looking furious. But I stare him down and he gives a small, curt nod.

'Well,' Alessandro says, looking at him angrily. 'Now is not the time for such stupid antics. Let us not play silly buggers. We are on a schedule and we have a film to make. Or has everybody forgotten this except me?'

He looks from me to Roman.

This time, I nail the scene. I am alive with Amelia's strength – her confidence in herself, even in the face of her fear. And a joy surges up inside me, remembering the expression on Roman's face when he stepped back from my hold.

I stood up for myself. And it felt good.

When I get back to my trailer – breathless and full of adrenaline after what just happened – I find Avi waiting for me. Standing outside, still in costume. Something about his posture gives me pause as I approach.

'Hi,' I say, my breath catching a little in my throat.

He looks up and an expression of pure and unadulterated relief passes across his face.

'Thank God you're okay,' he says. 'I heard some runners on the radio, talking about… you and Roman…' He can hardly get his words out he's so worried. Something shifts in me at the sight, but I push it away.

'I'm fine,' I say. 'Roman was just…' I pause. 'Being Roman. You don't need to worry about me.'

But I must seem a little rattled, because he follows me into my trailer.

'I do, though,' he says quietly, closing the door behind him. 'It's my fault he's targeting you so much. I shouldn't have blown up at him on that first day. Shouldn't have—'

'Stop, Avi,' I say, trying to keep my cool. 'It wasn't your fault. He was just taunting me.'

'Taunting you about what?' he asks. Always with the questions.

'It doesn't matter,' I say.

'Lara,' he says. 'If he's harassing you—'

And this time, I can't keep it in. It explodes out of me before I can stop it. 'You, Avi,' I say. 'He was taunting me about you.'

He looks down, confusion passing across his features. 'What about me?' he says slowly. Quietly.

I shake my head, not wanting to admit it.

'Lara,' he says. 'Tell me what he said or I swear to God I'll go to his trailer right now—'

And in this moment, any last sliver of control I had slips away.

'He was implying that…' I pause, my voice catching. 'That I had feelings for you.'

His deep-brown eyes snap up to mine, betraying surprise mingled with something else. The same gaze from the park, after the Olivier Awards. That I've been pretending I don't see too, when he looks at me after we kiss on-set. Because it's all wrong. And it's all too complicated.

'Do you?' he asks.

'I don't think that matters—' I say, trying to throw him off. Because I'm beginning to lose control of this conversation and I don't know what'll happen if I do.

'I think it does,' he says, taking a step towards me. 'In fact, I think it's the only thing that matters, right now. Lara…'

And, for a second, my breath catches. The words he's saying to me right now so reminiscent of Jackson and Amelia's dialogue the other day, I can hardly process them. And in the next, the dam breaks – everything flowing towards me.

A year of friendship. Jokes across the bar. Covering my shifts when I needed to attend auditions. Checking in on me when I didn't get the parts I wanted. Running lines with me late in the bar after shifts.

Him crossing the room to me at the Christmas party. Arriving like the star he was – at the time, his film about to be released. Everyone vying for his attention, wanting to talk to him. But he only had eyes for me. His low, deep voice, saying, 'I've missed you'. The night spiralling into the kiss that ruined everything.

His abrupt departure.

The texts the next day, telling me it was a mistake.

But then more comes rushing through. Him swinging a rat around Roman's trailer. Saving me from the light fitting falling. Looking at me the other night in the park, more vulnerable than I've ever seen him. Telling him that this film is the happiest he's been in a long time.

And a part of me still wants to ask him why – why he dropped off the face of the earth. Why he didn't want me to be in his life any more. Because I was angry, that he kissed me then decided it was a mistake. But that didn't mean I didn't want him to be my friend.

But as he's looking at me now, the past hurt starts to fade. And he's standing in front of me, his gaze pulling everything into a point like it used to, making me feel like I'm the only person in the whole world.

'I do,' I say, a tear slipping out. He closes his eyes, absorbing my words. His fist clenching almost imperceptibly at his side. Like he's trying to hold himself back. 'But I know it's my problem. And it doesn't matter, anyway, because you have a girlfriend. I just need to get over it…'

He closes the space between us.

'Lara,' he says. Tracing a hand slowly down the side of my face. Like he did yesterday in front of the cameras. Only this time, it's real. Just us. My heart thuds. 'Sienna is not my girlfriend.'

And then he kisses me.

14

His hand clenches around my shirt, pulling me close to him. And then I'm against the wall of the trailer, hearing something fall – one of the books from the shelf. But I don't care. Electricity flickers through my veins like it did the other day on-set. Igniting a flame in a way I haven't allowed it to until now. The on-set control melting away.

His lips are soft then firm on mine, his hand grasping the fabric of my dress like he can't get enough of me.

Like, somehow, he's been waiting for this.

For a moment I lose myself in him. But then I replay his words. *Sienna's not my girlfriend*. I pull away and he looks at me with such longing I can hardly see straight. But I force myself to step back. His chest is heaving. What we just did was insane. And, despite all my better instincts, all I want is to do it again.

'Avi,' I say. 'What do you mean she's not your girlfriend?'

He looks at me for a second, faltering, not immediately answering my question. That's when the regret hits. Memories crowding in – of the last time he looked at me like this. The last time he kissed me. The last message he sent me. *Last night was a mistake.*

But before the feeling can take hold, he starts talking.

'I never meant to end up in a situation like this,' he says. 'Honestly, it probably sounds insane to you. And it is. I know that. But...' He pauses, as if gathering his thoughts.

'LA is a strange place, and when my first film came out, the paparazzi were everywhere. I didn't know how to deal with it,' he says. 'At all.' His voice shifts, a little vulnerable. And despite the hurt I'm feeling, I find myself quiet. Listening. Because I've never really seen this side of him; he seems like such a pro now. And he never mentioned any of this in his postcards.

'Sienna was my neighbour,' he says. 'And one day, she knocked on my door and introduced herself. And, slowly, we started doing stuff together – grocery shopping, driving each other to auditions. It was nice – she was an old hand. Someone who had spent so much time in Hollywood because of her parents that she was already sick of it, which made her refreshing to spend time with. It really felt like she had her head on straight, you know? So I liked being around her.'

I nod, recognising again how poorly I misjudged Sienna when I first met her. Everything he's saying about her makes sense, aligns with the impression I have of her now.

'Last year, she was having a really hard time,' he says. 'Could hardly leave her apartment without being followed and it was really affecting her. And we spent – spend – so much time together, that the rumours have been going on for years. On and off. One or the other of us always denies it. But it always comes back around, eventually. And I'll be honest, it's been good for both of our profiles. So one day our publicists got together and suggested we start leaning into the rumours – and at first we thought it was insane. But the more we thought about it, the more we realised that it might be a good thing, to take some of the heat off both of us for a while. It made me feel safe, even. Because the photographers might still be hanging around, looking for snippets of my life, but I had some control over it. I could give this to them – a story to digest and dissect that wasn't real at all.'

I nod, slowly. Because there's logic to what he's saying. But I don't understand why he needed to keep up the act for me.

'So,' I say. 'All of it was a lie?'

He nods. 'Yes. Only our publicists know and a few of our friends.'

'Why didn't you just tell me?' I say.

He looks down. 'I know,' he says. 'I should have told you. In fact, I planned to as soon as we started working together. But then… When we got here, you seemed to find it easier for there to be some distance between us. And it didn't feel right, to burden you with it. To pull you into that mess, when everything was going so well. But then, after the Olivier Awards…'

He pauses and my pulse surges at the memory of that night. Our almost-kiss in the park, which I've been torturing myself over – apparently with no need at all. And some anger flares up, that he left me alone with those feelings. Because he was there too. He felt it too. And he didn't say anything.

'I started to think that maybe I should tell you. And so I made a plan – once the film was over, if you still wanted to spend any time with me, I was going to tell you everything. But it's been killing me, Lara – presenting this fake front to you. And then you told me you had feelings for me and…'

His eyes burn into mine and my anger is still there – but there's something else too. Something that keeps me stock still as he reaches up gently to push some hair from my face. My emotions warring inside me. And in the next second, I realise I can't do this – not right now. Because it's too much.

What am I doing?

'You know what?' I say. 'I'm not sure I can do this right now.'

'Lara,' Avi says, his expression shifting. 'Wait—'

But the way he's looking at me hurts too much. And I feel used, like someone he doesn't respect. Because if he did, he wouldn't have deceived me like this.

'No, Avi,' I say, my heart thudding. 'I need you to leave.'

'Okay,' he says, his voice betraying his emotions. 'You need some time. That's fine.'

I nod, my throat dry, but I don't say anything more in this moment. Because I'm not sure what I would even say. He waits for a few seconds, his eyes on mine. Then he turns and walks towards the door, opening it and heading out onto the set outside.

Once he's gone, I sit in a complete daze for I don't know how long. Trying to process the myriad of emotions running through me. Failing to make sense of any of it. Frozen, not sure what to do. We still have a week of filming left, but for the first time I'm not even thinking about the film – can't find it in myself to care about anything right now, except the feeling of his lips on mine a few moments ago. But I don't know if I can trust him. It's all too much. I pick up my script and run through the lines for tomorrow a few times, trying to distract myself. But it doesn't work. Still, I try anyway.

After probably an hour, when the words on the page stop looking like words at all, I slowly start to come to my senses. I need to get out of here, need time to think. I pull out my phone, ready to call George and ask for a lift back to the hotel, and find five missed calls from Alison. A text, asking where I am. If I'm okay. And the events of the last couple of hours disappear immediately, replaced by blind panic.

Oh, fuck, I think, a cold shock running through me. Alison's party. In all the chaos with Roman and now Avi, I completely forgot about it. I get up, my actions dictated by panic, and pull on the pieces of the lobster costume that was hanging in a garment bag by the door – one that's been in my eyeline for the last hour and I haven't even noticed. I throw the red Morphsuit, the claws and the red face paint she specially ordered into my bag, ready to put them on in the car. My stomach churning as I do – because I confirmed three times that I'd be there on time. Checking and re-checking my schedule to make sure. I promised.

I hurtle out of my trailer, tailed by a startled runner who looks more than a little alarmed by my probably maniacal expression. 'Can I get you anything, Miss Francis?' she asks. But I'm already running, shouting 'No, thank you,' over my shoulder. Pulling out my phone, calling George, who, mercifully, is still on-set, waiting for my call. He pulls out the front and I leap into the car, asking him to drive as quickly as possible.

I check the time on the clock on George's dashboard while squeezing myself into the Morphsuit, watching the seconds tick by as we pull into standstill traffic. There's a football match at one of the nearby stadiums today, so it's backed up. Once I'm no longer exposing my bra to George and have dragged the zip up my back I pull my phone out, pinging with a few more texts asking where I am, if I'm okay.

I'm fine, I type quickly. *So sorry – work stuff. On my way.*

A read receipt pops up but she doesn't reply, and a knot twists in my chest. I silently will the car to go faster, but we're stuck in gridlock. I busy myself by painting my face, jolting as George accelerates where he can. It's probably going to look like a total mess by the time I arrive, but it's the best I can do in these circumstances.

George manages to find a side street, which takes us a slightly longer route and avoids the main crush. But by the time I arrive at the party, I'm two hours late.

I rush through the door, sweating my make-up off and throwing my lobster claws on as I go, and find her, in the middle of a room surrounded by friends. Some balloons extending up to the ceiling. A large, sea-themed cake in the centre. With candles on it, wax dripping down from their black tips. And a few slices cut out at the bottom. *Fuck*, I think, my chest pinching. *I've missed the cake.*

She turns and looks at me. And my first thought is how beautiful she looks. A red wig, cascading down her shoulders. Shell-shaped bikini top. A long, foil tail. This costume must have taken hours. And she's been telling me about it for weeks, so I should've expected this. But I didn't understand the full extent she'd be going to.

Then I see the look on her face and I stop thinking about her costume at all.

'Ally—' I say as she approaches me.

'Not in here,' she says through clenched teeth. Grabbing my arm. Pulling me out into the corridor.

'You're late,' she says, putting her hands on her hips. 'And you said you'd be here on time. You promised. I was worried that that light fitting had fallen on you again and you were actually dead this time. Did something happen?'

'No…' I say, a flicker of guilt appearing as I do. Because something did happen. But it's not an acceptable excuse for being late.

'Are you sure?' she asks, examining me. Looking me up and down, as if checking for injuries. 'Are you sure you didn't break your leg, or fall, or have some horrible accident that would make this all much easier for me to forgive you?'

'No, Ally,' I say. 'I'm sorry – I ended up staying late at work.'

'Did you have to?' she asks.

And for a second, I want to tell a more elaborate lie. I want to tell her I was contractually obliged to stay, that Alessandro asked me to film some more scenes. Because that would be easier. But in this moment, I can't. I might not be able to tell her the full truth, but I can at least own this. It's my fault I'm late.

'No,' I say quietly. Shame spilling through me. 'I- I lost track of time, running lines in my trailer. I—'

'Okay,' she says, stepping back. Nodding. The shells of her bra bobbing slightly as she does. 'Okay. I don't want you here.'

What?

'I'm serious, Lara,' she says. 'I don't want you at this party.'

'Why not? I'm sorry—'

'Because you promised you'd be here and you weren't. Because you say no to literally everything I invite you to. Because your career comes first, always. And I'm really fucking tired of coming second. I've had enough.'

'You don't come second, Ally—'

'Yes, Lara,' she says. 'Yes, I do. Everyone does. You haven't even seen Mum and Dad for months, except to move your stuff into their garage. It's always the next script, the next audition. And that's if you even tell us about it. Everything is on your terms. And it hurts. Because it makes me feel like I'm more of an inconvenience than a sister to you.'

And I can't help it – I know I've fucked up, but anger comes out instead.

'You don't exactly make it easy for me to tell you things, Ally,' I say. She blinks for a second, looking hurt and surprised.

'What are you talking about?'

'I mean,' I say. '"Stop worrying, Lara", "Get a life, Lara", "Just do this and this and this and everything will be fine, Lara". Because everything is fine for you, all the time. Because you literally breeze through life with no worries in the world. Because it was me that sat in the kitchen with Mum and Dad and helped them go through their bills. Me who was isolated at pretty much every school we went to while you went off and made friends like it was so simple. Telling me I just needed to try harder. Rolling your eyes when I went off to read during break times. Like it was my fault – for not trying hard enough, or putting myself out there enough. When I was trying. People just didn't like me, Ally. And I know that's a foreign concept to you, but it's true.' My heart pounds as I say the words, the hurt spilling out. 'And I'm tired of feeling like you think I'm doing everything in my life wrong. And I know I can be laser-focused sometimes and I know I've fucked up this evening. But this – acting – is all I have. You have everything else.'

'No, I don't,' she says. 'I don't have a sister. And I haven't had one in a long time.'

This hits me in the chest and tears start welling up in my eyes. 'You don't mean that, Ally,' I say.

'Acting isn't all you have,' she says. 'Not by a long shot. And it makes me really fucking sad that you can't see that. And I think if you stopped holding everyone at arm's length for one second you might see that it's not true. But tonight, I've had enough. I don't want you here and I don't want to talk to you right now. I want to go back in there and have a nice time with my friends. I need you to leave.'

I stand for a few seconds, my chest heaving as I process the weight of her words.

'Okay,' I say, eventually. Nodding, even as my heart breaks. Because I can see that my presence here is making everything worse. Because I might feel angry, but I fucked up. And it's her birthday. And she deserves to have a nice evening, with or without me there. I hand her her gift – a necklace I spent the last few weeks looking for on Etsy.

Something she mentioned wanting from an antique shop a while ago, but it was too expensive at the time. I thought it might be a nice use of some of the money I'm being paid now. Was thinking about maybe buying her a holiday too – for all of us, with Mum and Dad – once filming was over. Because I might not have spent enough time with them lately, but I want to give them the life they deserve. Because I do love all of them in my own way, even though I'm not always good at showing it.

But Alison doesn't want to hear any of this right now. So I let go of the bag, leave it in her hands and head towards the door. I reach up to open it with my hand, which is still encased in a papier mâché lobster claw. Alison sent them to my hotel and I realise now she made them by hand. I try and fail to grab hold of the handle a few times, eventually pulling the claws off and sticking them under my arm. I go for the door again – but I can feel that she's still there, watching. And so I turn back, tears welling up again. Spilling down the red face paint in streaks.

'I'm sorry, Ally,' I say. She doesn't respond. Just wipes a tear from her own eyes, paints a smile on her face and goes back into the party.

★ ★ ★

When I get back to the hotel, I find Avi waiting outside my room. I didn't even know he knew my room number; he must've asked at Reception or something. *Fuck*, I think. *Not this. Not now.* My heart thuds against my chest as I approach him, because after the confrontation with Alison just now, he's the last person I want to see. Because I haven't yet worked out how I feel about anything he's thrown at me today. Because, despite myself, the first thing I think when I look at his face is how it felt for him to push me up against the wall of my trailer earlier today. And how I want to do that again.

'Are you okay?' is his first question. Then, 'What are you wearing?' I look down. I almost forgot I was still in full costume. I must look an absolute mess – full red Morphsuit, face streaked with red face paint. He's looking me up and down like I might've actually lost my mind. But in this moment, I don't care.

'Now's not a good time,' I say to him, approaching the door with my room key.

'Please, Lara,' he says. 'Five minutes. I-I feel like I need to explain myself more. To apologise for some things. I didn't say enough earlier.'

And I want to say no – am about to. But I'm tired and worn down. Angry with myself, with

Alison. I don't have the strength to turn him down right now.

'Five minutes,' I say, opening the door and letting him through.

He sits down on a chair and I sit down on the bed opposite, dropping my bag and the lobster claws by the door on my way.

'I should have told you, Lara,' he says. 'I owed you that, owed you a lot more, honestly. And I've been thinking about it a lot, the things I should've said, from the beginning. That I haven't. So, if you'll hear me out, I'd like to say them now.'

I nod. Because honestly – despite the terrible timing – I want to hear them.

He looks down at his lap for a second, gathering his thoughts. 'I need you to know,' he says. 'When I left, back then – I was stupid. I shouldn't have told you it was a mistake that I kissed you. Should have dealt with it better, when you told me I shouldn't have put our friendship on the line. Because you were right – it was my mistake. But that was my own stuff.'

I blink. I wasn't expecting this. I find myself wondering what he means by 'stuff'. A few of the things he's said coming to mind: about his agent, about the pressure on him, about letting the opinions of others in. I begin to wonder if that might've had something to do with it. But before I can say anything, he continues.

'Your postcards kept me going, those first few months – they were a tether to home. They made me feel… normal. And when I came back for the Christmas party and saw you, all I felt was that I'd missed you so much. And you were the only person I wanted to talk to. I hadn't planned to kiss you and I freaked out. So I left and thought I could make it up to you the next day. By apologising. By telling you it was a mistake. Honestly, I thought you'd agree.'

What? I thought I was being so obvious, honestly – was sure that half the bar knew I had a crush on him, even when we were working together.

'Why would you think that?' I ask, incredibly confused.

'Because,' he says, letting out a breath. 'I don't know… you're… you, Lara. You're brilliant and beautiful, and so talented. But there were so many times back then that I had no idea what you were thinking. And when I kissed you, and you pulled away and looked a little freaked out, I thought I'd got it all wrong.'

I blink, searching my memories of that night. Avi and I in the corner of the pub. Everyone milling around us. The electricity I could feel, pulsing between us. And then him leaning in, our lips pressing together like it was fate. Like it had always been that way. But then, a flicker of fear. A moment of wondering what would happen, how it would all work with him being so far away. The immediate, clear decision that it didn't matter. That it was what I'd wanted for a long time and we'd figure it out. And I was about to say all this, once my brain got back into gear after one of the most head-spinning kisses of my life. But what I saw as a momentary flinch, a momentary wavering, seemed to him like a rejection. Then the confusion – him apologising, immediately. Saying he'd had too much to drink. Leaving the party. Then the text the next day. Telling me it was a mistake. All of it now suddenly thrust into a new light.

I was convinced it was regret. That he crossed the line, then decided he didn't want me.

But it turns out he thought it was the other way around.

'And then you were telling me – rightly – that I'd risked our friendship. That I should've thought more about what I was doing. And you're right. I should have. But I could see, in that moment, how much I'd hurt you. And I thought I'd ruined it.

That I'd fucked everything up and that I should just take myself out of the picture entirely.'

I look down at my hands in my lap, hurt twisting in my chest. Realising as I look down that they're still red – I'm still in the Morphsuit. *Oh, my God*, I think. This is so embarrassing. I can't believe I'm having this conversation, dressed like this, probably looking completely unhinged. But then I glance up and he's gazing at me from across the room. Eyes full of remorse and pain. And I've been trying to keep control. To not lose it. But I lost control earlier – or, rather, I let go – and the world is spinning just as it was before.

The person in front of me, right now, looks incredibly sorry for what he's done. Seems to genuinely want me around.

Maybe that's enough.

'I accept your apology,' I say quietly, flicking my eyes up to his. Tracing the flecks of yellow in their dark brown.

'Do you mean that?' he asks, still looking like he's not sure. But I realise in this moment that I do – I want a clean slate.

'I do,' I say, nodding. My heart thuds. And all I want to do, right now, is close the space between us and kiss him again. But something stops me.

He must sense the hesitation or see it on my face because he stands up and heads for the door. 'I think my five minutes is up.' he says, opening it. 'I'll leave you – give you some time to think.'

'Avi,' I say. 'Wait.' The only thing I know right now is that I can't let him leave.

He turns and looks at me.

Before I know what I'm doing, I'm standing too. Crossing the room. Inches between us. And he freezes in place, as if he's hardly daring to move. Then slowly, awkwardly, I place my hand on his hip, my fingers grazing the fabric of his jacket. I look up at him, my heart thudding at a thousand miles per hour.

And he looks down at me, his eyes burning with desire. With permission. And so I tilt my face upwards and press my lips against his. Like a prayer. And the final brick falls away from the wall I've built between us.

He leans in, deepening the kiss. His hand clenching around my waist, holding on for dear life as our bodies press together. My body flush against his as he pushes me against the door he just tried to leave through.

I kiss him again and he reaches behind me, looking at me for permission before gently pulling down the zip of my Morphsuit. Pulling it down my shoulders. And when I'm out of it, he looks at me for a second with an expression that makes my heart thump in my chest. His eyes simultaneously fiery and almost disbelieving that this is really happening – everything I'm feeling in this moment too. And then his lips crash against mine, hand running down my back. Fingertips grazing against my skin as he unlatches my bra.

He kisses my neck and a shiver runs across my skin. I undo the buttons of his shirt slowly and he lets it drop to the floor. I take a second to slide my hand down the curve of his arm. Taking in his form: strong, perfectly sculpted. Then, as if he can't wait any longer, he kisses me again and lifts me up, my legs hooking around him. Feeling how much he wants me.

He carries me to the bed and sets me gently on it. Brushing my hair away from my face in a gesture that is so tender and vulnerable I feel overwhelmed for a second.

'Are you sure you want to do this?' he asks, noticing my expression. I nod. 'One hundred per cent?' he says, a furrow appearing in his brow. And I pull him towards me. Tracing my hand down his back, feeling the dimples at the base of his spine. His back arching at the sensation.

And, in turn, his hands move down my body in a way that feels like small lightning flashes crackling across my skin. He pulls the elastic of my underwear gently down my legs, kissing the edge of my hipbone. Looks up at me, to which I nod infinitesimally, so turned on I can hardly breathe.

And then his tongue is there, moving across me, sending more small shocks through my body. Pleasure building to a peak until I can't stand it – I need more. I run my hand down his back to get his attention, pulling him towards me. Want burning through every cell of my body. Finding his length – running my hand along it over the fabric of his trousers so he lets out a shaky breath.

'Jesus, Lara,' he says. 'You have no idea how long I've wanted this.'

'I think there's an uneven distribution of clothing here,' I say, gesturing to his chinos, and he laughs. I pull them off, slowly. Throw them and his Calvin Klein underwear to one side. I take hold of his shaft and move my hand in a way that looks like it might be about to drive him completely insane.

'You are something else,' he says and pulls me down onto the bed, on top of him, kissing me like he can't get enough. Like air doesn't matter.

He grips my hip, his length sliding against me in a way that makes me feel insane. And then he's reaching for his trousers on the floor, opening his wallet. Pulling out a condom. And something flickers – some wondering how long that's been in there, who it might have been in there for. But then he's opening it with his teeth and I roll it over him, and he looks at me with such intensity it sets my skin on fire. And then I'm gently sliding over his length, my breath catching in my throat with how good it feels. And a second later he's inside me and I'm on fire.

His hand reaches over to grasp the headboard behind me as he thrusts into me, his hips rising to meet mine as I grind over him, the sensation increasing until I'm almost blinded by it. A vague thought that I can't believe this is actually happening floating through my mind as I meet his thrusts with my own, angling my hips so his length slides into me further.

'Oh, my God,' he says, sounding like he's about to lose control. The look on his face is addictive, sending waves of pleasure through my whole being.

He takes hold of me, his hands pressing into my skin, guiding me, slowly rising and falling, the sensation deliciously slow. And then he moves his thumb, circling me. Reaching up with his other hand to gently caress my breast, flicking his hand over my nipple and driving me slowly insane.

'Avi,' I whisper, as the sensation rises to its peak. And in this moment, something lifts, some weight I've been carrying for the last few weeks. I feel free to let go of all my anxieties, all the pain and worries I've been holding on to. They all seem to float away, disappearing into a feeling of bliss that comes over me in waves. And a few seconds later, he moves his hands back to my hips, his grip tightening with his final few thrusts, everything in me on fire as he surges into me and lets go too. A deep moan, his whole body shivering. And then he pulls me close, holding me to him for a few seconds. Our bodies pressed against one another. He kisses my shoulder, then rolls to one side, looking up at the ceiling.

'Lara Francis,' he says, breathless. 'I think you might be the death of me.'

15

The next day I wake up to my 5 a.m. alarm to find Avi gone. I panic momentarily, wondering where he is, but then see a piece of paper on his pillow – he's left a note. *Had to get to set. Didn't want to wake you. Talk later? A x*

I pick it up and fold it over, putting it on the nightstand. My heart is in my throat after what happened last night – because it was reckless and stupid. Outrageous behaviour.

But it was also incredible.

And I feel lighter today for it. Less worried that something's going to go horribly wrong. Because I've let go of control, completely. And I'm beginning to wonder if it was my attempts to hold on to it so tightly that were causing problems in the first place. It's a relief to finally allow myself to feel… however I'm going to feel around him.

Alison is still in the back of my mind. I text her, telling her I'm sorry, again. Asking if she'll call me back later, at a normal time. But I don't have much hope of a response at this point – I've never seen her this angry. Worry coils in my chest at the thought. But I have to give her space. She'll come to me when she's ready.

Besides, I'm still a little angry with her too.

Some of what she said might've had some truth in it. But it doesn't mean it was fair. And I've had enough of her making judgements about how I choose to live my life.

My parents are visiting set today, which I've been excited about for weeks but forgot about in the chaos of what happened yesterday. I call them to check on their progress, but get to set to find them already waiting outside the fencing where I said I'd meet them. Looking – bless them – just how I expect I look: like they got up at 4 a.m. and have barely had any coffee yet.

'There she is,' my dad says, pulling me into a tight hug. I return it with interest. Despite everything else, Alison's comment about me not visiting them lately hit home.

'I've missed you guys,' I say. 'I'm sorry I haven't seen you much lately.'

'We've missed you too, sweetheart,' my mum says. 'And don't you worry – you've been hard at work.'

I swallow, a flicker of guilt flaring up again about the things Alison said last night. But before I can say anything more, David rushes over.

'Lara, my darling,' he interjects. 'Are you ready to head over to WHAM?'

'Hello,' my mum says, and David snaps his head sideways like he hadn't realised there was anyone else here. Taking in my parents – in their hiking boots and Fair Isle knitwear, looking like they're about to climb a mountain in the Scottish Highlands.

'Hello,' he says, a little confused. 'Who are you?' His gaze flickers to my own outfit – which, minus the boots, is pretty close to what my parents are wearing – and I see a flash of recognition pass.

'We're Lara's parents,' my dad says. 'I'm Andrew and this is Louise.'

Before David can say anything my dad is shaking his hand vigorously, which seems to snap him out of his usual stressed-out state momentarily.

'Oh, how wonderful to meet you,' David says. 'I'm so sorry – I must've missed the memo that you were visiting set today.' I know someone's going to get it in the neck later for not informing him.

'If you'll come with me, we'll get you some passes.' He clicks his fingers and another runner appears, as if out of nowhere. He directs them to take me to WHAM.

I fight a smile at how nice he's being, even if my parents do still look a little scared. They don't understand that, for David, who probably has a million more important things to worry about than a set visit for my family, this is pretty much superhuman levels of kindness.

'I'll see you guys later,' I say, waving my parents away as they're marched – at an impressively slower pace than David usually keeps – through the crowds.

Today we're filming at Brompton Cemetery, a hauntingly beautiful graveyard in West London. Arched sandstone walkways rise up on either side of us, with stairs leading to crypts down beneath them. Up ahead, there's a round building, an active church that holds services for funerals. It's a little creepy, honestly – but in a good way. This is a particularly intense scene we'll be filming today: one where Amelia has had a grave exhumed to search for evidence. A chill runs down my back as I approach, the graves framed by the grey, moody sky. The chill mingles with the anticipation I'm already feeling about seeing Avi. For the first time since last night.

Tailed by David I head to my mark, the ruffles of my dress bouncing behind me. Once I'm there, I look around to see if I can spot my parents; I find them right by the director's chair, in deep conversation with Alessandro.

I smile despite myself. Of course they'd have found the most important person here and already charmed him. They've always been that way. Like Alison.

'Lara!' Alessandro waves me over.

I walk over towards them, holding up the folds of my dress so it doesn't drag along the floor. Avi isn't here yet – he had a scene to shoot in the main lot this morning, hence his early departure. So I'm assuming he's on his way, a fact that should be making Alessandro tense about timings. But he doesn't seem to be worried about that right now.

'I have just met your wonderful parents,' Alessandro says. 'Now why did you not bring them to set sooner?'

'Oh, you're too kind,' my dad says dismissively. 'But you really must try that wine I recommended – please allow me to send you a bottle.' This is one of my dad's pre-retirement hobbies – he's thinking of starting a wine business in his spare time to keep himself busy once he finishes work.

'Pah,' Alessandro says. 'I will not even think of it. But if you are ever in the Tuscan region, you must look me up, no? We will go to a wine tasting together.'

I almost laugh. I've spent the last few weeks keeping a respectful distance from Alessandro, hardly engaging in conversation with him at all beyond his directorial comments. But my dad has met him for five minutes and is already planning a trip to a vineyard with him. A surge of pride rises in my chest, curbed slightly by a twist of jealousy. The same confusion as always: that my parents are so good at this. And yet somehow, I never picked it up.

'And you, Lara,' Alessandro says, turning to me. 'My Amelia. Bambina mia. You will come to the wine tasting too, yes?'

I pause momentarily, surprised that he's included me too.

'Of course,' I say.

'She is a real marvel, your daughter,' Alessandro continues, turning to my dad, and my stomach twists. 'I am lucky to have her.' After everything I've been through to get – and keep – this role, I can't quite register that he's saying this. It's all I've wanted to hear for weeks now.

'We feel lucky too,' my dad says, giving me a kind look. *Oh, God*. I'm going to cry and ruin all my make-up.

'Thank you,' I say to Alessandro while reaching for my dad's hand and squeezing it.

'Now,' Alessandro says, rubbing his hands together before I can get too overwhelmed. 'Shall we make some movies?'

As I turn to head to my mark, I see him approaching across the grass. Eyes locked on mine. In a way that can't be too obvious because he's publicly still, technically, dating Sienna. Because it would be reckless to make eyes at each other right now. But still – there's a burning in them. A want that sets me on fire.

'Ah, our altra estella has arrived,' Alessandro says, interrupting my reverie. I look away, a blush creeping across my cheeks, and am suddenly incredibly grateful for the many layers of make-up I'm wearing.

'Avi,' I say, clearing my throat a little to hide how aware I am right now of his presence. 'These are my parents.'

'Oh,' he says, looking a little surprised; I forgot I didn't tell him they were visiting today. And a second later the surprise has gone and he is vigorously shaking their hands.

'It's wonderful to meet you,' he says, and he sounds like he actually means it. I swallow. 'I'm Avi.'

'We know,' my mum says, and I cringe internally. 'I've seen all your films.' Avi smiles.

'Well, then, I can only apologise,' he jokes. And everyone laughs. But there's a flicker of something behind it, something I saw when we were talking about his career at the Olivier Awards – some part of him that actually means it.

But before I can analyse it further, Alessandro calls us over to set.

I say goodbye to my parents at 4 p.m., after we've wrapped for the day. It was so lovely to see their faces light up as they watched us film, but it felt strange too, like two parts of my life crashing into each other. A reminder of how much I've given up, for this one. Alison's words flickering into my mind occasionally between takes when I'd catch their eye or they'd wave at me. They don't mention Alison at all except to tell me to send her their love if I see her before next weekend. *I'm not sure I will,*

I think. *It seems like she'd rather swallow live eels than see me at the moment.* But I promise anyway. This is between me and her. They don't need to know about it – they'd only worry.

The filming was intense, to say the least. Alessandro was happy with the chemistry, but asked for 'a little less sexual tension when we are standing over a dismembered corpse, please'. But I couldn't help it – every time our eyes met, I was thinking about last night. His body, pressed against mine. Kissing me like he couldn't ever get enough of me. But we didn't get much time to talk, either between takes or once we wrapped – Alessandro was too keen to get the scene nailed before the weather shifted, so we could make the most of the grey skies. Still, we got a take he was happy with, and Avi and I managed to arrange to meet at his hotel room later this evening while Alessandro was adjusting camera angles.

I head back to my trailer after my parents have left – coming back via the main lot to pick up the pages I left there yesterday so I could rehearse my lines ahead of tomorrow. But when I enter, I see something unexpected. A bunch of lilies on the table. A note attached to them. I walk over to the table, slightly apprehensive – worried this might be a prank gift from Roman, and that he'll have filled the vase with raw meat or something. But they're just normal flowers. In a vase. I frown, picking up the note.

My dearest Amelia, it reads. *With apologies for any psychological distress I may have caused you.*

It's signed with the name of Roman's character.

What the fuck? I think. I'm still half-expecting something horrible to crawl out of one of the flowers. But this seems... nice. Remorseful, even if it's still in the voice of his character. *Maybe I got through to him the other day.* And the thought lights something up inside me. I used my voice – stood up for myself. And it actually worked.

I head back to the hotel, feeling unexpectedly light. I knock on Avi's door, the nerves from before surging up again, and he opens it, wearing a half-buttoned shirt and some crumpled linen trousers. My heart rate increases and this time I enjoy the feeling – the thrill. Because there's nothing standing between us now.

I look around his room – it's the first time I've been in here. It's incredibly neat, like his trailer. In my room (and trailer) there are bits and pieces everywhere: a jacket here, a pile of books there.

He has books, but they're stacked neatly on the desk by the window. His script in a neat pile too – compared to mine, which is flung all over. There's so much… order. And that's sort of how he's always been – he had systems for sorting glasses behind the bar, which he followed religiously. But there's something about this level of it that feels strange. Like I've walked onto a film set rather than someone's room.

'So,' he says, as I sit down on the bed. 'Drink?'

I nod, and watch as he opens the minibar and pulls out a bottle of wine. Opening it, pouring two glasses.

He hands one to me, my fingers brushing over his as he does, and sits down at a respectable distance from me. Too respectable, if you ask me. But he looks serious, so I don't want to push anything. Want to let him speak.

'Last night was…' He pauses, shaking his head as if he can't find the words.

I'm pretty sure by his expression that it's a positive speechlessness rather than a 'what the fuck did we just do' speechlessness. Relief passes through me at the sound of it.

'I agree,' I say.

He takes a long sip of his wine.

'But I do think we need to get some things straight,' he says. 'Make sure we do this right.' And he sounds so serious. And I don't need him to be serious right now. I just need to know what he's already told me, basically: that he doesn't regret it. That he's not about to up and leave.

'Avi—'

'Obviously, there's the stuff with Sienna…' he says over me and I open my mouth, ready to interrupt him. But he keeps talking before I can. 'And we still have a few days of filming left. So we should probably have a plan for that. And…'

He looks more flustered than I've ever seen him. I reach over, placing my hand over his.

'Hey,' I say. 'Seriously, you sound so worried. You really don't need to be.'

'I…' he starts. 'I really like you, Lara. I don't want to let you down. I want you to know I'm serious this time. That I'm not going to—'

'It's okay,' I say, my heart clenching. Because he looks so vulnerable right now, so remorseful. And I don't need him to feel this way, like he still has something to make up to me. Because when I kissed him yesterday, it felt like a decision. To leave the past in the past. To take a step forward into the present. Just a step, though. I don't need any big leaps just yet. 'Really. I know this is complicated and there's stuff to work out, but I don't need a plan right now. I don't need anything, really. I think we should just take it a day at a time, keep going until the end of filming. And then, when the film is over, we can figure stuff out. Okay?'

He exhales. 'Okay,' he says. But he still doesn't look convinced.

'Besides,' I say. 'I like the idea of this being just between us for a while.'

He looks up, catching my eye. Something moving in his expression. Like there's some hope there. 'And what, exactly,' he says, putting his wine down, 'is "this", to you?'

I don't answer. Just take a sip of my wine. Then shift over on the bed, so I'm closer to him. He traces his hand gently along my jaw. Taking the glass from my hand, placing it on the table next to us. Looking at me like he's never wanted anything more in his life. And then his hand clenches, lifting my chin up. Tilting it towards him. And he leans down and kisses me. Gently sliding his hand down my thigh. And then I climb onto his lap, straddling him.

★ ★ ★

The next few days, Avi visits my hotel room every night. Sometimes we fall into each other, sometimes we just stay up talking. Watching old films – like we used to, on the projector in the pub theatre. Reminiscing about old times. And there's an occasional pinch in my chest when we do, a lingering hurt from when he left. But more and more it starts to dull. Replaced by something else: hope. Hope that once this film is over we might be able to continue whatever's happening between us. Hope that, this time, he won't leave – or, at least, if he has to go back to LA, we'll stay in contact. Figure it out.

But I don't turn that hope into anything approaching a conversation yet. For now, I want to stay in the present.

In the privacy of his hotel room, this fragile, early thing between us feels pure, like no one is going to stick their nose into it. Like it belongs to us.

And it spills on to set too; I've completely let go of any inhibitions around Avi, so our scenes are electric. Easy and fiery. Alessandro is happier than ever, saying that whatever drug we're taking, we should keep going with because the footage is brilliant. I catch Avi's eye at that statement and have to dig my nails into my palm to avoid imagining the 'drug', which involves us spending a lot of time pressed up against each other in his hotel room. Even, sometimes, in his trailer when we're feeling particularly bold. But that only happens once or twice.

We've shot most of the closing scenes of the film now, including one where Amelia and Jackson chase Roman's character down to his secret bunker in the sewers of London. It's a scene I was feeling nervous about filming, because of my altercation with Roman the other day. But the energy between us is different since the flowers. Respectful, even. The scene goes really well. It honestly feels like everything I've worked for has come together. I'm on a professional and personal high, and don't imagine coming down from it anytime soon.

The night before our last day of filming, Avi and I order room service and watch *Casablanca*, one of my favourites. We're in bed, his arm lazily draped around me. As if it's the most natural thing in the world.

'There's something I need to discuss with you, ahead of tomorrow,' he says. I look up at him and he looks a little nervous. I frown, wondering if now's the time to have this conversation about us going forwards. Because it feels like our time might be up, as far as sneaking around in this bubble goes. And I'm not ready for the talk. For now, we still have tonight. And tomorrow. And everything else will come after.

'What is it?' I ask.

'I heard from Sienna earlier. She's in town this week for a shoot and she asked if she could come to set tomorrow.'

Oh, I think. That wasn't what I expected.

'So it'll be a little weird,' he says. 'If I say yes, she and I will have to act as usual, I guess. There are a few photo opportunities, too, that our PR team have been discussing. It'll seem odd if she's in London and we're not seen in public together a few times.'

This is so strange, I can't really wrap my head around it.

'It's fine,' I say, a little too quickly.

'Lara,' he says. 'Are you sure?'

'I think so,' I say, the cogs turning in my mind as we speak. 'I mean, I was the one that said we didn't need a plan. That we'd figure things out once shooting was over. So I think it's only fair that you proceed like before until we figure that all out.'

'Okay,' he says. 'I'll tell her.' He reaches for his phone and texts her.

'But I promise,' he adds, looking up. 'We will figure something out. Even if you want to move slowly with this, we can look at a timeline. Ways to keep it between us. It won't be easy, probably. But we can work it out as we go.'

I nod, feeling suddenly overwhelmed by the prospect of more people knowing about us than just us. Like imagining our relationship – if we can even call it that – is suddenly on a world stage. Everyone looking at us. At me. Scrutinising me, maybe. Comparing me to her. *How do people sustain things like this in the public eye?* I think, my panic lessening a little as he meets my gaze. His eyes softening. My heart slowing in my chest.

'I was thinking…' he says, putting his phone down, his tone shifting. 'Maybe I'll tell my agent I'd like to stay in London after this. Spend some time with you. Maybe…' He hesitates. 'Maybe do some theatre.'

And even despite my anxieties about what might happen, despite still not knowing what exactly the future will look like, despite still having some questions – questions I'm not going to ask right now, because I want this one last perfect night — something lights up inside me. At the thought of him going back to theatre. At the thought of a future between us.

'That's great, Avi,' I say, a rush of emotion coming through.

16

The following morning, I wake up and Avi's side of the bed is empty. No note this time. The sheets crumpled where he was lying last night, after we stayed up probably way too late making the most of our last few hours together in this hotel room. Though our call time is a little later today – 8 a.m. – so the late night doesn't matter so much. I'll be coming back after filming to pack everything up, then I'll be moving in with my parents for a while until I can sort out my living situation.

I have a call scheduled with Nat later this week too, to discuss future projects. Apparently she's already had some interest, but has been keeping them at bay until I'm done filming. One more day. And that should be at the forefront of my mind right now. The shoot, and the fact that everything we've been working towards for the last few weeks is about to culminate in one final scene. But I'm not focused on that. I'm worried about where my scene partner might be.

I sit up, a little confused and slightly concerned. *Maybe he just went to get breakfast*, I think. But it's weird – the last few days, he's stayed until I've woken up. Said goodbye before heading to his room, to take his separate car to go to set. I look around the room. His clothes are gone, any trace that he was here last night erased.

I roll up the sleeves of the shirt I'm wearing – his shirt, which I fell asleep in. An Armani shirt that probably costs more than my entire wardrobe. I reach for my phone on the bedside table, in case he's texted me. And when I look at it, I find myself blinking hard. Trying to make sense of what I'm seeing.

Avi and I had our phones on 'do not disturb' last night. We wanted to close off from the outside world for our last night before the film ended. To spend some uninterrupted time together. And usually I have very few notifications anyway. So I assumed it would be fine to take a night off. Alison and I still aren't talking, and for the sake of my sanity and her space I've decided to leave that resolution until the end of filming. So that leaves my parents, and Hannah and Spencer, who are used to my sporadic reply times over the last few weeks. At most, I thought I would have a couple of texts. But looking at it now, I have three missed calls from my parents. A flurry of texts from Hannah and Spencer, saying they've seen the news, asking if I'm okay. *What the fuck?* I think, as I scroll through them. A sudden anxiety hitting me that something might have gone wrong with the film.

I open Google and type out the film's name, and find an article – several, actually. Which aren't about the film at all. They're about me. And Avi. *Oh, my God,* I think, clicking into the first one. Staring at the photo at the top of the page.

A small, grainy photo of Avi and I kissing on-set. One taken through the window from outside my trailer. Another of me leaving my hotel room the other day, wearing his shirt – I only went out to get coffee and a part of me thought it was stupid at the time. But the hotel has been blocked from paparazzi for weeks. I've not seen a single photographer. So I thought that I'd be okay – that even if someone happened to take a picture of me, I could claim the shirt belonged to someone else. I flick my eyes upwards, horror curdling in my stomach, to see a headline screaming in my face, all caps: ROMANCE WITH SIENNA ON THE ROCKS? AVI KUMAR AND CO-STAR CAUGHT KISSING ON-SET BEYOND THEIR CUE.

'Oh, fuck,' I say, my breath catching in my throat. I feel like I can't breathe.

I scroll through the comments:
What the fuck is he doing with her?
Massive downgrade imo
Man didn't know what he had – he fumbled badly
Who even is she?!?!?!

And then more comments, worsening as I scroll. Calling me a homewrecker. A whore. I open my Instagram messages to find a barrage of death threats, messages saying I'm evil, that I've ruined the best relationship in Hollywood. That I'm a fame-grabbing slut with no talent.

This is bad, I think, a stone sinking in my stomach. *This is really bad*. And then the next thought I have is: Roman. A crashing realisation that this must've been him. I kick myself for how stupid I've been – to take his silence, those flowers, as evidence that everything was okay. That I'd finally won. Because of course I underestimated him. I threatened him with press exposure and he must have sent the flowers to put me at ease so he could get me back without me suspecting him.

'Oh, my God.' I take a deep breathe, the panic hitting me like a train now. 'What have I done?' Because I haven't ever dealt with anything like this before, this feels irreparably bad. Like my career might end before it's even properly begun. Like I might be for ever known as someone who was just trying to use Avi's fame to boost my own profile. And it will be awful for Avi too – and Sienna. My heart clenches as I remember all the reasons they were in a fake relationship to start with, how hard everything has been for both of them. Right now, wherever she is, she might not even be able to leave her hotel room. I head over to the window, which overlooks the street below. My throat constricts – it's full of photographers. And I'm high enough up that they can't see me right now. Won't be able to tell that it's me. But there's no way I'll be able to leave the hotel by the front entrance today.

Fuck, I think. *Fuck, fuck, fuck.* Regret seeping through me – not for anything that's happened with Avi. But for not thinking through the potential consequences. For being stupid enough to feel safe, when we clearly weren't.

I click out of the article and open my contacts, scrolling down to Avi's number. Calling him. It rings through. And then I look for Alison's number. Hovering over it. Almost clicking on it. But in the next second, I decide against it. I know she's been googling me pretty much daily because she's told me and if she didn't see it, one of her friends would have sent it to her. Something tightens in my chest. *She must be angrier than I thought*, I think. I consider calling Nat, but it's early – I'll try her from the car.

My eyes flick up to the time and I see that I'll be late if I don't hurry. So I get up and get dressed quickly. At the very least I need to discuss this with Avi first. Before I freak out completely. Then, maybe, we can work out a plan. Besides, it's the last day of filming and I need to get to set. Whatever might be waiting for me there.

My throat dries up as I go to leave my room, worry landing in my stomach about what Alessandro will think of all this. The whispers on-set today. Everyone will know about this. Everyone will have seen it.

But I have no choice.

And so I exhale, set my nerves and walk through the door.

★ ★ ★

I get into the car and George's 'How's it going today, Miss Francis?' is even more comforting than usual, despite the fact that there's no way in hell I can answer that question honestly.

'Pretty rough, I'm afraid,' I say, giving him a half-truth.

'Sorry to hear that, love,' he says. 'Still, though – last day. You must be proud of the work you've done.'

I try to summon anything but panic, and can't. So I just nod. Scrolling through my phone contacts, checking the time. Waiting until it's an appropriate hour to ring Nat. But I don't have to – her name pops up on my screen.

'Hi, Nat—'

'Lara,' she says, cutting me off, her tone gentle but belying a light panic. 'Would you mind telling me what the fuck is going on?'

'I'm so sorry—'

'I've just had Alessandro on the phone,' she says, cutting me off again. 'He is pissed, to say the least. And I realise you told me about this history you had with Avi, but I'm not sure I expected that anything like this would happen. You're a professional, Lara. This is your first big project with a major director. I don't think I need to tell you how potentially catastrophic this is.'

I close my eyes, blinking back tears. 'I know,' I say. 'I fucked up. I'm sorry.'

'Don't apologise to me,' she says. 'Apologise to Alessandro. And look – you're my client and I have your back. Always. So we'll figure this out. But in the meantime, I need you to get to set and do the best job of your life today. Please.'

I nod, my hand shaking a little as I hang up the phone. For Nat to sound angry with me, I need to have really, truly, catastrophically fucked up. And – it seems – I have.

'Darling!' David says when I get out of the car. We're filming on the river in Greenwich today. It's cold and the air whips across my face. I can hear the distant sound of ships in the background. 'Happy last day. How are you feeling?'

And for a second I wonder whether maybe he hasn't seen it. But then I catch the way he's looking at me and my stomach drops. He's nervous, clearly. *Oh, God*, I think. He escorts me to my trailer and I try to pretend I don't see people looking at me as I walk past. Try to ignore the pit that's forming in my stomach – at everything Nat said on the phone just now. The prospect of seeing Alessandro. The fact that Avi hasn't called me back yet. Hasn't even texted me. But I have to keep it together. Alessandro is probably going to be apoplectic. The least I can do is show up to set on time.

Sarah isn't in WHAM today, so I have my make-up done by someone else, which is something of a relief because I somehow feel like I'd be disappointing her. And I can't explain, yet, that it wasn't cheating, because that'd be putting Avi and Sienna at even more risk than they already are. So I absorb the glances in the mirror from the girl doing my hair. The sideways looks from runners as they pass. I feel like I'm in hell, being judged for a crime I didn't commit. And to add to my anxiety, there's still no sign of Avi.

I was hoping I'd have time to go via his trailer, but I'm pretty much rushed straight to set from Hair and Make-up. When I arrive, neither Avi nor Alessandro are there yet, so I stop at the food table while David is on the phone and try to choke down some toast, to settle my nerves. But instead I find Roman. Spearing some melon with a fork.

'Hello, Amelia,' he says, his voice impassive.

'Don't even try it, Roman,' I say. 'I don't want to fucking talk to you right now.'

'What do you mean?' he says, fake-clutching his chest.

I lean in, incredulous that even now – even after what he's done – he still thinks this is all a game. 'I know it was you,' I say.

He frowns. 'I don't know what you're talking about.'

I pull out my phone and open my browser. Turning the screen towards him. He looks at it and blinks a few times, surprise and shock passing across his face – coming out of character for the first time since we met.

'Shit,' he says. 'Honestly, that wasn't me.' And his facial expression seems so genuine, so earnest that something falters in me for a second. But there's no way it was anyone else. And this man can slip in and out of character so easily – he's made it very clear to me that I can't trust him.

'Right,' I say. 'Because you've given me so many reasons to trust you. Why would I ever believe you? And besides, who else would it have been?'

'Seriously, Lara,' he says and I baulk – because that's the first time he has ever called me by my name. Because I can see genuine concern on his face and it's throwing me for a loop. 'I didn't do this.'

But in this moment, I have bigger things to worry about. Like Avi, who has just shown up, flanked by Sienna. Her blonde hair perfectly coiffed. *What is she doing here?* I think. Surely it will only make things worse – for her as well as Avi and me. And I can already see it: the crew members looking from me to her with great interest, as if waiting to see what's about to unfold. But there's no time to even process this because then Alessandro arrives too. An expression on his face that sends a boulder into my stomach.

Shit.

I swallow the lump in my throat and cross the set. Trying, for the moment, to ignore the fact that I feel like I'm living in a parallel universe, and to do as Nat suggested and offer a grovelling apology to Alessandro for what happened. But he is in deep discussion with the first AD. And, after a few minutes, Avi and Sienna separate and he makes his way to his mark. She moves off to one side, positioning herself among the runners. Sitting in a chair and opening a magazine as if none of this is of any concern to her.

'Hi,' he replies. His tone off – cold, almost.

'Where were you this morning?' I ask. 'And what's Sienna doing here?' Trying not to sound too needy, too hurt. But the sudden shift in his demeanour — and the fact that he arrived here with Sienna — is really freaking me out.

'Damage control,' he says. Shifting on his feet a little. Not giving me any more information than that.

'Okay,' I say, the worry starting to rise. 'Is everything okay?' A stupid question — because I know it isn't. But I'm not just talking about the article. He shakes his head, slowly, and my heart drops.

'I have a plan, though. Let's just get through filming first, okay?'

I nod, my heart hammering. And I'm about to say that I want to know more. Because he's more important to me, in this moment, than anything else. But then Alessandro clicks his fingers and shouts at us to get on our marks, and my voice dies in my throat. I look over at him and see the thunder in his expression — and realise that right now I have to find that commitment. Everything I've been relying on, up until now, which feels incredibly faint in this moment. Because Amelia needs me still. Because what Nat said was right. My responsibility is to Alessandro and this film, even if my heart is somewhere else. Even if hurt and worry might be spilling through every part of me right now. We still have work to do. I have to draw on her strength – have to find a way to get through the next few hours – to do justice to the reason why I'm here, even if Alessandro is going to hate me either way. Until we can talk.

I look up and meet Avi's eye. He nods, his expression placid, then moves to his mark. I follow suit.

'Right!' Alessandro shouts. 'Let us rehearse.'

I breathe in, and out, trying desperately to get back into my body. Waiting for his cue – flinching as it comes.

It's time.

A few run-throughs later, we're ready to shoot. I'm still feeling shaky on my feet between takes, and it's honestly incredibly hard not to focus on the fact that Sienna is sitting only a few metres away and there are clearly runners whispering about us. But by some miracle, some of Amelia's presence is filtering into me when the cameras are on – I'm finding her. Relying on her more than I ever have. Her steadiness. Her strength, to carry me through. Even as I feel like I might be about to completely fall apart.

We've managed to go in chronological order just as Alessandro wanted to, so this is the final scene of the film. And it's a fitting finale, a farewell between Amelia and Jackson as he travels back to America.

'So,' Avi says, once the cameras are rolling. 'I suppose this is goodbye, Amelia Blackthorn.'

'I suppose it is,' I say, finding myself all of a sudden holding back tears.

Because in this moment – even though Avi and I haven't spoken yet, even though it might be irrational – I can already feel him pulling away. I can feel the meaning underneath that goodbye. It's not just Jackson saying it.

And I have a horrible feeling that everything is about to go wrong, all over again.

17

Somehow we pull through. Manage to get a shot Alessandro is happy with. And then the room explodes: everyone celebrating that Avi and I have wrapped. Joy that I should be sharing in too, as the culmination of everything we've worked for. The film that was my dream, that I've been feeling so proud of for the last few weeks. A dream which, right now, feels like it's turning into a nightmare. I look around. Beyond the hugs and high-fives of the crew is Alessandro's face, serious and stoic.

I look around for Avi and spot him across the room, talking to Sienna. Alessandro taps me on my shoulder.

'Bambina,' he says, his tone not betraying any of his feelings. 'I have spoken to Avi. I would like to speak to you too. If you please, could you come to my trailer before you leave set today.'

★ ★ ★

Alessandro's trailer is sparsely decorated and notably different to my trailer. I try to settle my nerves by looking around. My eyes focusing on each aspect of the room as I enter. Two chairs and a coffee table set up by the door, for entertaining – a tea set meticulously arranged on it. Then, to the left, what looks like a camping chair, and a lamp next to it. A side table, scattered with sections of script, his notes scribbled over them in red pen. A board that looks like that of a police detective or conspiracy theorist, different coloured threads winding around pins. My Polaroid from casting up there, next to Avi's. Notes about each of our characters. It's the trailer of a genius – which he is.

But then my distraction tactic ends, because he clears his throat. Gestures to a chair, which I sit down in. My stomach churning with worry about what he might be about to say. He sits down opposite me, pouring us tea. Takes a sip, as if composing himself.

'I want to thank you for your work these last few weeks, Lara,' he says. And I let out a breath of relief – wondering if, maybe, this is going to be better than I thought. 'But I am also very angry and very disappointed.' My stomach drops.

'I'm sorry...' I try to think of a way to apologise. To explain myself in a way that won't implicate

Avi or Sienna. But I can't think of anything and he holds his hand up before I can get any more words out.

'I do not want to hear the excuses,' he says. 'Avi has already given me enough. And I have to say I would have appreciated a visit from you this morning too. But that is by the by now. What I want to say to you is this: when you spoke to me about wanting to be Amelia – because you loved her, because you wanted to do her justice – I thought, this is someone I can rely on. A professional. But this…' He pauses, taking another sip. 'This, I do not know if I can forgive. You have caused a press scandal because of your own personal feelings. Which might be the downfall of this film. And for that, you have let me down. You have let yourself down. And bambina, I am afraid you have let Amelia down.'

Oh, God. My chest tightens, the panic gripping me now. And I feel sudden huge regret for how stupid I've been, how neglectful not to go straight to Alessandro's trailer this morning and apologise for what happened, and for what it might do to his film before it even wrapped. This is my worst fear come to life – that everything in this film would be messed up. Would fall apart. Because of me.

'I hope you can learn from this, Lara,' he says. 'But I am afraid that because of this I am not sure if we will work together again. I want professional values on my set. Respect for the project. For what we are doing here. And I am afraid you and Avi have shown me the opposite.'

Fuck, I think, his words hitting me like a ton of bricks. *What have I done?*

And I scramble, to try to find something to say. Something that will make this okay. But he simply puts his tea down, the cup clattering into the saucer, and gestures towards the door.

'I would like you to leave,' he says.

The same assistant from this morning takes my make-up off, asking me about my plans now, what I think I'll do next. I give her pretty much one-word answers. Because I don't know now. Because I got everything I ever wanted and I fucked it all up. And I have no room for any thoughts or feelings beyond shame and anger at myself.

By the time I make it back to my hotel, I'm completely defeated. I go straight to Avi's room, checking the corridor first to make sure there's no one there. I find him waiting for me. Sitting on the bed wearing an expression that matches how I'm feeling on the inside. And he starts speaking before I can.

'I'm so sorry, Lara,' he says. And there's such genuine remorse, such concern in his expression, that the nerves from this morning flash up again. It feels like he isn't just apologising for what happened – which isn't his fault anyway. But for what he might be about to say.

'It's not your fault,' I say. But his expression doesn't change. 'We both made those choices. We both thought it would be fine.'

But he shakes his head slowly. 'I should've known better,' he says. And despite myself, despite the fact that I know we fucked up, that I know we're facing the consequences – because we were reckless and stupid, and didn't think them through – this lands like a familiar arrow to my chest. *Last night was a mistake.*

'Look,' he says, breathing out. I lean forwards, ready to hear what he's saying. Hoping it'll lift some of the weight off my shoulders. 'Sienna and I had a meeting with our publicists this morning. I'm sorry I couldn't explain more earlier, but she came to set with me today as planned because we all agreed that the best thing to do is to proceed as usual. To keep up our appearance of being a united front. And for me to release a statement saying that what happened between you and I was a gross error of judgement – a one-off that won't happen again.'

I blink for a second, processing his words. Trying to figure out how I might've misheard them in the daze I'm in. Because there's no way he said what I think he just said.

He looks at me, as if waiting for me to agree. One second passes, then the next. The reality hitting me like a truck. That he's serious. That this isn't all some horrible elaborate joke.

'What the fuck?' I say instead.

'Lara,' he says slowly. 'You don't understand how this stuff works. This is the best plan, for all of us.' And I bristle as he says it, some hurt coming up from before now too. Because I thought I'd forgiven him, but there's one thing that's still unaddressed. A thorn in my heart that I feel pressing in further now. He's deciding what's best for me again. Like he did before when he thought my life would be better without him in it, so just disappeared entirely. Giving me no choice.

'If I say this now, then maybe in a few months Sienna and I can release an official statement saying we've broken up, and—'

'Then what?' I ask, anger rippling through me and mingling with the hurt.

'Then we can…' He gestures between us, his words trailing off. 'Figure something out. I promise, Lara. We'll do it properly this time. Make sure we go through all the channels. We just need to give the public enough time to forget about it, so we don't end up having a scandal following us around.'

And I know that it was me who didn't want a plan, who thought it would be okay just to continue as before, not to put any pressure on this fragile thing we were building that now feels like it's been blown to pieces. Me who pushed Roman too far, who might honestly be to blame for all of this. But in this moment, I can't believe that it really seems that simple to him. That I'll just go with it.

'Look,' he says, taking in my expression, which must show the horror I'm feeling. 'This stuff isn't real. But it has a tangible impact on our careers, Lara. Yours especially, being so new to the scene.' Another flash of anger, weighed down by a crushing disappointment too. Because I know – I've read the comments, I just spoke to Alessandro. The impact on my fledgling career is at the forefront of my mind. I just didn't imagine I'd end up being rejected and discarded so publicly by him too.

'Please don't patronise me by talking about my career,' I say quietly.

'You don't understand, Lara,' he says, his voice breaking a little. And I look up, and see an expression on his face that makes my heart stop momentarily. 'I am under so much pressure, all the time. If I don't do this – if I don't keep this balance – then I could lose everything.'

And I can see it: the fear, written all over his face right now. Fear that his career is going to crumble over this. And something shifts in me, breaking through my anger and hurt. What he said to me in the park, about how important it is to him to inspire British-Indian kids like him, to show them they have a place in the industry. To be a role model. And I find myself in his shoes, thinking about the pressure he's under. About all the reasons why he can't lose everything he's worked so hard for – reasons that aren't just about him. And it surges up now, replacing everything else. Because I can see that he's scared and as much as I want to take that fear away, I know that I can't. This is bigger than me. And the realisation hits me, with a crushing sadness: I have to agree to this. But I can't watch him leave a second time. Even if this time he says it's only temporary.

'This is really what you want?' I ask. He nods.

'I don't see another way,' he says.

'Okay,' I say, trying to keep my tone level. Something clicking into place.

'Okay,' he says, his posture relaxing a little. 'Great. So I'll go ahead with the statement and I'll probably have to go back to LA for a bit. But in a month or two we'll release another statement saying we've broken up, then maybe I can come to London and…' He trails off as he catches my expression. I shake my head, slowly.

'No,' I say, my voice cracking.

'What?' he asks, and I can hear the concern in his tone now.

'You and I both know two months is too soon to start a relationship after a statement like that,' I say, sadness coursing through me. Because I might not be a PR expert, but the public's memory is longer than he thinks. I know that if we start dating in a few months people will dredge up these articles, the statement Avi made. It will follow us around, just as it has now – but probably worse than before because we'll both look like liars.

'And I understand this isn't real for you,' I say, struggling to keep my composure. Sadness spilling through every part of me. 'But it's real for me.

And I can't do this, Avi. I want you to release the statement – because I trust you, if you think it's the right thing to do. I want to protect your career too. But I can't keep feeling like I'm a mistake. And if you release this statement, that's all I'll ever be. The press will talk about your gross error of judgement every time we're photographed together. And I know that I'm to blame for this too – that we should've been more careful. That I can't ask you to blow everything up for me, especially when Sienna is involved too. But I can't face that. It hurts too much. I want you to do this, if it's really what you want, because I care – about you, and our careers. But as far as our relationship goes, I'm done.'

'Lara…' he says, his voice thick.

'I'm sorry, Avi,' I say, getting up. Making my way to the door. 'I can't wait for you any more.'

18

I call Alison a few times in the next few days. But she doesn't answer. Hasn't replied to any of the texts I've sent her in the past two weeks. But at least I'm not losing my mind alone in a big hotel any more. After shooting wrapped, I moved straight back in with my parents. So I'm losing my mind in my childhood bedroom instead. And it's been pretty good, as far as hideouts go. I needed somewhere the paparazzi – who hounded the hotel when I arrived to pick up my things – wouldn't find me. Hertfordshire is probably quite low on their list of locations to search for disgraced film stars, if I can even call myself a film star at this point. Especially where my parents live, in the middle of a comfortingly anonymous suburb.

And so, in the absence of Alison in our childhood home, I do my best to stay busy. To keep any thoughts of Avi out of my mind. I keep reading the scripts Nat's sending through to me – at least a few people still seem interested in working with me in the wake of the press storm. She also calls me most days, to check in. To see if I've been through the list of publicists she sent me. To prepare for the press tour, she says. It might be a good idea. But I feel stagnant. Stuck in my hurt. In my disappointment in myself. I stay up late instead, reviewing script after script. Focusing on the one thing I can control, the one thing I can hold on to. Ignoring the emptiness I'm feeling. And I try to stay offline, as much as possible. I've basically deleted every social media account I own.

Spencer and Hannah text me pretty much daily to see how I'm doing; I reply to every few, not wanting to give away too much information. I can't – because of Sienna, because of the statement that's going to be released imminently. But also because I'm ashamed and I don't really want to talk to anyone about it. Except, maybe, Alison. But she isn't returning my calls.

This is why you shouldn't have listened to her, I think, in a dark moment. *Your world was fine before. Now everything is messed up, because you stepped outside of it.* But even then I push the thought away – I know it's not her fault. I'm just sad, and let down, and looking for someone to blame for my own stupid behaviour. I know screwing my co-star wasn't what she meant by expanding my horizons. I just wish she'd talk to me; for once, I want her critical eye. I want her to tell me I'm an idiot. I want her to tell me what to do with my life. But I'm worried I've upset her so badly that something might be irreparably damaged between us now.

On the third or fourth day of my self-imposed isolation, I break. Open my laptop, scroll through the articles. Looking for the statement that Avi said he was going to put out. But there's nothing – just a few more gossip column profiles entitled *Who even is Lara Francis anyway?* and *Meet the woman who might've destroyed Hollywood's most beloved couple*. One or two articles with paparazzi photos of Sienna and Avi out in London, hands lightly entwined. Pictures that – even though I know they don't mean anything – make me feel sick. The headlines: *Trouble in paradise? Avi and Sienna spotted in London looking serious*. Once I've scrolled through enough to make me feel incredibly unwell, reading comment after comment about how relieved people are that they're still together, about how ugly and B-list I am, I close my laptop. Put down the script I'm reading. Pick up the copy of *A Murder in London*

Spencer and Hannah gave me, with the note inside it. The list of life goals. My heart twists when I look at it. The words I scrawled down – filled with hope, for a career I've now potentially destroyed. Words that don't seem to mean anything any more.

You have let Amelia down – Alessandro's words ring through my mind.

'I'm sorry,' I whisper, and I throw the book on the bed and walk through the door.

I leave my parents' house in sunglasses and a hat. Though I do feel a bit silly taking such measures, it makes me feel a little safer on the Tube. More anonymous. Less like the homewrecking whore who stole Avi from Sienna, and more like an ordinary commuter. And on the journey I start to feel a little better – because I might've screwed everything else up, but this, at least, is something I can fix… I hope. I've let Amelia down, and myself. But maybe this will help. Maybe this will be a step in the right direction. I text her flatmates again to make sure that they're still okay with my plan – that they'll be there to let me in.

I stop at a supermarket en route, picking up a cake, some candles, a few birthday hats and some confetti.

And when she gets home from work, I'm waiting.

The candles lit. A bright red birthday hat on my head.

But she throws her bag down on the sofa and sits down on it. As if I'm not there.

'Ally?' I say, my tone careful. I hoped she'd be surprised – happy, even.

'I don't want to see you, Lara,' she says. 'How clear can two weeks of not replying to your texts be?'

'I'm sorry…' I say, but she just looks at me sharply.

'Is this about me, or is this about the fact that your life is falling apart around you right now and you need someone to talk to about it?'

Something pinches in my chest. Because she's not wrong.

'It's not about that…' She looks at me for a long second. I sit down next to her.

'Okay,' I say. 'Okay – I let you down, Ally. And I'm really sorry for it. And I hoped you might see how sorry I was, with the cake—'

'I don't need a fucking cake, Lara,' she says. And then she breaks down. Crying, her make-up running down her face. 'I need my sister.'

When I put my arm around her, she leans into my shoulder. Sobbing. Something I haven't ever seen. Because she's usually so bright. So completely fine, all the time.

'What's wrong?' I ask. She shrugs.

'Everything.' And then she tells me – that she thinks she's about to be fired. That her new boss basically hates her and undermines her work every chance she gets. That her friends have created a group chat without her in it to plan a holiday that she's not invited to. That the last person she dated and really liked – the French guy she told me about – moved back to France without telling her. That she feels like she's treading water the whole time and nothing really clicks into place for her. That she's never felt as passionate in her life about anything as I do about acting. That she feels like she's drifting, purposeless – life just happening to her day by day. And she sometimes can't find any meaning in it any more.

And when she's done, I sit there completely gobsmacked.

'So you see,' she says. 'Everything does not come easy to me. The opposite, in fact.'

'Ally, I'm so sorry—'

'You're not the only one who struggled when Dad lost his job,' she says. 'I did too. I might not have been there for some of those conversations, but

I heard them. I knew how bad it was. And I hated moving schools, too – every time I made a group of new friends I had to say goodbye to them within a year. I could never let anyone too close because I knew I'd be leaving soon. And I knew how much it would hurt to say goodbye if I did. So I had lots of friends, but they were all surface-level friendships. And when I came home and felt the tension and stress, I smiled wider. Told Mum and Dad about everything that was going well at school – because that was what they needed to hear. Because they needed me to be the golden child, because you were in your room the whole time. Buried in a book or a script. Or at play rehearsals. And so I played that role. And I've been playing it my whole fucking life – and I'm just so incredibly tired.'

And I can't help it – some tears start to escape. 'I had no idea,' I say.

'I know you didn't,' she says. 'Because you were in Lara-land. But the day of my birthday, I'd had the worst day at work. And Pierre had just texted me back and told me that he didn't want to see me any more. That he'd never been interested in me. And about fifteen people had cancelled last minute. And I just thought—' She cuts herself off to catch her breath, another tear falling.

'I just thought that maybe my sister would show up for me. That I'd see you and I might feel okay. But you were so late, Lara. And it hurt so much, to hear that I'd come second to your work again. I'm sorry,' she says, wiping away the tears. 'I think I've been holding on to this for a long time and I've overreacted. And I've definitely been judgemental towards you, which wasn't fair. But I just thought that maybe if I could get you out of your shell a bit…' She looks at me, her eyes wide and innocent. 'Then I might get my sister back.'

And I pull her towards me, holding her while she cries herself out. Kicking myself for being so caught up in my own world for such a long time that I never stopped to think that Alison might have her own stuff going on. For believing the image she was putting out – of success, and ease, and sunshine. For being jealous of it, even.

I realise I've been doing it to her too. Hiding things. Trying to seem fine, in my own way. Not telling her what's been going on in my life. Because somewhere along the way I picked up the same fear – the same idea that I had to hold it together, no matter what. And for me, that looked like disappearing into books and acting. For Alison, it looked different. But that doesn't mean we weren't both struggling in our own ways. All this time I was waiting for her to hear me – see me. Resenting her for not being able to. For being stuck in her own ways. But I was so stuck in mine that I wasn't looking closely at her, either. Wasn't seeing beneath the surface of her seemingly perfect life. I feel awful, that she's been struggling so much. That I was so thickheaded I couldn't see it.

'I'm so sorry, Ally,' I say.

'Dad's fine now,' she says. 'You know, they haven't had any issues with money in a really long time. And I think – I think maybe they don't need us to do this any more.'

'You're right,' I say, nodding. Thinking about how happy my parents have seemed in the last week, even when I've been shutting myself in my room on the pretence of dealing with this PR catastrophe and reading scripts, and only really emerging at meal times. Something lifts as I think about it.

'So,' she says. 'I don't need a cake. I just want you to put the fucking scripts down and come and visit me sometimes. And I want you to tell me what the fuck has been going on. I've seen the articles, Lara – it's been so hard not to call you. And I've been stupid not to. And I'm sorry. I was just… angry.'

'It's okay, Ally,' I say. 'I understand.'

And then I tell her – about Avi and I meeting for the very first time, at the pub. About him becoming my friend, and my favourite person. About the feelings I developed for him, slowly and then all at once. Feelings I thought maybe he had too. Feelings that, recently, I was sure he shared. Feelings that blew everything up between us. Twice, now. That might potentially, this time, have ruined my career. The conversation I had with Alessandro. Sienna showing up on-set. The pictures, the articles. The statement that they're about to put out.

Everything going wrong, all over again. And me being the one that's left behind.

She looks at me for a long second when I'm done talking.

'Jesus,' she says.

'Yeah,' I reply.

'That's rough, Lara,' she says, leaning on my shoulder. 'I'm sorry. What are you going to do?'

'I don't know,' I reply.

And she frowns, like she's making a decision. Then reaches for her laptop – pulls it from her bag, lying next to her on the sofa. Opens it and looks at me with an expression that sends warmth surging through my chest.

'Right,' she says. 'Let's make a plan.'

19

The next morning I call Alessandro to apologise, again – phase one of the new plan. And he's more open to speaking to me than I expected. Still clearly angry. But he tells me about an idea he's had, for some damage control: an early press obligation for the film – an interview with Avi and I that he has secured with a friend in the business, who has promised no questions about our relationship. A chance to pull the focus back towards what we're really here for, to establish a narrative. Get ahead of the negative press, rather than reacting to it. I say yes, even though every inch of me feels nauseous about doing it.

With Alison's help and support, I'm in the process of hiring a publicist and reactivating my socials, ready to take this job seriously, but I'm still incredibly nervous to see Avi. Because even though the media storm is calming – we're down to one or two articles every couple of days now – I still haven't seen anything approaching the statement we discussed him making. It feels like a grenade I'm expecting to go off at any moment, shattering my heart into a thousand pieces. And I haven't spoken to him since the last day of filming, ignoring his calls and messages.

On the day of the interview, I arrive at the shiny *Teen Vogue* offices five minutes early. The receptionist asks me to wait and so I take a seat in a large turquoise chair by the window.

Then I hear the door open, hear someone come in. I look up and meet his eye.

'Hi,' he says.

'Hi,' I manage to get out.

But before I can say anything else, the receptionist comes over.

'They're ready for you,' she says. And so I swallow, my throat dry – and without looking back, follow her into the building.

We're taken down the corridor into a room where the interviewer is waiting – three microphones set up to record us and then put it in print. Avi's publicist is present, standing in the corner of the room, looking pretty fierce. I have hired someone too, but she can't start until next week. So for today, I'm on my own. A fact which has me feeling more than a little unwell, especially when I look at the interviewer and have a flash of recognition. It's the same one from the red carpet, at the Olivier Awards. A colourful claw clip pulling her hair back from her face. Her eyelashes perfectly curled. *This can't be Alessandro's friend in the industry, can it?* I think, confused. Because of all the interviewers I spoke to that night, she was by far the most terrifying.

'I understand you were scheduled to meet my colleague Veronica today,' she says, before the recording has begun. 'I am afraid she has food poisoning, so I'll be conducting the interview instead. But not to worry – I'll still be respecting the, uh, boundaries that were agreed to beforehand.' She raises her eyebrows a little as she says it, as if she disagrees with them, and Avi's publicist clears her throat.

'But before I start the interview, off the record – are you guys seeing each other?'

I falter, my throat seeming to close up. And Avi's publicist frowns, looking like she's about to step in. But before she can, Avi starts talking. 'If you have a listen to the *Behind the Scenes* podcast interview that should be dropping…' – he looks at his watch – 'about now, you should get the information you're looking for.'

What the fuck? I think. *Behind The Scenes* is a famous podcast, aimed at lifting the curtain on what happens on-set in Hollywood. I feel sick at the thought that he and Sienna might have gone on there to confirm their story, to make the statement we discussed – for some reason, that's so much worse than the idea of reading it in print.

'Interesting,' she says, and I can see her restraining herself from picking up her phone and searching for it right this second – an impulse I'm fighting right now too. 'I'll have to check it out.'

'You should,' Avi says, smiling with the same look on his face he had at the awards ceremony – glossed over. A half-glance in my direction betraying his slight vulnerability right now. But I can't do anything except stare at the white wall across from me and wish I was literally anywhere else.

Avi's publicist clears her throat again, a sound I believe to be aimed this time at Avi too, and the interviewer reaches over to hit record on the sound set-up.

'So,' she says. 'Why don't you both tell me what being in this film means to you?'

I get through most of the interview in a fugue state — doing my best to stay on track, to keep my promise to Alessandro. To speak about our hard work, our commitment to the role. Steering away from any answers that paint my relationship with Avi as anything other than strictly professional. For anything that gets too personal, Avi's publicist steps in and deflects. Keeping the conversation on track — about acting, about our craft, about working with Alessandro. The interviewer asks me about my relationship with Amelia and the book, and I answer candidly. Opening up about how much I used to love her as a child. About how much I wanted to do her justice in this film. And as I do, I catch Avi looking at me. His eyes softening in a way that makes me want to look away.

When we get out of the interview, Avi's publicist, Sam, introduces herself and shakes my hand, giving me her card. But all I can think about is the podcast interview. I need desperately to know what they both said.

'Lara...' Avi says. But I don't want to hear it, not until I know.

'I have to go,' I reply. And I practically run out of the building.

As soon as I'm out, I see a text from Alison that came through during the interview. Because of course she's on top of this – she might be at work, but she's my number-one spy for Avi content. Sifting through it, giving me the highlights. *You need to see this*, it reads. A link underneath. I find a park bench to sit on and click on the link. It's a video on YouTube.

The title jumps out at me straight away: *Living a lie: the damage the Hollywood machine can do to you.* I read it a few times. *He can't have*, I think. *Surely he can't have blown it all up like that.*

But then I start listening, playing it out loud in the park. Unaware of the people milling around me, my focus sharpened to a point. Sienna starts. Describing her career in Hollywood as a child. Attending parties where drugs were present. Being exposed to grown-up issues, long before she should've been. Being followed down the street by paparazzi. Having to hide out inside her house for days at a time. The psychological damage it did to her. How it made her feel like her life wasn't her own. Then Avi starts talking and I zoom in to the screen – watching his facial expression. Serious. Determined.

'When I moved to Hollywood,' he says. 'I kind of lost my mind.'

The interviewer laughs. 'It'll do that to you.'

'Yeah,' Avi, says, fidgeting. His hands twisting in his lap. 'It hit me hard, actually. Being in a new world. Away from friends, from family. The hours on-set were demanding, the directors sometimes abusive. And I was expected to put up with it. Because I was lucky to be here. Because I was a role model. Because my mental well-being came second to everything else. And, eventually, I started putting myself second too.'

And a stone lands in my stomach – because he's said things that have hinted at this. But I didn't realise how deep it went. He continues, talking about how he became depressed. How he isolated himself from people he cared about, because he didn't want to complain. Because he didn't think they'd understand. How lonely he felt, being followed around by press every second of every day. My heart twists as I hear about it. Because even though I'm still hurt by our last interaction, I feel awful for him. The glimpses I saw over the last few months suddenly thrown into stark relief – he hasn't just been struggling a little, trapped between the life he wants and the life that's been created for him. He's been dealing with much more than that. I think about the postcards he sent me back then – the glittering image he presented. An image that he's completely shattering now.

'All of this is important context,' he says. 'But it's not the full story. The reason we came on this podcast is to get something straight.' He takes a deep breath, looking at Sienna, and she nods. Reaching for his hand and giving it a reassuring squeeze. 'Sienna and I have never been together.'

Oh, my God.

'That's quite a revelation,' the interviewer says, struggling to hide his shock. 'Can you elaborate?'

Avi nods, swallowing. My heart thuds in my chest. He continues, explaining what I already know. That when people started spreading rumours about him and Sienna, they decided to lean into them. Because two successful actors dating each other was a better headline than him being cast for diversity reasons rather than for his talent. Because it gave Sienna a break from being torn apart for going out drinking with her friends and being a 'party girl'.

'So it was all a lie?' the interviewer says.

Avi nods. 'It was. Lara Francis and I did have a romance on-set, but it was entirely outside of my relationship with Sienna. She and I have only ever been friends.'

'Wow,' the interviewer says. 'And what would you have to say to fans who might feel betrayed by the revelation of this information?'

Avi looks over to Sienna and she nods.

'I would apologise to any of our fans who feel let down by the fact that we weren't telling the truth,' she says. 'Who trusted us, and feel that trust has been betrayed. We never meant for that to be the impact of all this. We're just two humans who were trying to protect our private lives as best we could.'

'And why now?' the interviewer asks. 'Why are you coming forward with this?'

'Because I hurt someone,' Avi says. 'Badly. And none of this was her fault – it was all mine. It was an error of judgement. But only in the sense that I pulled her into something she never asked to be involved in in the first place.'

'Lara Francis?'

He nods, slowly. 'And I hope she doesn't mind me talking about her when she's not here to speak for herself. But I just want to say, so it's clear: she did nothing wrong. She is not at any fault here. The fault is all mine. And I'm lucky and grateful that Sienna agreed to come on this podcast, so I can set the record straight. For Lara's sake too.'

And the segment ends. I click out of the video, my hand shaking.

'Oh, my God,' I say to myself. A text pings in from Alison, saying pretty much the same.

I sit on the bench for what feels like an hour, just staring into space. Processing Avi's words. What he's just done – for me. And I get up, not sure where I'm going to go. Realising how wrong I was about it, all of it.

And, like magic, I see him, across the other side of the park. His eyes flicking up and meeting mine.

I cross the park to him. My heart thumping in my chest. Because I don't know what the outcome of this conversation will be – but I know that I want to talk to him, right now, more than anyone else.

'Did you follow me here?' I ask. He nods.

'I…' he starts. 'I had an inkling from the look on your face when I mentioned the interview that you might listen to it. So I thought I'd wait until you'd seen it. See if afterwards you maybe wanted to talk…'

He looks down, as if he's gathering his thoughts. Trying to think about what to say. But before he can speak, someone interrupts us. An older woman, pulling off her sunglasses. 'Are you Avi Kumar?' she asks, squinting at him. Avi opens his mouth to tell her – presumably – that, yes, he is, but we're in the midst of a private conversation. Before he can, she leans in towards him. Pulling out her camera and snapping a selfie. I watch her take it, Avi's expression thunderous, and she turns to walk off. But then she catches sight of me. For a second she looks at me and my heart thuds, wondering if she might've recognised me from some of the press. But instead she just says, 'Sorry, dear, I didn't see you there,' and walks off. A rush of relief passes through me and I almost laugh.

'Watch out,' he says. 'Once this film is out, that'll be you too.'

'I've been thinking about buying some wigs actually,' I joke. 'But it seems like that won't be necessary. That woman had literally no idea who I was.'

He laughs, and then his face darkens momentarily. The reality of our situation crashing back in through the levity.

'Did you hear about David?' he asks, and I frown.

'What about him?'

'The leak,' he says. 'It was him. I hear he's going to do a tell-all about it tomorrow – my publicist somehow managed to get wind of it. Probably either a cash grab or a career move. We managed to move the podcast date up to get ahead of it.'

What the fuck? I think, the knowledge sinking into my chest. Trying to reconcile the image I had of David – businesslike, bustling – with something conniving like this. His attitude did seem strange, now I think about it, on the last day on-set. Like he was more worried about my well-being than usual. Guilt, maybe. And I think of Roman, the picture becoming clearer by the second. The flowers, perhaps meant as an olive branch. His confusion and seemingly genuine assertion that it wasn't him: both things I dismissed at the time. And I feel suddenly bad for how I spoke to him, that last day: because he treated me terribly on-set, and there was no way I could've known. But I know better than anyone what it's like to be accused of a crime you didn't commit.

'I thought it was—'

'Roman,' he says. 'I know. Me too.'

'Wow,' I reply. I can't quite wrap my head around this – I feel like my world is tilting on its axis for the millionth time in the last few weeks.

'I'm so sorry, Lara,' he says, through the silence. And his face breaks, and my heart clenches at the sight.

'Avi—' I start, ready to say… honestly, I'm not sure what. Because, in this moment, the avalanche of my emotions is crashing back in. And I'm not sure I can put it into words.

'Please,' he says, before I can find them. 'Let me finish.' I nod, letting out a breath. He looks at me, an intensity in his eyes that makes me almost want to look away. But I don't – keeping my gaze fixed on his.

'I never meant to make you feel like a mistake,' he says, his voice full of emotion. 'Not when I left, the first time. Not this time, either. I have never, ever thought of you that way. Both times, I thought I was doing what was best – for you. Maybe also for me. But I can see now that I fucked it up.'

I let out a breath, asking the question I should've asked at the time. The one I think I know the answer to, now. But still, I need to hear him say it.

'When you said a few weeks ago that you thought my life would be better without you in it,' I say. 'What did you mean?'

He looks at me, the expression in his eyes so devastated I want to reach over and take his hand.

'I was losing it, Lara,' he says. 'I was in such a dark place. I honestly… I couldn't see anything good about myself. I was drowning. And then I saw you at the Christmas party and it felt like a light came on.'

I close my eyes, remembering – the look on his face, like the sun had come out. Feeling like I was the only person in the room. Like the last six months without him just melted away, because he was finally there. He swallows.

'But then when we met the next day and I could see how hurt you were, I fell back there. Into stupid thoughts – ones that convinced me I was going to drag you into the hole too. That I needed to cut things off between us. Because I was only going to hurt you if I didn't.'

'Avi…' I say, my throat constricting. Because it's heartbreaking that he felt that way. And it's so far from the truth it physically hurts. *We've lost so much time*, I think.

'I'm so sorry. But you know that wasn't true, right? I just…' I pause, gathering my thoughts. 'I was angry. That you crossed that line, then took it back. But that didn't mean I didn't care when you stopped talking to me. It didn't mean I didn't want you in my life. My life…' I take a breath, looking at him. Trying to find a way to put everything

I'm feeling right now into words. 'It was so much better, always, with you in it.'

He looks at me for a long second, his expression filled with an emotion I can't quite place.

He nods. 'I could see how stupid I'd been when you lost it at me after the audition. And there's no excuse for the way I treated you. Not now, not then. And this time, I was being stupid too. Because I couldn't see how trapped I was – how much I was willing to sacrifice my own happiness. Yours, too. For the sake of something that wasn't even real to begin with.'

He stops for a minute, takes a breath. Whatever he's about to say must be big.

'I've had a lot of time to think over the last week and I feel like I'm seeing more clearly now than ever. That those expectations I felt don't have to define me. That I get to define myself. To choose what I want. That my priorities can change and it's not going to ruin everything. I can do both. Go after my own happiness and inspire people too. It doesn't have to be one or the other. But I have to be honest, with myself and with other people, in order to do that.'

He's smiling now, grinning really, and my heart soars – because this is all I could have wanted for him. And selfishly I wonder whether there might be hope, still, for us. That maybe this means he'll come to London. Do some theatre, like he said. I take his hand, my heart thudding. 'Okay,' I say. 'So be honest with me, now. What do you want?'

He looks up at me, his eyes burning with something. 'Honestly? You, Lara.'

I close my eyes, the truth of it hitting me full in the chest. Because that's all I want too. But before I can say anything, he starts talking again.

'But,' he says. 'I need a little time to figure out what I'm doing. And I can't risk putting you in any kind of a situation like that again until I know. I'm sorry.'

Oh, I think. My heart breaking as he says it.

'But, if you'll consider it,' he says. 'I'd really like to be a friend to you again.'

I nod – a sadness pulsing through me for everything that's been lost. The time we could've spent together, still being friends. Being something more, even. But that won't be possible, right now.

'I would like that,' I say.

When I'm home, I find the house empty. I shut the door behind me, still processing the conversation I just had with Avi, and head straight up the stairs to my childhood bedroom. The poster of Deborah is still up on the wall. Acting manual after acting manual on the shelf. No pictures of friends, or tickets to events – the kinds of things I know are still littered in Alison's room. The box of postcards from Avi – the only evidence of any friendship I really had, outside of work – long gone by now. And for the first time, looking at it, I realise that it doesn't look like a home.

And as I look around – at the acting books, the scripts I printed on my parents' printer, none of which gave me comfort while I was hiding from the world – I find myself thinking about the house share I lived in before the film. Spencer and Hannah's things thrown around the place. His sheet music, marked up in blue pen. Her hand-crocheted blankets thrown over the sofa.

I cross the room to the book Spencer and Hannah gave me. I open it, carefully pulling out the note that sent me over the edge the other day. I fold it out, looking at it again. The list of things – what I thought I needed – to have the life I wanted. The goals that, once I achieved them, would fix everything.

1. Pursue acting with everything I can, not letting anything get in my way

2. *Get my first role in a film*
3. *Not care about what anyone thinks (especially Alison)*

I've spent my life narrowing my vision down to a point. Always transitioning, never putting down roots.

But slowly, over the last few weeks, some of that has been chipped away. To let other people in. To expand the world beyond the four walls of my room.

I think about Amelia, about how much of her confidence I've embodied in the last few weeks. Her sense of self. Her ability to walk into most rooms and command them. And I realise that I've been afraid, for so very long.

But maybe that's just it: the difference between Amelia and I.

She has always been willing to take bigger risks. Because she has always known her worth. Because the rewards can be really high, if you're just willing to put yourself out there. To try. And perhaps I can let go of the version of myself who holds back. Who hides. Because that's what I've been doing: hiding behind my career. Stubbornly seeing it as all I would ever have to offer. But Alison was right:

there was always more to me than that. I just didn't want to see it. Didn't want to open up, to let it out. Because I was afraid that other people wouldn't like it — that they wouldn't see it, too.

I took a risk, opening myself up to Avi. Then, and now. And it hasn't worked out the way I wanted it to. But the feeling I have now — of having been honest and true, of having given something a chance. That's worth the risk.

And before I know it, I'm picking up a pen. Tearing a new sheet of paper from a notebook on the shelf. A feeling of determination and peace coming over me. And I press the tip of the pen to the sheet, the words flowing through me as if coming from somewhere else. A new list: a fresh start.

1. *Keep giving everything I can to this dream.*
2. *Make sure I have a life too.*

20

SIX MONTHS LATER

'You're going to be late!' Alison shouts at me from the kitchen. And she's right – I am. My new publicist is meeting me at the event in about half an hour and I'm still in the spare bedroom of Alison's flat, putting the finishing touches on my eyeshadow.

I was offered the full works for this evening – a stylist, hair and make-up – but I said no. I thought it would be more fun for it to be just me and Alison. The marketing agency Alison is working for has a few luxury-clothing clients, so she managed to source a dress from a relatively unknown French designer for me. It's black, with beading embroidered all over it. A corset at the top. And I've done my make-up myself. Using tips Sarah gave me, the last time we met for coffee.

I step back and take a final look in the mirror. The dress looks incredible. Like something Amelia would wear, if she lived in the present instead of in the 1800s. But the final effect isn't of her. I don't feel like someone else. I feel like me. I snap a picture and send it to my group chat with Spencer and Hannah, and they reply immediately. Hannah tells me the kids at her school will be so excited to see the official pictures – I'm giving a talk there next month and she's incredibly jazzed about it.

'Seriously, Lara!' Alison yells. And I stumble down the stairs, almost stacking it in the heels she lent me.

She sighs. 'Finally.' She's dressed up too – she's coming as my plus one. I offered tickets to my parents too, but they're coming to the LA premiere next week instead. Alison's wearing a dress by the same French designer, in a midnight blue. Stars embroidered across it.

'You look beautiful,' I say.

'We don't have time for this,' she says, rushing me over to the door. And we run together down the stairs.

This time, I feel more prepared – for the photos, the interviews. I grew pretty well-versed in the press training Alessandro insisted on sending me to before the press tour, so I wouldn't say anything stupid. And for the most part, I didn't. Although it was a little weird to spend so much time sitting next to Avi, dodging pointed questions about our relationship, we managed. Georgia, my new publicist, has been helping a lot too.

Still, I blink a little as the cameras flash in our faces when we get out of the car. Alison takes my hand firmly, though, and we walk up towards the red carpet.

We get to the main crush of people – crowds milling around. People in glittering jewellery and beautiful dresses. And Alison keeps grabbing my arm, telling me she thinks she's seen Jonathan Bailey. Who I know for a fact is not here – he's currently filming on-location in Bali, on a project I was offered an audition for a few months ago. I'm searching the crowds too – for my publicist, namely. But also for someone else.

And then I see him.

He's talking to an interviewer, but mid-sentence he looks up and catches my eye. Excuses himself and makes his way through the crowd to me.

'Hi,' he says.

'Hi,' I breathe.

'I, uh… I'm going to go and check out the bar. Over there,' Alison says, slipping away.

'How have you been?' he asks. He means since the tour – the last time we saw each other. Which was nice, but strange. The time we spent together between interviews charged, somehow.

Like now. A shiver running down my skin as he looks at me that tells me he's not just my friend. But he has to be. Because that's been our official line for the press and the one we're sticking to personally too.

'Good,' I reply. 'You?'

'Great,' he says. And I try to build myself up to ask the only real question I want to ask. Which is whether or not he got the part in the play he auditioned for, on Broadway. Because if he did, he'll be in New York for the next few months. And I will too – I got a part in a new TV series. One Sienna has actually been cast in as well. We've been texting each other about the script already, making plans for our characters. After the podcast interview went live, I texted her to say thank you – for being so kind to me, for sacrificing her only protection from the press. And since then we've been talking. It was actually me that put her forward for this series.

But before I can get the words out, a hand lands on my arm – my publicist, Georgia.

'There you are,' she says. 'I've texted you about eight times. We should get going on the press circuit.'

'Sure,' I say, looking up at Avi.

Georgia is a true professional – she rushes me along, through interview after interview. Stepping in where needed. Flashing me a look if an answer runs too long. Avi is a few people behind me and I find myself aware of his presence.

We make it to the end of the line and I catch the last few sentences of Avi's interview: '…it was an honour to work with her. She's inspiring. When she enters a room, when she's on, you can't look at anything else.'

Oh, my God, I think, feeling suddenly overwhelmed with emotion. Because he's talking about me.

'And what's next for the both of you, personally and professionally?' the interviewer asks, and I tense up immediately.

'I don't know,' he says. 'But…' My breath catches and it takes every fibre of my being not to turn and look at him. 'I've learned recently that I don't think you ever really know what's going to happen in life. You just have to be honest and hope things fall into place.'

I blink, processing his answer. *What can he mean by that?* I think.

But right now I have a job to focus on. So I allow Georgia to pull me towards where the cameras are set up. Where Alessandro is waiting.

'Bambina,' he says. 'I am so glad to see you.' And relief soars through my chest. Because even though we've made up over the last few months, I still feel awful about how things went down between us. And so to see him tonight – to have made it so far – fills me with joy.

When Avi and Sienna's podcast was released, he called me up to say that he was still angry that I was so impulsive – especially given that I knew about their arrangement and the potential damage it could cause to the film – but that he was sorry, for speaking to me more harshly than he needed to. And grateful too, that I reached out to him after filming, that Avi and I were willing to do that interview. That perhaps, at some point, we could look at a future project together – which is looking maybe likely, because I've heard rumours that the studio might be funding a sequel. Turns out that *no publicity is bad publicity* is more true than I'd thought; people have been so caught up in the drama around this film that it's having a much buzzier release than even the studio expected. And the early reviews have been good – encouraging. A few four stars, and even one or two fives. Praising the direction, the scenery. I only know this from Alison, because I've been trying not to get distracted by all that. To keep my focus on the next project, the next script Nat sends through.

But still taking time to enjoy the journey while I can. The life I've been building in the meantime – late night takeaway with my sister, pub trips with Spencer and Hannah. Everything I avoided for fear I couldn't have it, because it wasn't for me.

I take my place in the photography line-up next to Roman, who is looking more dressed up than I was expecting; he has a tradition of appearing at premieres either woefully underdressed in a T-shirt and jeans, or with a paper bag over his head. But tonight, he's apparently on his best behaviour. Wearing a luxury custom suit with blue silk lapels.

We greet each other cordially.

I might not like Roman still – we will definitely never be friends – but over the press tour, we've been civil. And over time I've realised that, though I hate to admit it, we weren't as different as

I thought. We both had the same drive to succeed. His just came out in incredibly bizarre ways.

We take the group photos, then Roman, Sienna and Alessandro move along to the edge of the carpet, and Avi and I have centre stage.

Avi winds his arm around my waist, like he did last time. And this time, I look where Georgia has trained me to: just above the cameras rather than right at them.

'You look beautiful,' Avi whispers, leaning down. His breath tickling the edge of my neck. The cameras flash, capturing the moment I smile shyly at him.

And when the screening is over – and everyone has clapped, and Alessandro has given his speech, and made a joke about the PR surrounding the film, and thanked all of us – I head out with the crowd spilling into the night air.

He locates me and I find myself noticing how beautiful he looks in this moment. How much like himself. Even in these clothes. The difference I was seeing before was never the clothes or the flashy lifestyle. It was him – he looked distant from himself. Unhappy.

He doesn't look that way any more.

'You seem... like you're doing well,' he says, smiling. 'Taking to this fame stuff like a natural.'

I nod. 'I am,' I say. 'I've got the right people around me. You seem good too.'

He nods. 'I am. I've been thinking a lot lately. About my life. What I want.'

I catch my breath, trying to figure out exactly what he means. But then he continues, looking at me in a way that makes me feel like I'm on fire.

'I got the part in New York,' he says.

Oh, my God, I think. A rush of joy flashing through me. It spills through every part of me, getting bigger the longer I look at him.

21

THREE MONTHS LATER

I reach the theatre about fifteen minutes before the show is due to start and rush through the back halls to his dressing room. He's in there already. Full stage make-up.

'I was beginning to think you weren't coming,' he jokes. Standing up, pulling me in. Kissing me like he hasn't seen me in weeks — when really he saw me this morning before I left for work.

'It's your first night,' I say. 'What kind of girlfriend would I be if I missed it?'

'A terrible one,' he agrees. 'But right now I need you to leave this room. Because I'm about five seconds away from tearing your clothes off.'

'Noted,' I say. 'You like the red dress, then?'

'Lara,' he says, warning in his tone. 'That's not even a question.'

I kiss him again one more time. Then I pull back and he looks a little nervous.

'You're going to be great,' I say, squeezing his hand. 'And I'll be right there the whole time.'

I leave him with his script and head up the stairs to my seat. In a box, off to the side. One Sienna is already waiting in.

'You were great today,' she says – we had a long day shooting, but she wrapped a little earlier than I did. And I smile and tell her about a girl I met on the subway who asked me to sign a copy of *A Murder in London*. Sienna reaches down and roots through her bag, pulling out her own copy – I got it for her birthday a few weeks ago.

'Started it last week,' she says. 'It's so good – I can't believe I've never read it before.' And we talk a little about it. Gratitude spilling through as we do. For the friendship we've been forming in the last few months.

The lights go down and a rush of pride surges through me as we turn our eyes to the stage. Pride for Avi – because he found a way to choose himself over the huge pressures placed on him. And for me too – because I've been keeping the promise I made to myself. The list, that's currently framed in my trailer. The life, that encompasses

Spencer, Hannah and Alison – all due to descend on the studio apartment I'm renting next week. That has now expanded to include Avi, and Sienna too. Within a matter of days of Avi and I arriving in New York, we ended up falling into bed with one another, all sensible plans of being friends falling apart as soon as the distance between us was closed.

If I've learned anything over the last few months, it's that the dream will never be enough. You need everything else too.

And we watch as the curtain pulls up on the stage and he delivers his opening line.

Three weeks later, I walk up another set of stairs. To another audition studio. But this time, I don't wait to be called into a room. I know where I'm going.

I open the door and find a table of people – some of the same faces I was so terrified of, what feels like a lifetime ago now. Alessandro. The producers. My eyes scan across them, looking up at me expectantly. Greeting me warmly. And then the one I've been waiting to see: Avi. He smiles as I enter and shut the door behind me. I take my place next to him.

I pull the script for *Amelia 2* – already marked up with my notes – out of my bag. Notes that aren't just for me this time, because everyone here wants to hear them too. Avi finds my hand under the table, his fingers interlacing with mine. And a thrill runs across my skin at his touch. Like always. And this time there's no fear, no worry. Only joy – to be here, together. His presence a certainty, among other things. Like my certainty of who I am. What I have to offer.

'Right, bambini,' Alessandro says. 'Shall we begin?'

Read on for the first chapter of Bianca Gillam's bookish enemies-to-lovers romance…

Bad Publicity is available now

1

'Fuck.'

Not a word I expected to come out of my mouth on the first day of my new job. In my first conversation with my new boss. From the look on her face, she wasn't expecting it either. My hand flies up to my mouth but it's already out there, in the air, floating around. *Fuck*, I say again, this time in my head.

'Is something wrong?' She's all wide eyes and concern, which is better than judgement, at least. I look back down at the list between us, squinting, making sure. The name is still there, clear as day. Jack Carlson. Jessica follows my gaze.

'Ah, I see. Nerves, right? He is a big name. I get it – I felt that way when I first started working on bigger authors.'

I open my mouth to correct her, then realise that explaining the actual reason would be infinitely worse. Five years ago at university, Jack Carlson screwed me over so catastrophically that I made a promise to myself I'd never have to be in the same room as him again. And until exactly this moment, I was pretty sure I'd sooner light myself on fire than break that promise.

'I thought he wrote non-fiction?' I say, trying to keep my tone neutral.

'He does, usually. But his editor persuaded him over to the dark side last year, so you'll get to be the publicist for his first novel. Once you're over the nerves it's actually a very exciting campaign!'

She starts telling me about the campaign, while I stare at the list of authors I will be representing in my first senior publicist role. The role I was so excited about until my big chance turned into my worst nightmare. I emerge from my stupor when I hear the words 'book tour'.

'What did you say, sorry?'

Jessica looks momentarily confused, then repeats herself without a hint of irritation. I like her very much. It's a shame I'll have to quit immediately.

'I said, you'll have time to get over those nerves when you accompany him on his book tour.' *Shit.* I grip the edge of the desk to hide my reaction, while Jessica tells me that there are a few events planned in New York, then a European leg.

'Europe?' I say, trying desperately to gather my thoughts. As Jack's US publicist, Europe is not my remit.

She nods and continues, her smile widening. 'He's extremely successful in France, Germany, the UK and Ireland, and our sister companies publish him in those territories, so we've arranged a tour.' I silently pray that this explanation isn't going where I think it's going. 'We did the same thing for Jack's last non-fiction book, but there were a few hitches on the tour – miscommunication between publicists in different countries, missed flights, etcetera. So this time, to keep things clean, his agent has insisted that we stick to one publicist. One schedule. One person to make sure things run smoothly.' She pauses, her expression expectant. 'That would be you.'

Oh, good. It can get worse. My knuckles are practically white from gripping the desk at this point, and Jessica waits as I force a smile which probably comes out more as a grimace and try to think of an appropriate response. I am sure she's expecting enthusiasm – and why wouldn't she? It's any book publicist's career dream, to run a global tour for a world-famous author. I should be excited – this should be the culmination of all the work I've done so far, an opportunity to show what I'm made of.

I manage to choke out a strangled 'Oh?' from my throat, which suddenly feels like it has closed up. Fortunately, Jessica smiles gently, interprets my response as concern about planning such a large tour, and reassures me that they have already handled the flights and accommodation, and nailed down the schedule. All I have to do is go and make sure the tour goes off without a hitch. Which would be fine, if there wasn't already a hitch: a fucking huge one. I excuse myself in a choked voice to go to the bathroom.

As soon as I find it, I lock myself in the nearest cubicle and let out a long breath. 'Fuck. Fuck!' I say, out loud, to no one in particular. It's been bad enough, watching Jack's stratospheric rise from a distance – *New York Times* bestseller this, literary award that. Historical documentaries, radio interviews. Viral threads about how hot he is, thirst traps, video compilations of him running his hand through his hair while he's describing some battle that happened 500 years ago. Now, not only do I have to be aware of his success, I have to *travel around Europe with him facilitating it*. There are not enough swear words in the world to do this justice.

I want to scream. But, somehow, I have to try and calm down. As disastrous as this reality is, it's not going away any time soon. *Come on, Andie. You can handle this.*

Can you? a small voice inside me asks, and suddenly I'm dangerously close to being pulled back to that last semester at Edinburgh. To telling Jack I never wanted to see him again, and meaning it. To the weeks afterwards, when my world was smashed into pieces. But I shut all that in a vault long ago. If I'm going to get through this, I have to keep it there, somehow.

I clench my hands into fists at my side and start doing the meditative breaths my dad taught me. A fresh pang of grief appears at the image of him in his yoga trousers on the deck of my family home, but then the breaths start to work, clearing the cloud of emotions into an almost-calm. My eyes flutter open, bringing me back to the present. I check my watch: it's been ten minutes. I'd better return to my desk, so Jessica doesn't think I've disappeared completely.

I take one more deep breath, and leave the cubicle.

As I navigate through the office, my professionalism starts to take over, gradually replacing my earlier panic with a temporary resolve. For today, for this week, I need a plan. There are lots of other authors on that list. Perhaps until I can process this and strategise properly, I can focus on those.

Jessica is still at my desk when I return, sipping her tea as if I haven't just sworn at her and had a near-meltdown. I sit in my new swivel chair, at my new desk, and – for a second – feel a flash of pride. I've made it here, to senior publicist in one of the most prestigious publishing houses in New York. The Andie who moved here from London as an intern would hardly be able to believe this.

Unfortunately, this lasts about three seconds before Jessica starts talking about Jack again and I almost fling my pen across the room at the sound of his name. I'll have to get better at that.

'As you'll see there's quite a list of authors here, but most of them are under control – your predecessor lined up a lot before she left. So your focus will mostly be on Jack's campaign for the next few months.' I swallow the sound of frustration that moves up my throat and plaster what I hope is an excited expression on my face. So much for focusing on my other authors. 'The book publishes this week,' she continues, 'so we have events in the city spread over the next few weeks. The first event is this Thursday, actually. It would be a great chance for you to meet him.'

'This Thursday?' I say, my voice about three octaves higher than usual. I overcorrect my tone and my 'Great!' comes out in a baritone. *Jesus Christ, Andie. Get it together.*

'Wonderful,' she smiles, still seemingly unfazed. 'I'm sure he'll be delighted to meet you.'

Or he's about to get the shock of his life.

Acknowledgements

This book is the thing I am most proud of that I have ever done. It was also not without struggle. I say this to provide proper context for the thanks that follow. Because the people (angels, really) who had a part in this book weren't just supporters; they were much more than that.

To Elizabeth Counsell first, my agent who has now moved to different shores as an Editor but who will be (I hope!) a lifelong friend. For calling me every morning in those last deadline weeks. For being a voice of support, always. For believing in me, always.

To Darcy Nicholson, for your unfailing support. For being there to listen. To discuss. To understand. To encourage. To help me shape. To find everything behind the barriers I was placing in front of myself and help me polish it into something that shone.

ACKNOWLEDGEMENTS

To Jeramie Orton, for believing in this book too. For taking a chance on it. For having me into the offices for the best day ever in NYC, and reminding me why I love being a writer in the first place.

To my sisters – Charlotte Gillam, for supporting me so entirely from the other side of the world (including booking me a spa weekend). For always encouraging me to be less hard on myself. Lucie Gillam, for always being there to listen about the challenges of a creative career. For coming to hang out in my flat on the days where I was too frazzled to leave the house.

To my parents – my mum, Dr Amanda Gillam, for being there with reminders that you were proud of me. For days in the London Library when you read the early pages of this book and gave me the confidence to carry on. My dad, Martin Gillam, for your listening ear – always on the other end of the phone. Always there to remind me to keep going. That I could do it.

To Andrew Grassick – I don't know really how to summarise this except with the image of a rock in the ocean, and a rope tied around it. You gave me something to tether to. Somewhere to rest. My dedication says it all: I couldn't have done this without you.

Many other thanks are due, too: to the Bloomsbury team including Maisie McCormick, Fabrice Wilmann, Caroline Hogg, Ben Chisnall, Charlotte Phillips, Amy Donegan, Abigail Walton, and the team at Penguin Pamela Dorman.

To Diane Banks and Martin Jensen. To Ayushi, and Himani Sharma for not only helping me to shape Avi's character, but for your kind and incredibly helpful feedback on your beta reads which made the book infinitely better.

To Jack Bardoe, Bianca Bardoe and Grace Edwards for giving me insights into your very cool jobs. To Lucy Johnson for going above and beyond, even as far as reading the whole manuscript and giving me pointers as to how to bring it closer to reality. Any mistakes or discrepancies are my own.

To Henry Taylor, for being my most constant friend.

To the person reading this – thank you for giving my book a chance. I hope you found a home in its pages.

And finally – to my grandma, Anne Willett, for being the roots of the tree that I am so grateful to be a branch of. You were a light in this world. I want to keep shining that light for as long as I can.

B xx